# Beneath the Ashes

Bekka Scott

Published by Bekka Scott, 2024.

This is a work of fiction. Similarities to real people, places, or events are entirely coincidental.

BENEATH THE ASHES

**First edition. December 18, 2024.**

Copyright © 2024 Bekka Scott.

ISBN: 979-8227739568

Written by Bekka Scott.

# Table of Contents

Chapter 1 .............................................................................. 1
Chapter 2 .............................................................................. 7
Chapter 3 ............................................................................ 13
Chapter 4 ............................................................................ 19
Chapter 5 ............................................................................ 25
Chapter 6 ............................................................................ 29
Chapter 7 ............................................................................ 35
Chapter 8 ............................................................................ 39
Chapter 9 ............................................................................ 45
Chapter 10 .......................................................................... 51
Chapter 11 .......................................................................... 57
Chapter 12 .......................................................................... 63
Chapter 13 .......................................................................... 69
Chapter 14 .......................................................................... 73
Chapter 15 .......................................................................... 79
Chapter 16 .......................................................................... 85
Chapter 17 .......................................................................... 89
Chapter 18 .......................................................................... 95
Chapter 19 ........................................................................ 101
Chapter 20 ........................................................................ 107
Chapter 21 ........................................................................ 113
Chapter 22 ........................................................................ 117
Chapter 23 ........................................................................ 123
Chapter 24 ........................................................................ 127
Chapter 25 ........................................................................ 133
Chapter 26 ........................................................................ 139
Chapter 27 ........................................................................ 145
Chapter 28 ........................................................................ 153
Chapter 29 ........................................................................ 161
Chapter 30 ........................................................................ 167
Chapter 31 ........................................................................ 171

| | |
|---|---|
| Chapter 32 | 177 |
| Chapter 33 | 185 |
| Chapter 34 | 191 |
| Chapter 35 | 197 |
| Chapter 36 | 203 |
| Chapter 37 | 209 |
| Chapter 38 | 223 |
| Chapter 39 | 227 |
| Chapter 40 | 233 |
| Chapter 41 | 237 |
| Chapter 42 | 243 |
| Chapter 43 | 249 |
| Chapter 44 | 257 |
| Chapter 45 | 259 |
| Epilogue | 273 |

For my feral one. I love you.

The difference between a garden and a graveyard is only what you choose to put in the ground. —Rudy Francisco

# Beneath The Ashes
# By Bekka Scott

All rights reserved. No part of this publication may be reproduced, stored or transmitted in any form or by any means, electronic, mechanical, photocopying, recording, scanning, or otherwise without written permission from the publisher. It is illegal to copy this book, post it to a website, or distribute it by any other means without permission.

This novel is entirely a work of fiction. The names, characters and incidents portrayed in it are the work of the author's imagination. Any resemblance to actual persons, living or dead, events or localities is entirely coincidental.

Bekka Scott has no responsibility for the persistence or accuracy of URLs for external or third-party Internet Websites referred to in this publication and does not guarantee that any content on such Websites is, or will remain, accurate or appropriate.

Designations used by companies to distinguish their products are often claimed as trademarks. All brand names and product names used in this book and on its cover are trade names, service marks, trademarks and registered trademarks of their respective owners. The publishers and the book are not associated with any product or vendor mentioned in this book. None of the companies referenced within the book have endorsed the book.

ASIN B0DJ9G8R5M

**ISBN:** 9798227072832

Copyright © 2024 Bekka Scott All rights reserved.

For my feral one. I love you.

The difference between a garden and a graveyard is only what you choose to put in the ground. —Rudy Francisco

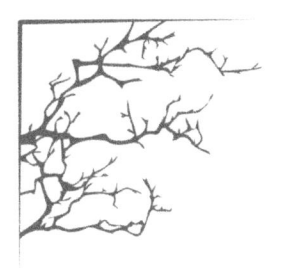

# Chapter 1

Emma Dawson's hands moved with a practiced grace, her fingers deftly adjusting the IV drip as if it were an extension of her own body. The sterile room hummed with the incessant beeps of monitors, the rhythmic pulse of machines keeping time in a space where time often seemed suspended. To the untrained ear, the sounds might be a reassurance—a sign of life, of stability—but to Emma, they were a constant reminder of how fragile that life truly was. The steady beat of a heart, the rise and fall of lungs, all hinging on the fine balance she maintained with every careful adjustment.

She had mastered this delicate dance long ago, her composure now so deeply ingrained that even the turmoil churning within her couldn't break through the surface. To her patients, she was a beacon of calm, a figure whose steady hands and soothing presence were as much a part of the healing process as any medicine. It was her kindness, her gentle touch, that they loved most—how she managed to make them feel seen, cared for, even when they were fading.

But the air in the room was thick with more than just antiseptic. Despair hung in the space between them, invisible yet suffocating, settling over Emma like a shroud. It clung to her skin, filled her lungs, weighed her down as she leaned over the frail man lying in the hospital bed. His body, once strong and vibrant, was now withering beneath the relentless assault of age and illness. His skin, pale and paper-thin, barely seemed to contain the man he once was. His eyes, once bright with life, now flickered with a dull, muted resignation.

He looked at her, and in that gaze, Emma saw not fear but acceptance. Not hope, but the quiet understanding that his battle was coming to an end. His breaths came slow and shallow, each one a labored effort, as though even the simple act of drawing air was too much for his worn-out body to bear. The inevitability of it weighed on them both, though neither spoke the words aloud. They didn't need to. It was written in the lines of his face, in the way his chest barely moved under the thin hospital blanket.

Emma felt the familiar ache in her chest, the one that came when she saw someone slipping away—someone she could only comfort, not save. She had seen this too many times to count, yet it never got easier. How could it, when every patient was someone's father, mother, sister, or child? She had learned to keep her emotions at bay, to stay strong for those who needed her. But inside, the pain of watching another life fade away left a bruise on her soul that never fully healed.

She adjusted the man's pillow with tender care, her fingers brushing against his cool skin. "Is that better?" Her voice, soft and warm, filled the room, offering what little comfort she could. Her words were a lifeline, even if they couldn't change the inevitable.

He gave a small, almost imperceptible nod, his lips twitching in what might have been an attempt at a smile. It faltered, turning into a grimace of pain before fading back into weariness. Emma's heart clenched, but she kept her expression steady, refusing to let the emotion show. She couldn't afford to break. Not here. Not now.

This was her calling—to ease the suffering of others, to be the constant in a world full of uncertainty. But no matter how many times she performed this ritual of care, no matter how many lives she touched, there was always that lingering feeling of helplessness. The knowledge that she could only do so much, and sometimes, that wasn't enough.

Emma checked the machines again, her movements efficient, automatic. Her mind, though, was far from the task at hand. It drifted to her own life, to the turmoil waiting for her outside the hospital walls. The doubts that gnawed at her, the cracks forming in her marriage, the weight of responsibilities that threatened to crush her. In here, she was in control, every action purposeful, every decision clear. Out there, her life was unraveling, thread by fragile thread.

She brushed a lock of hair behind her ear, her hands steady as always, though her heart was anything but. The man's breathing slowed, his body sinking deeper into the bed, and Emma felt a familiar sense of loss, even before the end came.

In the sterile, artificial world of the hospital, she could hold despair at arm's length, but it always found a way in. It crept into her thoughts, into her bones, until it was as much a part of her as the care she gave. And in moments like this, as she stood at the bedside of a man quietly slipping away, she wondered how much longer she could carry it without breaking.

The steady hum of machines and chaos of hurried footsteps echoed throughout the halls. Doctors and nurses rushed by their faces etched with the gravity of life-and-death decisions. The sound of an approaching ambulance sent shivers down Emma's spine, a constant reminder of the never-ending stream of emergencies that awaited. The cries of a new baby just born in the Emergency Department, a reminder of the circle of life. We're born, we do our best to live and we die. Everyone has the same story, some just live better than others.

Amidst the chaotic scene, Emma navigated with a sense of calm and control, like a seasoned captain steering her ship through stormy waters. But beneath her composed exterior, a tempest raged within her. Every step she took felt like another crack in her carefully constructed armor, and each breath reminded her of the storm brewing in her personal life - a storm she could not outrun.

In the break room, Emma sank into a worn chair that groaned under her weight. She closed her eyes, trying to shut out the rising tide of thoughts and emotions that threatened to overwhelm her. Her once steady hands now trembled as she pressed them against her temples, trying to silence the voice that haunted her more than any patient's cries for help.

The relentless question sliced through Emma's mind like a jagged knife, bitter and unrelenting. Am I enough? No matter how many lives she touched, how many souls she eased, the doubt lingered, gnawing at her insides. She couldn't silence it, even as she buried herself in her work at the hospital.

But thoughts of her husband Carlos invaded her mind like a haunting specter. His late nights and growing distance had become a constant ache in her heart. She longed for his love, his honesty, but all she received was cold indifference. And now, it felt like she was asking for the impossible.

His phone calls that ended too quickly, the secretive glances at his screen - they all screamed betrayal. But instead of loud fights and slammed doors, their marriage fell apart in silence. With secrets.

Blinking away tears, Emma tried to hold herself together. She was a nurse - she healed others. It was what she did. Yet the pieces of her life seemed irreparable.

Her fingers traced the cool metal of her wedding ring, once a sacred symbol of their love, now feeling like a cruel joke. How could something so small weigh so heavily on her heart? Biting back helplessness, she turned it around her finger.

With a deep breath, Emma stood up from the chair and smoothed out the wrinkles in her uniform as if trying to smooth out the fractures in her heart. Beyond the door lay a world that needed her - patients in pain, lives hanging by a thread. There was always someone worse off than her. And so she would go on, pushing herself forward.

As she stepped back into the fluorescent-lit hallways of the hospital, Emma's expression hardened into one of practiced professionalism. The hospital swallowed her back into its rhythm, and she followed without hesitation. But inside, each step forward felt like it carried her further from herself, from the life she once knew, from the love she had freely given but no longer recognized.

Deep down, the question lingered, taunting and unforgiving. Am I enough?

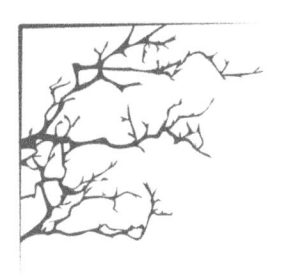

# Chapter 2

The sterile hospital lights hummed softly, flickering ever so slightly as Emma Dawson walked through the narrow corridors. The soft squeak of her shoes against the linoleum floor was the only sound that accompanied her racing thoughts. She was just about to reach the exit when her phone vibrated in her pocket, snapping her out of her reverie. The screen lit up with a familiar name: Carlos.

"Em, where are you?" Carlos's voice was low, but there was an unmistakable edge to it that made Emma's shoulders tense.

"Just finishing my shift," she replied, keeping her tone neutral even as she gripped the phone tighter.

"Make it quick," he said, his words more of a command than a request. "Dinner better be ready when I get home."

"Of course," Emma managed to say before the line went dead. She slipped the phone back into her pocket, feeling the weight of expectation pressing down on her like a heavy blanket.

Pushing through the hospital's double doors, Emma stepped into the crisp evening air and took a deep breath, trying to steady herself. Her mind was already racing ahead to the role she'd have to play for the rest of the night—the perfect wife, the perfect mother, all while keeping the cracks in her life hidden. Outside the walls of Oakdale General Hospital, a palpable energy filled the air.

At home, the routine unfolded with practiced precision. Emma moved through the kitchen, chopping vegetables with the same mechanical efficiency she used at work. The rhythm of the knife against the cutting board was sharp and quick, a staccato beat that matched the forced smile on her face. She stirred the pot on the stove, but the savory aroma couldn't cover the sour taste of anxiety that lingered in her mouth.

"Smells good, Em," Carlos remarked as he walked into the kitchen, his eyes briefly meeting hers before darting away, as if the connection was too much to hold.

"Thanks," she murmured, her voice hollow, the words feeling as empty as the space between them.

"Is Jaxon asleep?" Carlos asked, his question more of an afterthought as he poured himself a drink, the sound of liquid splashing into the glass echoing in the quiet kitchen.

"An hour ago," she replied softly, her voice barely a whisper against the clinking of ice cubes.

"Good," he said, his tone light but lacking warmth. "We need our time too."

Emma nodded, serving dinner with a practiced hand, each plate a small offering to the fragile peace she was desperately trying to maintain. As they ate, their conversation skimmed the surface of safe topics, avoiding the deeper currents of tension that threatened to pull them under. Emma spoke of mundane things—Jaxon's school, the weather—while her mind circled around the unspoken truths, suffocating in the silence.

Later, as she stood at the sink washing dishes, she watched the soapy water swirl down the drain, mirroring the whirlpool of emotions that threatened to drag her under. Her reflection in the window above the sink showed a woman with tired eyes and a forced smile, her features worn from years of pretending everything was fine. Emma reached out, touching the cold glass, tracing the outline of her face as if searching for the person she used to be.

"Everything okay?" Carlos's voice called from the living room, distant and distracted.

"Fine," she replied automatically, the word a shield against the questions she was too afraid to ask, the confrontation she knew she wasn't ready for.

"Good," he said, the single word carrying the weight of expectation, the assumption that she would continue to play her part.

Emma dried her hands on the dish towel and hung it up with deliberate care, each action a way to keep herself grounded, to maintain the fragile order of her world. But the tightness in her chest and the tremor in her fingers betrayed the storm brewing inside her.

Later that night, as Emma stood in the dimly lit hallway, she watched through the crack in the bedroom door. Carlos was hunched over his phone, the screen casting an eerie glow on his face. His fingers moved quickly, typing messages that would never be meant for her. She watched as a small smile crept onto his lips—a smile she hadn't seen directed at her in months.

Emma's breath caught in her throat, and she stepped back into the shadows, the creak of the floorboard beneath her foot sounding like thunder in the silent house. The air felt thick with secrets, every breath she took suffocating under the weight of unspoken truths.

Carlos's muffled laughter filtered through the door, cutting through her like a knife. Her green eyes, once bright and full of life, now reflected the cold reality of her situation. He didn't laugh like that with her anymore—not since the late nights had become routine, the excuses paper-thin, and the distance between them an unbridgeable chasm.

She retreated to the guest bathroom, closing the door behind her as softly as she could. Leaning against the cool marble sink, Emma stared at her reflection in the mirror—a woman on the verge of falling apart, holding herself together with sheer willpower. Her hands shook, betraying the calm exterior she fought so hard to maintain.

"Confront him," she whispered to the woman in the mirror. "You deserve to know the truth."

But then she thought of Jaxon, her son, and the disruption it would cause if she were to leave his stepfather. Could she really shatter his world by tearing theirs apart? The image of Jaxon's bright smile and carefree laugh cut through her resolve like a knife.

"Denial is easier," she countered, gripping the edge of the sink until her knuckles turned white. "Keep the peace, protect this broken family."

But the thought of continuing to live a lie, of sharing a bed with a man who was already halfway out the door, filled her with a deep, gnawing despair. Anger and sadness churned inside her, a toxic mix that threatened to overflow.

"Is it worth it?" Emma asked her reflection, but the woman in the mirror didn't answer. She just stared back with those same tired, green eyes, silently pleading for a way out.

"Mama?" A sleepy voice interrupted her thoughts. Jaxon's body filled the space of the doorway, rubbing his eyes with one hand, his hair tousled from sleep.

"Everything okay?" he asked, his voice huskier than normal from sleep and full of concern.

Emma swallowed hard, pushing down the bitter taste of her lies as she reached out to hug her son. His lanky body in her arms was a comforting weight, grounding her in the present, pulling her back from the edge.

"Everything's fine, sweetie," she whispered, standing on her tiptoes to kiss the side of his face. "Let's get you back to bed."

She led him down the hallway, the familiar surroundings of his room a stark contrast to the turmoil in her heart. The walls were covered in posters of fast cars and sleek motorcycles, a young man's world of adventure and excitement, so far removed from the painful reality Emma faced.

As she tucked Jaxon into bed, smoothing the covers over him, she felt the pull of two choices—confrontation or complacency. The duality of her existence churned within her, a storm on the brink of breaking.

She lingered in the doorway, watching Jaxon as he drifted back to sleep, his breathing steady and peaceful. In his world, everything was still okay. But in hers, the time for pretending was running out.

Tonight, she allowed herself one last moment of indecision, one last night of holding on to the illusion before the dawn forced her to face the truth.

THE NEXT MORNING, THE kitchen was quiet, thick with unspoken tension as Emma set two mugs of coffee on the table. The steam curled up from the cups, a calm contrast to the storm of emotions swirling inside her. Carlos sat across from her, his face hidden behind the morning paper, a barrier as solid as the distance that had grown between them.

"Carlos," Emma began, her voice steady despite the sleepless night of turmoil. "We need to talk."

He lowered the paper slowly, his eyes locking onto hers, a faint smirk playing at the corners of his mouth as if he found the situation amusing. "About what?"

"About your late nights...the secretive phone calls," Emma said, her heart pounding in her chest like a drum. She watched his expression shift from feigned ignorance to something colder, more calculated.

"Emma, you're overthinking things," Carlos said smoothly, his tone condescendingly calm. "You're always getting worked up over nothing."

His words were like a knife wrapped in velvet, designed to soothe even as they cut deep. Emma felt the familiar sting of self-doubt, the insidious gaslighting that had slowly eroded her confidence.

"I'm not imagining it," she insisted, but her voice wavered, revealing the cracks in her resolve.

Carlos leaned forward, his brow furrowing in mock concern. "Emma, you've been so distant lately. Maybe you're the one hiding something."

His accusation hung in the air, a cloud of doubt that seeped into her, poisoning her thoughts. He reached out to touch her hand, but she pulled away, the gesture feeling like a betrayal.

"Stop it, Carlos. Just stop," Emma whispered, a tear slipping down her cheek. She saw the flash of victory in his eyes, confirming the painful truth she had been trying to avoid.

"Call your mother," Carlos said abruptly, standing up and brushing off any attempt at sympathy. "She always knows how to calm you down."

The door closed behind him with a soft click, the sound echoing in Emma's mind like a gunshot. Alone in the quiet kitchen, she wrapped her arms around herself, trying to hold onto whatever strength she had left.

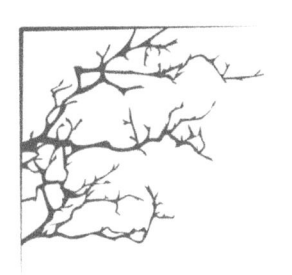

# Chapter 3

Emma's hands trembled slightly as she tucked a strand of hair behind her ear, the sensation of the smooth lock slipping through her fingers momentarily grounding her in the whirlwind of her thoughts. She leaned against the kitchen counter, the cold marble pressing into her back, a stark contrast to the warmth of the simmering pot on the stove. The aroma of sautéed garlic and onions filled the air, but Emma barely noticed, her mind elsewhere.

The phone buzzed on the kitchen counter, its vibrations cutting through the quiet, the screen flashing with a name Emma knew all too well: "Ma." She stared at it for a moment, her hand hovering over the phone as if it were some fragile thing that might shatter if she touched it. With a heavy sigh, she swiped to answer.

"Mama..." The word slipped out, brittle and broken, catching in her throat. She swallowed hard, trying to hold herself together. "I just... I don't know what to do anymore."

A brief silence followed, filled with the faint static of the call, then her mother's voice broke through, steady and no-nonsense as ever. "Emma, baby, you've gotta stop letting this man walk all over you. Enough is enough."

Emma bit down on her lip, her eyes burning as she sank onto the couch, pulling a cushion into her lap like it could somehow protect her from the truth. "I know, but..." Her voice faltered, barely a whisper. "What if I'm wrong? What if it's all in my head?"

Her mother's sigh came through the phone, long and weary, tinged with a familiar blend of love and frustration. "Emma, honey, you're not wrong. You've been second-guessing yourself for so long, you've forgotten what's real. This man—he's been making you doubt your own worth. You don't need to put up with that."

"I'm scared, Ma." Emma's voice cracked again, the admission dragging something heavy from her chest. "What if—what if he's really trying? What if I'm just overreacting?"

"You've always been the one giving, Emma. Always making excuses for him, trying to see the best. But look where it's gotten you." Martha's tone softened, but there was no missing the edge of urgency. "You've got more to think about than just him. You have a son. You have yourself."

The words hit Emma like a slap, her breath catching in her throat. She clutched the cushion tighter, her nails digging into the fabric. The truth was, she had known for a while now, deep down, that something had to change. But the fear—the fear of being alone, of making the wrong choice—kept her trapped, tethered to a life that no longer felt like hers.

"I don't know if I'm strong enough." The confession slipped out before she could stop it, her voice small, like a child's.

"Emma," her mother said, her voice gentle but firm. "You've always been strong. You just forgot. This isn't about whether he's trying or not. It's about how long you've been waiting, how long you've been losing yourself. Don't let him take any more from you."

Emma pressed her lips together, her eyes squeezing shut as her mother's words settled deep into her heart. She felt a flicker of something—something she hadn't felt in a long time. Not confidence, exactly, but resolve. A quiet, simmering resolve that began to replace the doubt gnawing at her.

"Okay, Ma," she breathed, the words soft but filled with the weight of a decision she wasn't sure she was ready to make. "I'll talk to him."

"Good," Martha said, her voice losing its sharpness. "But remember, talking isn't enough if nothing changes. You deserve more than what he's giving you, baby girl, and you're stronger than you think. Just remember that. Remember, you aren't alone in this, either. You have me and Jaxon.. Don't forget that."

Emma nodded, even though her mother couldn't see it, her chest tightening with both fear and relief. "I won't."

As the call ended, Emma sat there in the dim light of the living room, the phone still clutched in her hand, the cushion pulled tight against her chest. The silence that followed was deafening, but in it, she could hear the echoes of her mother's voice—the voice that had always been her lifeline, her anchor in moments like this. And for the first time in a long while, Emma allowed herself to imagine a life where she wasn't weighed down by fear and doubt, a life where she could finally breathe. She wasn't there yet, not by a long shot. But maybe, just maybe, she was on her way.

"That's my girl," Martha said, her voice softening, as if she could sense the tears welling up in Emma's eyes. "If you need me, no matter what time, day or night, I'll be there. I'm driving in now, and I'll be home in a few hours. "

Emma nodded, even though her mother couldn't see her, and after they hung up, she sat in silence for a long moment, the weight of the conversation settling on her shoulders. She glanced at her reflection in the kitchen window, seeing the hint of steel that had crept back into her green eyes.

The front door banged open with the familiar sound of Jaxon's arrival, snapping Emma out of her reverie. She quickly wiped her eyes and forced a smile as her son burst into the room, his school uniform disheveled and his hair sticking up in all directions.

"Hey Mom, what's for dinner?" Jaxon asked, his voice bright and full of the energy that only a sixteen-year-old could muster at the end of a long school day.

Emma ruffled his hair, feeling a pang of guilt at the thought of what her uncertainty might be doing to him. "Your favorite, spaghetti. It's almost ready, kiddo. Why don't you wash up?"

As Jaxon disappeared down the hallway, Emma returned to the stove, stirring the sauce with renewed focus. The rhythmic motion was soothing, a temporary distraction from the storm brewing in her mind. She heard Jaxon's voice in the distance, asking about Carlos, and her grip tightened on the wooden spoon, her knuckles whitening.

"Is he going to be home for dinner?" Jaxon asked.

"Maybe," she replied, her voice catching in her throat as she forced the words out. "He's always busy with work, honey."

Jaxon's response was lost in the clatter of dishes as Emma set the table, arranging the silverware with the same precision she applied to everything else in her life—a desperate attempt to maintain control in a situation where she felt anything but.

Later, as they sat down to eat, the silence between them was heavy, the usual chatter about school and friends reduced to monosyllabic answers. Emma tried to engage, but her mind was miles away, tangled in the web of suspicions and fears that had kept her up at night.

After dinner, Jaxon retreated to his homework, and Emma found herself standing alone in the laundry room, folding clothes with mechanical precision. The soft hum of the washing machine was the only sound, its steady rhythm a counterpoint to the chaos in her mind. She paused, a pair of Jaxon's socks in her hands, and stared blankly at the wall, her thoughts spinning.

The doorbell rang, jolting her out of her trance. She hesitated for a moment, her heart skipping a beat, before she wiped her hands on a dishtowel and went to answer it.

Rachel stood on the doorstep, her face a mix of concern and uncertainty. "Hey, Em. I was in the neighborhood and thought I'd check in on you."

Emma forced a smile, stepping aside to let her friend in. "Thanks, Rach. Come in."

They settled on the couch, the same one where Emma had sat earlier, clutching her phone like a lifeline. Rachel's presence was comforting, but it also brought the reality of the situation crashing back down on her.

"You seemed off at work today," Rachel said gently, her eyes searching Emma's face. "Is everything okay?"

The words tumbled out of Emma before she could stop them, a torrent of emotions and fears that she had kept bottled up for too long. She spoke of the late nights, the phone calls, the growing distance between her and Carlos. By the time she finished, her voice was hoarse, and tears had begun to slip down her cheeks.

Rachel reached out and took Emma's hand, her grip firm and reassuring. "Emma, you need to trust your gut. If you feel like something's wrong, you have to find out the truth. You owe that to yourself and Jaxon."

Emma nodded, wiping her eyes with the back of her hand. "I'm just... I'm terrified, Rach. What if I'm wrong? What if confronting him makes everything worse?"

Rachel's gaze was steady, her voice calm. "And what if you're right? You can't keep living in limbo, Em. Whatever happens, you'll get through it. And you won't be alone. Can I help with anything?"

"No, no, I'll be ok. Thanks though Rach, really. It means a lot to me that you are here for me to vent to."

Emma looked at her friend, seeing the truth in her words, and felt a wave of resolve wash over her. It wasn't much, just a spark, but it was enough to start rekindling the fire she thought she had lost.

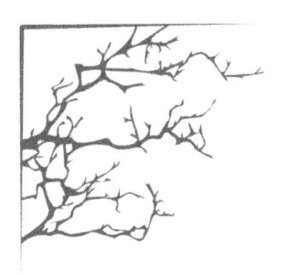

# Chapter 4

Emma stood in the dim hallway, the coolness of the wooden floor pressing against her bare feet as she stared down at the crumpled receipts clutched in her trembling hand. The thin papers, smudged with ink from countless re-reads, were evidence enough—hotel stays, dinners for two. Her fingers tightened, crinkling the receipts further as the reality of Carlos's deceit closed in around her like a vice. The house, usually a sanctuary, now felt like a suffocating cage.

Downstairs, the muffled sound of the TV barely registered through the thick fog of her thoughts. Carlos's laughter drifted up to her, a hollow, mocking echo that cut through the silence. It was a sound that once filled her with warmth, but now it was laced with a bitterness that made her stomach turn. How long had she been blind to the truth? How long had he been crafting these lies, thinking she would never notice?

The creak of the floorboards behind her made Emma turn, her heart lurching. Jaxon stood in the doorway; his tall, lanky frame still unsteady with sleep. His dark hair, tousled from bed, fell into his eyes as he rubbed them, trying to focus on his mother.

"Mom? What are you doing?" His voice was soft, concerned, cutting through her spiraling thoughts. "Are you okay?"

Emma's breath hitched. She forced a smile, one that didn't reach her eyes, and nodded, tucking the receipts behind her back. "I'm fine, Jax," she lied, her voice barely above a whisper. "Go back to bed, sweetheart."

But Jaxon didn't move. His eyes, so much like hers, searched her face, picking up on the tension she tried to hide. "Mom...You sure? You look... upset. What is it?"

She hesitated, fighting the urge to break down in front of him. Instead, she reached out, brushing his hair back from his forehead, her touch lingering a moment longer than usual. "I promise, it's nothing you need to worry about. Just... go back to sleep, okay?"

Jaxon studied her for a moment longer before nodding slowly. "Okay," he mumbled, turning back toward his room. But the worry in his eyes told her he wasn't convinced.

Emma watched him hesitate and look back before he disappeared down the hall. Her heart aching with the knowledge that she could no longer shield him from the storm brewing in their lives. As soon as his door clicked shut, her facade crumbled. She clutched the receipts tighter, feeling the sharp edges of her fingernails dig through the papers and into her palm.

She couldn't let this continue—not for Jaxon's sake, not for her own. Her body, still trembling, carried her down the stairs. Each step felt heavier, the weight of what she was about to do pressing down on her with relentless force. When she reached the living room, Carlos barely looked up from the television, his attention absorbed in the screen.

"Carlos," she said, her voice steadier than she felt, as she stepped into the room. He glanced up, a casual smile on his face that faltered when he saw her expression.

"What's up?" he asked, muting the TV. His eyes flicked to the papers in her hand, the color draining from his face as he realized what she held.

Emma said nothing at first, just walked over to the coffee table and laid the receipts down. One by one, she spread them out—hotel bookings, expensive dinners, purchases that couldn't be explained away. Each one was a nail in the coffin of their marriage.

Carlos stared at them, his jaw tightening. "You've been going through my things?" His voice was low, a dangerous edge to it that made Emma's heart race, but she didn't back down.

"Yes, these were in your jeans pockets. I was emptying them to wash. " she replied, her voice cold. "I think you owe me an explanation."

The tension in the room crackled like static. Carlos's hands clenched into fists, his eyes narrowing as he looked back at her. For a moment, neither of them moved. Then, without a word, he grabbed the papers and his jacket and stormed out of the house, the door slamming behind him with a force that rattled the walls.

Emma stood there, the echoes of the door reverberating in her chest. She felt a strange mix of relief and dread—relief that the confrontation had finally happened, and dread for what would come next. The silence in the house was deafening, pressing in on her from all sides.

THE NEXT MORNING, AS Emma sat at the kitchen table on a video chat with Martha, the remnants of evidence of Carlos's betrayal lay spread out before her. Emma's usually steady hands shook as she picked up one of the many unopened credit card statement envelopes. She slid her nail under the flap, her movements deliberate, almost ritualistic, as if she were unveiling the full extent of the damage for the first time.

Emma sat across from her mother on the screen, her face pale and drawn, her eyes swollen from the tears she'd been holding back all evening. She watched her mother's reaction, every small twitch of her mouth, every flicker in her eyes. "Mama, he didn't come home last night. I don't know what to do. I went through his desk and found letters written in Spanish, pictures of a girl, all of the credit card statements. Am I wrong for searching for things? Should I open the bills?" Emma asked her mother. "Yes, open them and see what kind of charges are there. They are all in your name aren't they?" Martha asked. Emma nodded. "Yes, he has no credit at all. I am going to send you copies, that way I have somewhere safe to keep them... just in case." Emma said with glistening eyes.

"Oh, baby girl..." Martha's voice trembled as she scanned the photos of the girl, the letters and images of credit card statements sent to her by text. The numbers, the dates, the names—they painted a picture more damning than any words could. "This... this is worse than I thought. What on earth..."

Emma said nothing, just stared at the table, her hands clenched in her lap. She felt numb, as if the enormity of what she'd uncovered was too much to process all at once. The betrayal wasn't just emotional—it was financial, personal, deep. Carlos had torn apart the life they'd built, brick by brick, lie by lie.

Martha looked up, her eyes locking onto Emma's. "He's been lying to you about everything," she said, her voice hardening with anger. "And you need to protect yourself and Jaxon. First thing we should do is get someone to translate these letters, figure out who this woman is and decide how to handle this."

"Oh mama, what am I going to do?" Emma cried. "We will figure it out, let's get things in order so we have an idea on what needs to happen first though." Martha said.

After hanging up the phone, Emma sat for a long moment, letting the weight of what lay ahead settle over her. The numbness that had been her constant companion for months was beginning to lift, replaced by a slow-burning anger and determination. She wasn't entirely sure where the strength was coming from, but it was there, pushing her forward. Her mind raced through the details she'd need to handle—the divorce attorney, the meeting with Carlos, and, eventually, the confrontation with "B," the woman she'd only recently discovered. There was no use pretending anymore. The late nights, the secret phone calls, the growing distance between them—it all pointed to the same devastating truth. He wasn't just pulling away from their marriage; he had already left in every way that mattered.

Emma felt a surge of anger, not the raw, explosive kind, but something colder, more calculated. Carlos had underestimated her. He probably thought she would quietly accept his lies, that she would stay for the sake of their son, Jaxon, or out of fear of what divorce might mean for their already precarious financial situation. But he was about to learn how wrong he'd been.

Jaxon. The thought of her son caused a lump to rise in her throat. She had to be strong for him, no matter how ugly things got. He was only seven, old enough to sense the tension but too young to understand the complexity of what was happening. Emma needed to protect him from as much of the fallout as she could, but she couldn't protect him by staying in a marriage that was crumbling from the inside out. The best thing she could do for him now was to show him what strength looked like—even if it meant walking away.

She rose from the couch, the cushion falling to the floor, and paced the living room, her mind spinning with possibilities. She would need to gather evidence—texts, emails, whatever she could find that proved Carlos's infidelity. If he wanted to play dirty, she would have to be ready. She wasn't naïve enough to believe that this would be a clean break. Carlos wouldn't make it easy.

Her heart clenched as she thought of the confrontation with him. Carlos had a temper, and the idea of standing face to face with him, accusing him of betrayal, made her stomach churn. But this time, she wouldn't back down. She couldn't. She would confront him, and she would leave. She would take Jaxon and start over, no matter how terrifying the prospect seemed right now.

Emma walked to the window, staring out at the sun-bathed street. In the reflection, she barely recognized herself—the worry lines on her face, the exhaustion in her eyes, the weight of years spent holding together a life that had been slipping through her fingers. But something new glimmered in her reflection too—resolve.

With a deep breath, she turned away from the window and grabbed her phone. The first step was to call a lawyer. Emma pulled up a number she had saved weeks ago but hadn't yet dared to use.

Her finger hovered over the call button. "For Jaxon," she whispered to herself, steeling her resolve. Then she pressed the button, and as the phone rang, she felt the shift inside her—the quiet, powerful realization that she wasn't going to be a victim anymore.

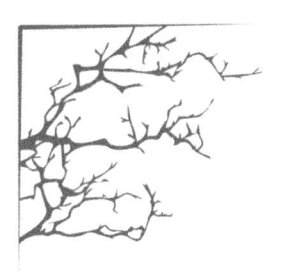

# Chapter 5

That evening, the steady simmer of a pot on the stove filled the kitchen with the rich, comforting aroma of beef stew. It hung in the air, clinging to the walls like a memory, but for Emma, the once-familiar scent brought no solace. She stood over the pot, wooden spoon in hand, stirring absently as if the motion itself might fill the hollow space inside her. Cooking, which had once been her refuge, was now just a mindless routine, a way to keep her hands busy and avoid confronting the storm brewing inside her.

Outside, the sun dipped below the horizon, long shadows creeping across the kitchen floor as dusk settled in. The ticking of the clock seemed louder than usual, each second dragging on, punctuating the silence that had settled over the house like a thick, suffocating fog. The light in the room dimmed, casting everything in shades of gray, reflecting the coldness that had seeped into her heart.

The lawyer gave her some good advice, gather up all of the evidence she could find. Phone numbers, screen shots of the texts from his phone, credit card receipts, every single thing she could gather. It would strengthen her case, forcing him to take financial responsibility for the debt he has created.

Her hands moved mechanically—chopping vegetables, adjusting the heat—but her mind was far away. As the knife sliced through the carrots, Emma imagined it cutting through more than just produce. Each chop felt like a symbolic act, a way of tearing through the layers of lies that had wrapped themselves around her life. The steady rhythm of the blade striking the cutting board became a silent release for the anger she kept bottled up, anger that simmered just beneath the surface, waiting for the right moment to spill over.

She glanced at the pot, watching the stew bubble, but instead of the satisfaction she used to feel when preparing a meal for her family, there was only a gnawing emptiness. The warmth of the kitchen couldn't thaw the icy knot of resentment in her chest. Every turn of the burner dial felt like the tightening of the screws in her imagined revenge against Carlos. She pictured him suffering, just as she had, though she kept her hands steady, her face composed. She couldn't let the anger show. Not yet.

In the growing darkness, Emma could almost hear the echoes of the life she'd once had in this very room—the quiet laughter, the easy conversations, the sense of togetherness that now seemed so distant. The ticking clock filled the silence where those moments had once been, and she realized how far she and Carlos had drifted. Now, there was only this—empty rituals and the suffocating weight of things left unsaid.

She paused, the spoon hovering over the pot as steam rose, curling in the dim light. A sigh escaped her, soft but heavy. The decision she had made earlier that day lingered in the back of her mind, a decision that felt both terrifying and liberating. The confrontation was inevitable. The thought sent a shiver of anxiety through her, but at least it would end the uncertainty, the constant doubt gnawing at her sanity.

She wasn't afraid anymore—not of Carlos, not of the fallout that would follow. As the stew continued to simmer, filling the room with warmth and fragrance, she realized that she wasn't cooking for him tonight. This meal, like the rest of her life, was hers now. She would no longer live in his shadow, no longer pretend that everything was fine.

The sharp clatter of the knife as it dropped onto the counter snapped her out of her thoughts. For the first time in months, she took a deep, steadying breath. The quiet, she knew, would soon be shattered by the confrontation that was coming. But for now, she allowed herself this moment of stillness, this brief pause before the storm.

The creak of the front door broke her reverie, and Emma stiffened. Carlos walked in, his presence heavy and imposing, breaking the fragile silence. He tossed his briefcase to the floor with a careless thud, the sound punctuating the tension that hung between them.

"Hey, babe," he said casually, planting a quick, perfunctory kiss on her cheek before heading to the fridge. He is completely oblivious to the turmoil swirling just beneath the surface, acting perfectly normal.

The familiar scent of his cheap cologne and the faint, unmistakable tang of whiskey wafted towards her, mixing with the stew in a nauseating blend. Emma watched him as he poured himself a drink, her stomach churning. How could he not see it? How could he be so blind to the fracture in their marriage, the abyss that had opened up between them?

"Dinner's almost ready," Emma said, her voice flat, devoid of any warmth. She set the pot of stew on the table with deliberate precision, the clink of dishes cutting through the thick silence. "Jaxon, dinner's ready." Carlos called out to the boy.

Jaxon took several long-legged strides and arrived at the table, noticing the tension in the air, he watched as his mother and Carlos did a silent dance of wills across the table.

They sat down to eat, the space between them at the table feeling like a chasm, a physical representation of how far apart they had grown. Emma's spoon trembled slightly in her hand; her grip unsteady as her mind raced. She thought about the confrontation, about what would happen when she finally told him she knew. The rush of relief she imagined felt distant, drowned out by the fear of what would come next—how it would unravel their lives, how it would affect Jaxon.

The image of the woman in the photograph flickered in her mind, taunting her. Ignorance isn't bliss—it's a slow poison, she thought, her chest tightening with the weight of her secret. But the fear of what lay beyond this revelation, of how their family might fall apart, kept her paralyzed.

They ate in silence, the tension thickening with each bite. Emma's resolve wavered. She could feel the truth pressing against her lips, begging to be set free, but tonight wasn't the night. Tonight, she would keep the peace, maintain the fragile facade of normalcy. For Jaxon. For herself.

Later, as they cleared the table and retreated to their separate corners of the house, Emma felt the weight of that photograph more acutely than ever. It seemed to hang over her, an accusation she couldn't ignore. Tomorrow, she told herself, steeling her nerves. Tomorrow, I'll face the truth.

But for tonight, she would allow herself the fleeting comfort of denial, a final moment of quiet before everything came crashing down.

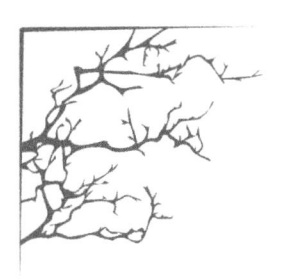

# Chapter 6

Three days passed in a blur of sleepless nights and tearful conversations with her mother, Martha. She had tried so hard to push her suspicions aside, but the more she thought about it, the more certain she became that Carlos was cheating on her. It was there in the way he looked at her—or rather, didn't look at her. In the way he always seemed to be somewhere else, even when they were in the same room.

"You deserve better, baby girl," Martha had said during their last call, her voice thick with anguish. "You're strong enough to leave him. I know you are."

But was she? Was she really strong enough to walk away from the only life she'd ever known? The life she'd built with her own two hands?

As she sits across from Carlos at the dinner table, the silence between them as suffocating as ever, Emma knows she can no longer stay silent. She has to know the truth—whatever the cost may be.

"Carlos, I won't live like this anymore," she says, her voice shaking slightly.

He looks up from his plate, brow furrowed in concern. "Is everything alright, mi amor?"

"No," she says, her voice gaining strength with each word. "I've been thinking a lot lately, and I... I think we have some issues we need to address."

Carlos's expression darkens, and he sets down his fork with a clatter. "What's going on, Emma? Are you having some kind of episode again?"

Anger and hurt well up inside her, but she pushes them down. "Don't do that, Carlos. Don't you dare try to gaslight me and make this about me."

"Then what is it, Emma? What have I done now to upset you?" he asks, feigning innocence.

"It's not about what you've done," she spits out. "It's about what you haven't done. You're always busy with work or 'client dinners,' but when I need you, you're nowhere to be found! You don't even come home every night."

Carlos sighs, rubbing his temples in mock frustration. "This again, Emma? I've told you a million times, my job is demanding. I work late nights and attend dinners because I need to provide for this family!"

"Provide for this family? Is that all I am to you? A person you need to 'provide' for?" The words tumble out before she can stop them, and she immediately regrets them.

Carlos's eyes narrow, and she braces herself for the explosion she knows is coming. But instead, he laughs—a cold, humorless laugh that chills her to the bone.

"You are unbelievable, you know that? I'm out there busting my ass to give you and this family everything we could ever want, and this is the thanks I get? Accusations and hysterics?"

He pushes his chair back from the table, causing it to screech loudly against the hardwood floor.

"I've had enough of this." He turns and storms out of the room, slamming the door behind him, leaving her alone with her jumbled thoughts and swirling emotions.

Tears welling up in her eyes, Emma stares at the untouched dinner, her appetite now gone. She knows this argument was different. There's no coming back from this one. She's finally had enough. Tonight, she'll pack her things and leave. She's not living like this anymore.

As she rises from the table, she catches a glimpse of her reflection in the window. In the darkened glass, she sees not only her own reflection but a distorted image of Carlos standing in the hallway, watching her every move.

THE MID-MORNING SUN spilled through the half-open blinds, casting long, slender shadows across the kitchen's tiled floor. Emma stood at the sink; her hands submerged in warm, sudsy water as she scrubbed at a stubborn stain on a breakfast plate. A steady rhythm of chores had always been her ballast against life's unpredictable currents. Her phone buzzed with the benign urgency of a daily reminder, but it was Carlos's screen that caught her eye from where it lay discarded on the counter.

A message preview flashed briefly before the screen dimmed, the words "Can't wait to see you again" etching themselves into her retinas. A prickling sensation crawled up her spine, her nurturing green eyes narrowing in suspicion. Emma glanced over her shoulder, ensuring the silence of the house affirmed her solitude. She reached for the device with a damp hand, hesitating only for a moment before drying her fingers on the apron tied around her waist and unlocking the phone with a swipe.

Curiosity coiled tightly within her, mingled with an anxiety that tasted sour at the back of her throat. The message was from a number not saved in his contacts, and the informality of the words gnawed at her like a warning. Should she confront Carlos? Demand answers from those hard, dark eyes that could turn from tender to icy in a heartbeat? The thought of his charm unraveling into aggression made her stomach churn.

But Emma couldn't unsee the message, couldn't unknow the seed of doubt now planted. With a breath that felt more like surrender than resolve, she delved deeper. Swiping through Carlos's messages felt like peeling back layers of deceit, each one a new cut against the fabric of their life together.

Then she found them—messages laced with longing, threaded with intimacy meant for another. There were photos too, images that seared themselves into her memory: the curve of a stranger's smile, the familiarity of Carlos's touch upon someone else's skin. Each pixelated betrayal twisted the knife a little deeper, confirming what the first message had only hinted at.

Emma's heart sank, a heavy stone dropped into the pit of her being. She stood motionless, the phone's glow casting a pallid light on her face. In the reflection of the darkened screen, she caught a glimpse of herself—a woman fraying at the edges, her warmth giving way to the weariness that now defined her features.

She looked away, the realization of the extent of Carlos's infidelity settling in. The evidence was irrefutable, stark against the backdrop of their seemingly ordinary life. It was there, in the quiet of the kitchen, that Emma understood the full weight of the truth she now held in her trembling hands.

The still air of the living room was suddenly heavy, charged with tension as Emma stood before Carlos. Her hands trembled, clutching the phone like a damning piece of evidence. She could feel her heart pounding in her chest, the rhythmic thuds echoing her turmoil.

"Carlos," she began, her voice barely more than a whisper, betraying the storm within. "Who is she?"

He looked up from his newspaper, his brows knitting together in feigned confusion.

"Who's who, Em?" His casual tone was a sharp contrast to the palpable anxiety that radiated from Emma.

"Don't play dumb!" The words erupted from her, louder and fiercer than she intended. "I saw your messages, the pictures... the naked pictures of you, of her. How could you?"

Carlos's eyes narrowed, a flicker of something dark crossing his face before his expression smoothed into practiced innocence.

"I have no idea what you're talking about," he said, setting the newspaper aside with calculated nonchalance.

"Stop lying to me!" Emma cried out, her resolve crumbling under the weight of her emotions. She thrust the phone towards him, the incriminating texts and images glaring back at them both. "This. This is what I'm talking about!"

There was an excruciating pause where only the ticking of the wall clock filled the void between them. Then, finally cornered, Carlos let out a sigh and his shoulders slumped—a gesture of defeat.

"Why are you going through my phone? Emma, Em, look, it was nothing—just a stupid mistake," he muttered, reaching for a thread of remorse that didn't quite reach his eyes. Taking the phone from her, he started to walk away.

"Nothing?" The word tasted bitter on Emma's tongue, acrid with betrayal. "You call this nothing?" Her voice cracked with a pain so deep, it seemed to bleed through the walls of the room.

Carlos shifted forward, the charm that once drew her in now repelling her like opposing magnets. "You're always working, Em. You are never around," he said, his words laced with an accusation that struck her like a slap.

"Is that supposed to justify what you did? What you are still doing?" Emma felt the rage bubbling up inside her, fighting against the sorrow that sought to drown her. "Am I to blame for your wandering eye? For your lies?"

His attempt to downplay his infidelity, to make her complicit in his deceit, only fueled the fire of her indignation. Every excuse he offered was a mirror reflecting back her deepest insecurities, suggesting that her dedication—to their son, to her work, to the life they'd built—was somehow the root of his straying.

"Emma, you know how hard it's been for me," Carlos continued, his tone softening in a ploy for sympathy. "I needed... I needed someone."

"Needed someone?" Emma echoed hollowly, her mind reeling. "And what about what I needed? What about our marriage? I am home every single night, waiting for you. I— I am always waiting for you."

The room seemed to close in on her, the walls echoing her escalating heartbeat. She searched Carlos's face for a sign of the man she married, but all she found was a stranger wearing his skin, his features twisting into a mask of self-pity and deflection.

Her own worth, once grounded in the love they shared, now felt like it was being called into question by the very person who vowed to uphold it. Emma's nurturing nature, her empathy—all of it seemed to crumble under the insidious suggestion that she was responsible for his failings.

"Your mistakes are not my fault," Emma stated, her voice steadier now, fortified by the shards of her shattered trust. "I won't let you put that on me, Carlos. Not anymore."

As she stood there, the woman with shoulder-length blonde hair and resilient green eyes, she realized that the warmth she once offered so freely had boundaries—and Carlos had just crossed them.

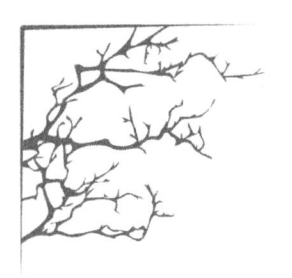

# Chapter 7

The silence that followed her declaration felt as cold and unforgiving as the steel of a knife edge. Emma's breath came in short, sharp intakes, slicing through the thick air between them. Carlos stood motionless, his eyes narrowing, calculating, as if he was plotting his next move in a twisted game only he understood.

Emma's gaze flickered away from him, traveling to the framed photograph on the mantelpiece—their small family smiling, a lie captured in pixels and glass. A sickening churn twisted her stomach, her mind awash with the confrontation's aftermath. Had she been wrong to confront him? What would this rupture mean for their son Jaxon, who looked to both of them for stability?

Her fingers brushed against her temple, an attempt to soothe the throbbing headache that pulsed in time with her racing heart. The doubts crept in like insidious shadows, whispering that perhaps ignorance would have been bliss. But the darkness couldn't unwrite the truth of Carlos's betrayal scrawled in digital ink.

"Em, don't. Don't do this," Carlos's voice broke through her spiraling thoughts, but it no longer held the same sway. "We can work it out, for Jax."

"Work it out?" she murmured, the words tasting like ash. Her insecurities clawed at her, the familiar specter of unworthiness that had haunted her since childhood. Was she so undeserving of fidelity, of respect? No. This wasn't about her shortcomings; this was about Carlos's inability to value their vows.

Emma took a moment to close her eyes and find the inner strength that had always been present, even when it was hard to hear over the doubts in her mind. She thought of Jaxon, her son with his striking dark locks and intense hazel gaze, who deserved a life free from the toxic effects of deceit.

"Jaxon needs more than empty promises," she said, her voice gaining strength as she opened her eyes and faced Carlos once again. "He needs honesty, integrity... things you've shown you're not capable of providing and haven't been for a long time."

Carlos's lips parted, but no sound emerged. He was unaccustomed to this version of Emma, the one who wielded her words with precision rather than comfort.

"Whatever happens next," she continued, the weight of her decision anchoring her resolve, "I'm doing it for me, for Jaxon. We deserve better, and I won't let your mistakes define our future."

In that moment, the woman who spent her life healing others decided to apply her care to the wounds within her own family, beginning with excising the infection of deceit. Emma Dawson, with her nurturing heart and newfound fortitude, stepped out of the shadow of her insecurities and into the light of her own worth.

Emma's fingers trembled as she dialed the familiar number, her heart thudding against her ribs in a rhythm that spelled trepidation. The phone emitted a trill before the line clicked, and Martha's voice, strong and immediate, filled the silence.

"Ma," Emma began, the single word a dam ready to burst.

"Emma, darling, what's happened?" Martha's tone shifted from warmth to alertness, a testament to her protective instincts.

Sitting at the kitchen table, Emma held the phone like a lifeline, the world outside the window reduced to a blur as she recounted the day's revelations. She spoke of the text messages, the confrontation with Carlos, the crippling uncertainty that now enveloped her.

Martha listened without interruption, the soft exhale of her breath over the line a steady presence. When Emma's words finally dwindled to a choked sob, Martha's response was immediate.

"Sweetheart, you're stronger than you realize," Martha said firmly. "You've weathered storms before, and this—this betrayal is no different."

Emma's trembling fingers reach out to trace the edges of her son's photo, her eyes brimming with tears as she imagines his smiling face. But Martha's words snap her back to reality, her grip tightening on the phone as she feels a surge of fear and determination wash over her.

"Jaxon needs you, Emma. You are his compass, his only hope in this darkness," Martha's voice crackles through the line, each word punctuated with a fierce determination that ignites a fire within Emma's soul. "You must steer both of you away from harm. You need to set the example for his future, you are the only parent he has."

A wave of emotion crashes over Emma, her heart racing with a mix of fear and courage as she realizes what she must do to protect her son. With newfound strength, she sets her jaw and vows to be the unwavering strength that Jaxon needs in this stormy sea of life.

"Leaving Carlos... it's not just about me, it's..." Emma's voice trailed off.

"About what's healthy for Jaxon too. He needs a stable environment, not one filled with deceit. You both do." Martha's words were a balm, soothing yet sparking a flame within Emma.

"I know. Thank you for reminding me, Mama," Emma said, a flicker of determination igniting in her green eyes.

"Remember who you are, baby girl, and the rest will follow," Martha replied before the call ended, leaving Emma wrapped in the quiet hush of the house.

In the stillness, Emma contemplated the gravity of staying or leaving. Staying meant preserving the façade of a family for Jaxon, but at what cost? Her mind conjured up images of strained dinners, forced smiles, and a boy caught between the crossfire of silent resentments.

Leaving, on the other hand, painted an uncertain picture, a blank canvas that was both terrifying and liberating. Could she rebuild their lives from the ashes of broken trust? Would Jaxon understand the reasons behind uprooting his sense of normalcy?

Each thought spiraled, entwining with fears and hopes, until Emma closed her eyes, taking in a deep, steadying breath. She envisioned a future where honesty laid the foundation, where she could look at herself—and Jaxon—with pride for having the courage to choose a path that led towards healing rather than festering wounds.

She reached out, her fingers brushing against the cool surface of Jaxon's photograph. Inside that frame lay the eyes of innocence the eyes of her son's perspective, unmarred by adult complications. For him, for that innocence, Emma knew what she needed to do.

Her decision, crystallizing amidst the chaos, anchored her. She would carve out a space free from lies, a sanctuary for her and Jaxon to grow, to heal, to rediscover the strength that had always pulsed within her.

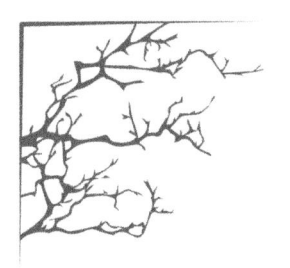

# Chapter 8

The air grew thick with newfound resolve as Emma Dawson, ensnared in the throes of betrayal, nestled close to the beating heart of her maternal instinct, ready to shield her cub from the storm that raged just beyond their door.

Emma paced the kitchen, each step echoing like a metronome counting down to an inevitable confrontation. The patterned tiles beneath her feet blurred as tears threatened to spill, but Emma blinked them back with a stubborn fierceness. She couldn't let her resolve crumble—not now, when the stakes were so high. The house felt eerily silent, a stark backdrop to the cacophony of emotions that clashed within her.

"Keep it together, Emma," she whispered to herself, clutching the edge of the sink for support. Her reflection in the window above was a ghostly specter, the early evening light casting shadows across her determined features.

The sense of duty that had always been her compass now warred with the raw pain of betrayal. Carlos's infidelity wasn't just a wound; it was a systematic erosion of trust, a relentless tide that had swept away the foundations of their marriage.

And yet, the thought of tearing Jaxon's world apart wrenched at her insides. The image of his joyful smile, so carefree and untainted, fueled her turmoil. How could she maintain the façade of a happy family when every fiber of her being screamed in protest?

But Emma Dawson was no longer the woman who would retreat into the shadows, shying away from conflict. The evidence of Carlos's deceit, once a leaden weight, now galvanized her spirit. She knew what must be done.

Steeling herself, she grabbed her phone, her thumbs hovering over the screen. This time, there would be no room for excuses or manipulations. She typed out a message to Carlos, concise and unyielding.

"Carlos, we need to finish this discussion. Tonight, when you get home. It's important."

Sent. The word flashed up briefly, an electronic verdict that sealed her intent.

Emma set the phone down, her gaze shifting to the picture of them on the wall—smiling, oblivious to the fractures that would soon cleave through their pretense of harmony. The frame seemed to mock her; a tangible reminder of happier times now tainted by lies.

She would confront him, yes, but not as the hurt partner seeking answers. This time, she would be the architect of her destiny, laying down the blueprints of a future where respect and honesty were non-negotiable. One where she could reclaim her self-worth from the ashes of deception.

In her mind's eye, she saw herself standing tall, resolute against the storm of Carlos's defenses. He would try to charm, to cajole, to shift blame—but Emma would not waver. She imagined her words cutting through his excuses, clear and sharp as shards of glass.

"Enough," she muttered under her breath, gripping the back of a chair. "No fucking more."

The setting sun cast long shadows across the room, painting the walls with hues of fading light. In that dimming glow, Emma found her clarity. She would draw the line, forge a boundary that Carlos could not cross.

It was time to salvage what remained—to build something new, not just for her sake, but for Jaxon's as well. A life free from the suffocating grip of falsehoods and manipulation.

As darkness crept into the corners of the room, a sense of purpose filled Emma to her core. Tonight, she would face Carlos—and whatever came next—with the full force of her newfound conviction.

Emma's hands were steady as she entered the living room where Carlos sat, his gaze fixed on the television screen. The ambient noise of some forgettable sitcom was a stark contrast to the tumultuous storm raging within her. She stepped in front of the TV, blocking his view, her shadow merging with the images flickering across the screen.

"Carlos," she said, her voice resolute, "we need to talk about what you are doing to this family."

He looked up at her, irritation flashing across his face before settling into a mask of feigned innocence.

"Oh my god, now what, Em?" he asked, rolling his eyes and attempting to skirt around the palpable tension.

"I am sick of all of this, sick of your lies," she replied, not taking the bait. "Sick of your cheating and sick of the disrespect. I know everything, you already know I do."

Carlos's eyes narrowed, a subtle shift from charm to menace as he realized the gravity of her words. He stood up, trying to loom over her, but Emma didn't flinch. She stood her ground, feeling an unexpected surge of power.

"Look, Emma—" he started, but she cut him off.

"No, you look," she interjected, her voice rising in force. "I have been accommodating, understanding, and forgiving. But there is a line, and you've crossed it. Repeatedly."

"Em, I—"

"That's enough of your fucking shit!" Emma's interruption sliced through his excuses. "This isn't about me needing answers or reassurance or even me being jealous, I'm not. This is about you respecting me, respecting my son, and the life we built together."

Carlos's expression faltered, his usual tactics crumbling under her assertive stance. "But Emma, I love you, you know that." He pleaded; his voice laced with desperation.

"Love isn't deceitful. Love doesn't hide behind lies or seek solace in someone else's arms," she countered, the realization of her own value igniting within her. "From now on, if you want this to work—if you want any part in my future or Jaxon's—you will respect the boundaries I set."

The air crackled with tension as they faced each other, an invisible chasm widening between them. Emma could see the conflict in Carlos's eyes, the struggle between conceding to her demands and fighting to maintain control.

"Emma, don't try to control me. That won't happen, I am the man of the house, and I won't be undermined." Carlos' voice was even but firm.

"You can either knock off this single man behavior or you can leave. There is no in between. Is that clear?" Emma demanded, her heartbeat echoing in her ears like the pounding of a drum.

"Crystal," Carlos said, his voice barely above a whisper, the weight of her conviction pressing down on him.

They remained locked in a silent battle, neither willing to break eye contact first. It was a standoff charged with the energy of unspoken ultimatums and the harsh reality of their fractured relationship.

As the silence stretched on, Emma felt something shift inside her. The woman who once tread lightly around Carlos's moods now commanded the space with an unwavering presence. The chapter of doubts and self-deprecation was closing, giving way to the narrative of a woman reclaiming her agency, her self-worth crystallizing with each passing second.

"Good," she said finally, breaking the silence. "Then we understand each other."

She turned away from Carlos, leaving him standing amidst the shards of his shattered facade. As she strode towards the doorway, Emma knew that this was the defining moment in their turbulent story. She had finally found her voice, one of courage, self-respect, and unbreakable strength.

The sunlight burst through the windows, illuminating the kitchen with a newfound determination. The storm may still rage outside, but Emma Dawson emerged from the shadows with a fierce resolve to weather it all.

Her fingers wrapped tightly around the door knob, her grip unwavering like a steel vice. In that moment, the truth would be exposed. She was no longer just a character in Carlos's twisted narrative.

He came up behind her almost like he was stalking his prey. Carlos's smirk evaporated, replaced by a cold, hard mask. "You don't just walk away from me, Emma. No one leaves me."

"Watch me," she retorted, her voice shaking but defiant. "I've been writing myself into your twisted story for too long, but not anymore. I'm taking back my life, my choices, my—"

Carlos sneered down at her as she stood tall before him. "That's right, Emma," he taunted with a wicked grin. "Keep talking and telling yourself that. Just remember, you're nothing without me."

A wave of fear washed over Emma's heart, but she refused to let him see it—not anymore. With every ounce of strength within her, she lifted her chin and locked eyes with him.

"Maybe you're right, Carlos. Maybe I've been nothing more than a pawn in your sick game. But I'm done being a character in your story. Effective immediately, I quit. From this moment on, I am done being a puppet in your story."

Carlos slept in their bed that night. Emma slept in the spare room across from Jaxon's. She didn't hear him get up and leave, she didn't know when he left. Maybe he went to her. She wasn't sure what to do now.

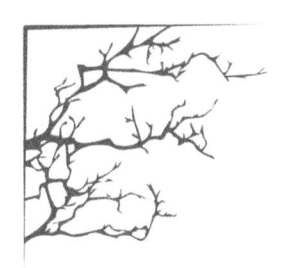

## Chapter 9

Saturday morning, an anger like Emma had never known jolted her from her fitful sleep. It surged through her veins like wildfire, obliterating the last remnants of uncertainty. Her chest felt tight with rage, and her trembling fingers could barely keep a grip on the phone as she dialed the familiar number. Her breath came out in short, ragged bursts, her heart pounding as if her body were preparing for a battle long overdue.

"Mama," she said, her voice trembling, though not from fear this time—no, it was from the barely restrained fury that coursed through her. "I need your help."

Martha's voice came through almost instantly, warm but laced with concern. "What do you need, baby girl?" There was a slight pause, as if Martha could sense something heavy looming between them. "What's wrong?"

Emma clenched her jaw, blinking away the hot tears threatening to fall. She'd been strong for too long—too long putting her pain aside for the sake of keeping things together. But now, it was all unraveling. "Carlos... he... he cheated on me again," she choked out, the words spilling like venom from her lips. The admission, though cathartic, cut her to the core, each word hammering the betrayal deeper into her chest.

Martha's sharp intake of breath cut through the line, her tone shifting from gentle concern to righteous anger. "That son of a fucking bitch. Emma, I knew it. I never trusted that man from the start. Honey, I'm so damn sorry you have to go through this." Her mother's fierce protectiveness radiated through the phone, wrapping Emma in a sense of comfort she hadn't realized she so desperately needed.

Emma let out a shaky breath, wiping at the tears streaming down her cheeks. She could feel the dam inside her breaking, years of pent-up emotions—betrayal, hurt, fear—all spilling out at once. "I don't know what to do, Ma," she whispered, her voice thick with exhaustion. "I can't just fall apart. I have Jaxon to think about. And I... I don't have anywhere to go."

Martha's voice softened, and Emma could picture her mother's face—strong, yet compassionate, the way it had always been. "Listen to me, Emma. You don't have to stay there another minute if you don't want to. You and Jaxon can come here. You know I've got room, and we'll figure out the rest later. Don't you worry about a thing."

The floodgates fully opened, and Emma sobbed quietly, overwhelmed by her mother's unwavering support. "Thank you, Ma. I just... I didn't know how to face this on my own."

"You don't have to, baby girl," Martha reassured her. "You've got me. Always. I'll be there in a few hours. Pack what you need for you and Jaxon, and we'll sort the rest out when we get you here. But you don't need to stay in that house a second longer."

Emma's heart swelled with a mixture of gratitude and resolve. Her mother's words were a lifeline, grounding her in the reality that she didn't have to face this nightmare alone. "I love you, Ma," Emma whispered, her voice raw with emotion.

"I love you too, Emma Carolyn Dawson. Don't you ever forget that."

When the call ended, Emma stared at the phone in her hand, a strange sense of calm washing over her. The world still felt like it was crumbling around her, but she had something she hadn't felt in a long time—hope. She and Jaxon would be okay. They would make it through this.

She wiped away the last of her tears just as she heard small footsteps padding down the hallway. She quickly pulled herself together, forcing a brave smile onto her face as she turned to greet her son.

"Morning, Mom!" Jaxon's bright, cheerful voice filled the air as he bounded into the kitchen. His face lit up with excitement. "Can we have pizza for lunch today?"

Emma smiled, her heart aching with love as she wrapped her arms around him. "Of course we can, sweetheart. Pizza sounds perfect." For Jaxon's sake, she would keep things as normal as possible, at least for now.

They spent the afternoon curled up on the couch watching movies and eating pizza, Jaxon laughing at his favorite scenes while Emma smiled beside him. But even as she tried to stay in the moment, her mind couldn't stop racing. Every time Jaxon giggled or asked her a question, the reality of her shattered marriage loomed in the background. How could she explain all this to him? How could she break up their family without breaking his heart in the process?

The fear of that moment—of having to tell Jaxon the truth—gnawed at her. She knew she had to leave, for both their sakes. But tearing apart their world, tearing apart her son's sense of stability, was the most terrifying thing of all.

As the afternoon wore on and Jaxon finally drifted off to sleep, Emma sat on the couch, staring at the blank TV screen. The confrontation with Carlos would come soon, and it would be brutal. But she had made her decision. For the first time in a long time, she felt sure of something.

Emma quietly made her way to the bedroom, her resolve hardening with every step. Tomorrow, she would leave. She would take Jaxon, and they would go. She wouldn't allow Carlos to destroy her any longer.

And when he came home that night, the conversation would begin. It was time for the truth to finally come out, no matter the cost.

As she tucked Jaxon into bed that night, Emma's heart ached with the weight of the decision that lay ahead. How could she possibly choose between her own happiness and the life she'd built with Carlos?

Once Jaxon was asleep, she crept downstairs and poured herself a cup of tea, her mind reeling. Her gaze drifted to the photo of her and Carlos on their wedding day, their faces radiant with promises of love and devotion. Tears blurred her vision as she picked it up, remembering the man he used to be—the man she thought she knew.

"How could you do this to us, you asshole?" she whispered, her voice raw with anguish.

With shaking hands, she reached for her phone and scrolled through their text messages, her heart twisting with every lie he'd ever told her. In the end, she found herself staring at a blank screen, her thoughts consumed by the same question that had been plaguing her all day.

Just after Jaxon had gone to bed, Martha arrived like a gust of fresh air sweeping through the house. "I'll stay here for a bit, but I want to get us all back to the house and set up the spare rooms for you and Jaxon. Have you talked to him about all of this yet?" She asked her daughter.

"Oh mama, thank you. I am glad you are here." Emma said, managing a forced smile that Martha knew wasn't real.

After half an hour, Carlos sauntered into the room. "Oh, oh... Martha, when did you—" His face showed his surprise at her arrival.

"Just this evening Carlos." Martha locked eyes with her son in law, successfully making him uncomfortable. Jaxon stood half-shrouded in the hallway's shadows; his piercing hazel eyes fixed on the spectacle unfolding in the living room. His long, curly brown hair fell over his forehead as he leaned forward, a silent sentinel to the familial storm raging before him. The tension was a live wire, buzzing through the air and wrapping around his chest like an unwelcome embrace.

"Emma, you're overreacting," Carlos's voice sliced through the thick atmosphere, laced with an insidious calm that didn't reach his eyes. Those eyes darted away from Emma's tear-streaked face—a telltale sign of evasion that Jaxon had come to recognize all too well.

"Overreacting?" Emma's response was a mixture of disbelief and hurt, her voice hitching on the edge of despair. "How can you say that when—"

"Enough!" Martha's voice thundered into the conversation, her presence filling the room despite her slim frame. Her long red hair seemed to flare with her rising temper, a visual echo of the fire within her. She stood between Emma and Carlos, a barrier as unyielding as iron.

"Martha—" Carlos began, but she cut him off with a sharp gesture.

"Don't 'Martha' me, Carlos. I have eyes, I see what you're doing to her." Martha's tone was as lethal as a blade, and Jaxon felt a shiver of both fear and admiration. "You think you can waltz in here and play these mind games?"

Jaxon's hands balled into fists at his sides, knuckles blanching. Each word from Martha's mouth was an echo of his own thoughts, his resentment towards Carlos growing with every heartbeat. Carlos, who had once been a figure of fascination, now embodied the chaos disrupting the hallowed ground of family.

"My mom doesn't deserve this," Jaxon muttered under his breath, the words lost in the cacophony of accusations and defenses.

Martha turned her steely gaze on Carlos, pinning him like a butterfly to a board. "If you care for this family, you'll stop this nonsense right now. Otherwise, you will have me to contend with."

A tense silence followed; one so heavy it almost had a sound of its own—a low, threatening hum that promised an imminent storm. Jaxon exhaled slowly, knowing full well that Martha meant every word. If there was a guardian spirit watching over their fractured home, it took the form of his grandmother's fierce resolve.

Carlos's jaw clenched, the only sign of his frustration. "This is between me and Emma, so butt out." he said finally, a clear attempt to dismiss Martha's influence.

"Family is never just between two people," Martha retorted, her voice steady as bedrock. "Not when you hurt one of us. Not when there's a child watching."

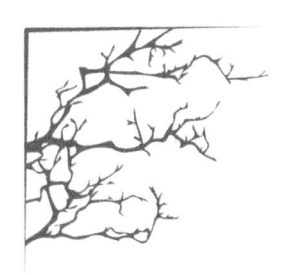

# Chapter 10

Jaxon's chest tightened with a cocktail of emotions, the most potent among them a burning desire to shield his mother from any further pain. He stepped out of the shadows, no longer content to be a mere observer. His lean figure might have appeared less imposing next to Martha's fiery stance, but his quiet intensity was no less formidable.

"Nana's right," Jaxon said, his measured tones cutting through the air. "I'm part of this family too. And I won't let you hurt my mom anymore."

The room seemed to hold its breath as three generations of Dawsons faced off against the man who dared to shake their foundations. In the stillness, Jaxon could feel the weight of decisions yet to come, the sense of a line crossed, and a battle line drawn. He stood ready, alongside Martha, to defend what they held dear, come what may.

Emma stood motionless, her back against the cool kitchen wall as if it could somehow absorb the heat of the confrontation. Her green eyes, usually so nurturing and warm, were now clouded with an internal tempest that threatened to spill over. The room felt like a pressure cooker, waiting for someone to twist the valve and release the steam.

"Carlos, how long did you think you could lie to me?" There was a tremor in Emma's voice, betraying the storm of vulnerability and insecurities raging within her. It took every ounce of her strength to confront him, but she stood her ground, the white-knuckled grip on her arms revealing a woman who was both frightened and resolute.

"Emma, this isn't what you think," Carlos replied, his voice oozing the charm that had once won her heart but now sounded hollow. His eyes darted away, avoiding her gaze, a subtle dance of guilt he performed all too well.

"Then what is it? Please, enlighten me. Because I've been trying to understand why you'd throw everything we have away!" Her voice climbed, edged with a newfound resolve that seemed to surprise even her.

"Your mother has always been in our business. She only knows your side of things. Maybe if we had some privacy—"

"Don't you dare put this on her!" Emma snapped, cutting him off. She could feel Martha's presence behind her, a silent pillar of support. "This is about us, Carlos. About me, and my son, and the choices you made." Her words were a scalpel, precise and sharp, dissecting the layers of deceit.

"Choices? You want to talk about choices?" Carlos's temper sparked, his tone shifting from defensive charm to something darker, more menacing. "You chose to ignore the signs. You chose this fantasy of a perfect family. If you wouldn't have gone through my phone..."

"Because I believed in you!" Emma's retort was a mix of pain and anger, a reflection of her internal struggle laid bare. Her usual desire to maintain peace was overridden by a need to protect not just her own shattered illusions, but also the young ears that hung on every word.

"Believed in me or wanted to control me, Em?" Carlos's question cut deep, twisting the knife of betrayal even further.

"Control? Is that really what you think this is about? That I'm like you?" Emma's retort came with a flash of insight. She was beginning to see through the fog of manipulation, her empathy no longer a blindfold but a lens sharpening into focus.

"Enough!" The single word resonated in the tense air, voiced not by Carlos or Emma, but by Martha. Her command was enough to momentarily pause the escalating argument, reminding them of the generations caught up in this struggle.

Emma's breath shuddered, a momentary lapse where her insecurities flickered across her face. But then, like a candle being lit in a dark room, her resolve returned, illuminating her path forward. She would navigate this conflict, for her son, for herself. Because at the end of this dark psychological tunnel, she glimpsed the possibility of light, of freedom from the chains of a love that had turned into a trap.

"Jaxon needs us to be strong, to show him what it means to stand up for yourself," Emma said, her voice steady now, a testament to her emerging resilience.

"Stand up for yourself? Or turn your back on the ones who love you?" Carlos's reply was a desperate attempt to regain control, to pull on the strings of loyalty he thought he still manipulated.

"Love doesn't hurt, Carlos," Emma whispered, a mantra for the battle-scarred heart. "And it certainly doesn't betray."

As silence fell, the tension remained, a living entity in the room, thick and suffocating. Yet amidst the turmoil, Emma stood a little taller, her vulnerability woven with threads of strength, preparing for whatever might come next.

Jaxon stood in the shadowed corner of the living room; his piercing hazel eyes fixed intently on the scene unfolding before him. He was like a silent sentinel, tall and lean, with an air of quiet intensity that seemed to ripple through the tension-laden air. His long, curly brown hair framed his face as he watched, his body tensed like a coiled spring, ready to unleash at the slightest provocation.

Martha's voice was a cutting blade, each word honed with contempt as she stood protectively in front of Emma. The silence around them was thick, but Martha's words shattered it like shards of glass.

Despite her slender frame, she exuded a fierce strength that was palpable. Her determined stance made it clear that she would not be easily intimidated or back down from a challenge. The dim light illuminated her fiery red hair, making it seem to glow like embers. It was a stark contrast to the cool air around them, a visual representation of Martha's passionate resolve. She was a force to be reckoned with, and Carlos could see that in her eyes as they locked gazes.

Emma, caught between her mother and husband, trembled slightly but held her ground. Jaxon could see the subtle strain in her posture, the way her expressive green eyes flickered with a turmoil of emotions. It pained him deeply, fueling the resentment that bubbled beneath his calm exterior. Carlos had inflicted this pain, and Jaxon felt a surge of protective instinct towards his mother, coupled with a growing desire to intervene.

"Carlos, you've caused enough damage here," Martha continued, stepping closer to him until her steely gaze locked with his. "I won't let you tear this family apart any further."

"Martha, I told you, this is between me and Emma," Carlos retorted, trying to sidestep her, but Martha was unyielding, a fortress standing between her daughter and the man who dared to hurt her.

"Carlos, everything you do affects all of us," Jaxon finally broke his silence, his measured tone cutting through the standoff. "You can't just expect us to stand by while you break her heart, day after day." His words were deliberate, revealing just enough of his burgeoning darkness, a warning of the storm that was brewing within.

Martha glanced at her grandson, pride mingling with concern in her gaze. She knew that look in Jaxon's eyes; it was the same determination she felt coursing through her own veins. They were kindred spirits, united in their purpose to shield Emma from more harm.

"Jaxon's right," Martha affirmed, turning back to Carlos. "You lost the right to privacy when you betrayed my daughter's trust. I won't let you manipulate her any longer."

The standoff intensified, an intricate dance of wills where each participant was acutely aware of the stakes. Jaxon's resentment towards Carlos grew with every passing second, a dark undercurrent threatening to spill over. He saw the pain etched into his mother's features, the battle scars of a love turned toxic, and he knew he couldn't remain a passive observer for much longer.

Martha's presence was a testament to her unwavering support, her willingness to confront the very source of her daughter's anguish. She was the backbone of their family, the one who had always seen through Carlos's veneer, the protector who would stand against any threat, regardless of the cost.

Jaxon mirrored her resolve, his own determination crystallizing into action. There was no room for passivity, not when those he loved were in pain. He stepped out of the shadows, ready to stand alongside Martha, to face Carlos head-on. Together, they would fight to safeguard the fragile peace within their fractured family, come what may.

Emma stood rigid, her back pressed against the cold kitchen wall as if she could meld into its plaster and evade the tempest swirling around her. Her green eyes were clouded with a turmoil that mirrored the gathering storm outside. The once comforting cadence of raindrops beating against the window now sounded like a drum roll to impending chaos.

"Carlos," Emma's voice was a whisper lost in the hurricane of her emotions, but she gathered the shards of her resolve. "How could you?"

Martha's gaze bore into Carlos, steely and unyielding. Jaxon, though silent, was an echo of his grandmother's defiance. Emma observed them both, torn between their protective stances and the remnants of a life she had cherished—a picture-perfect family that was now cracking at the seams.

"Emma, mi amor," Carlos began, his tone oozing charm as it always did when he sought forgiveness for sins too numerous to count. His dark hair, slick from the rain, seemed to match the shadow creeping over his face as he prepared to weave another web of deceit.

"Don't." The word cut through the air, sharper than they expected from her. "Don't call me that. Not now. Not after what you've done."

Carlos's eyes narrowed into piercing daggers, the softness that had briefly flickered in them vanishing as quickly as it had appeared. "You're letting them turn you against me," he accused, his voice dripping with venom as he gestured towards Martha and Jaxon. "We are a family, Emma. You, me, your son... we can fix this."

"Family doesn't hurt each other," Emma shot back, her tone laced with a fierce determination that seemed to emanate from somewhere deep within her, a wellspring of resilience she had almost forgotten existed.

"Everyone makes mistakes," Carlos countered, frustration seething in his words. "I'm trying to make it right."

"By lying? By sneaking around? By continuing to cheat?" Emma's fists clenched at her sides, knuckles turning white with anger. "I don't even know who you are anymore."

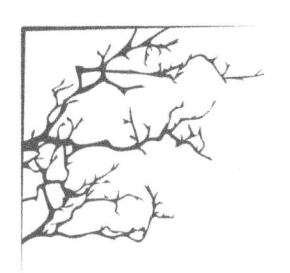

# Chapter 11

"That's enough!" Martha couldn't hold back any longer, her disdain pouring out in a rush of words. "This isn't about your mistakes, Carlos. It's about what you continue to do and who you choose to be, and you've shown us exactly who and what that is."

With a swift step forward, Carlos loomed over Emma, causing her to instinctively flinch despite herself. Jaxon moved too, not away but positioning himself protectively between his mother and the man who had once promised to cherish her forever. The tension in the room was palpable as all three stood locked in a battle of wills and betrayal.

"Let's not forget where we are," Carlos said, his voice low and dangerous. "In this house, my house, I will not be disrespected."

"Your house?" Martha scoffed. "Your house built on lies? You mean the house *I* own? You are so wrong, Carlos, this is Emma's house, you have no rights here."

"Ma..." Emma's plea was soft, barely audible, but it halted the escalating war of words. She looked at Carlos, really looked at him, and what she saw was a stranger cloaked in the familiarity of a husband she once loved.

"What happened to us, Carlos? To our vows?"

"Life happens, Emma!" Carlos's outburst filled the room, his hands balled into fists. "I fight every day in a world that doesn't want me, and I come home to more battles. Where is my peace?"

"Peace?" Emma's laugh was humorless, the sound of it foreign to her own ears. "Peace is built on trust, on love. Not whatever this"—she gestured helplessly between them—"has become."

The room fell silent, save for the relentless rain and the harsh breaths of four people caught in a web of betrayal and pain. Each one stood on the precipice of decision, the next words poised to either mend or shatter the fragile threads holding them together.

"Where do we go from here?" Emma asked, the question hanging in the air like a lifeline—or a noose.

The ticking of the grandfather clock in the hallway was like a metronome to Jaxon's rising pulse. He stood slightly behind his mother, his lean frame rigid with suppressed rage. The silence following Emma's question was a chasm that seemed to stretch and warp the very air around them.

"From here," Jaxon spoke up suddenly, each word slicing into the tension, "we start by talking about all of the wounds that can't be hidden under a band-aid." His hazel eyes, so much like his mother's, locked onto Carlos with an intensity that startled the older man. It was clear that Jaxon's patience had frayed, the threads of familial obligation unraveling with each passing second.

"Jaxon," Emma's voice was a whisper, a plea for restraint she wasn't sure she wanted him to heed.

"No, Mom. You've been quiet too long, we've been quiet too long," he said, his voice low but unwavering. His gaze never left Carlos, whose own eyes flickered with something akin to respect, or perhaps fear. "I've watched you break piece by piece because of him," Jaxon continued, motioning toward Carlos with a dismissive jerk of his head. "I won't stand by and watch it anymore."

"Jaxon," Martha interjected, her voice firm yet infused with warmth as she stepped closer to her grandson. She placed a hand on his shoulder, her touch grounding. "Your mother is stronger than you know, and she has us. We will navigate this storm together."

"My mama is right," Emma finally said, finding a thread of resolve in the midst of her turmoil. She reached out, her fingers brushing against Jaxon's, and then turned to face Carlos squarely. "Your choices have consequences, and we all bear them. But I'm not alone in this. I have my family, my real family."

"Family," Carlos repeated the word as if tasting a bitter fruit. His posture shifted, a subtle yet unmistakable sign of retreat. He glanced at the united front before him—Emma resilient, Jaxon resolute, Martha unyielding—and for a moment, the façade of control slipped.

"Guidance isn't just about direction, Emma," Martha said, addressing her daughter but keeping her gaze fixed on Carlos. "It's about support, about having someone who'll stand with you when the ground beneath your feet feels like quicksand." Her voice carried the weight of hard-won wisdom, a buoy in the tempest that raged around them.

"We need to sit down and have a real conversation," Emma demanded, her voice strong and determined, fueled by the support of her son and mother. "But not as enemies. Let's talk like two people who used to love each other enough to build a life together."

Carlos' response was strained, his emotions teetering on the edge. "Is there even anything left to say?"

Jaxon stepped in fiercely, his eyes boring into his stepfather. "Yeah, there's plenty left to say, starting with the truth about what you did to our family, what you keep doing."

The room felt colder, as if the storm outside had found its way in, weaving amongst them and chilling their bones. But within that cold, there was a fire—a fire kindled by Jaxon's courage, fueled by Martha's conviction, and stoked by Emma's emerging fortitude. They formed a circle, three points of light in the shadow of betrayal, each ready to face whatever darkness lay ahead.

Rain lashed against the living room windows, punctuating the charged silence. Emma moved to the center of the room; her hands clasped tightly in front of her as if she could physically hold together the fragments of their lives. Her eyes, a turbulent sea of green, settled on Carlos, whose presence seemed to both anchor and capsize her world.

"Carlos, please," Emma's voice was a soft plea, barely carrying over the storm's howl. "We can still talk this through, for Jaxon's sake. We can be adults about this, can't we?"

"Talk?" The word escaped Carlos like steam from a pressured valve. "You want to talk more after everything that's happened?"

"Emma's right. We need to stay calm." Martha's voice cut through, sharp yet steady.

"Stay calm?" Carlos scoffed, his gaze flitting between Emma and Martha, the contempt in his tone unmistakable. "While my own family judges me?"

Emma's words were laced with desperation as she tried to quell the rising tension between them. "This isn't about judging; it's about understanding and finding a way forward. That's what we owe each other."

"Owe each other?" Carlos sneered, his voice dripping with bitterness. "I owe you nothing after what you and your son have done to me."

Jaxon interjected, his tone firm and resolute. "I haven't turned against anyone. I just see the truth."

"Only what she wants you to see!" Carlos retorted, jabbing his finger in Emma's direction.

"Enough!" Emma's voice finally broke free, sharp with fear and anger. "Stop this, Carlos. Just stop. Can't you see? We're tearing ourselves apart!"

"Oh, is that what you think?" Carlos took a menacing step closer, his eyes narrowing. "That I'm the one tearing this family apart?"

"Isn't it obvious by now?" Emma's resilience flickered like a dying flame. She took a deep breath, trying to steady herself. "You've hurt us, Carlos. You've hurt me. And I... I still want to fix this, but not if it means destroying ourselves in the process."

"Destroying ourselves?" Carlos repeated, his voice dripping with disbelief and sarcasm. "Or just destroying me?" His words rang with a sense of betrayal and bitterness that cut through Emma like a knife.

Martha's words cut through the storm like a knife, her gaze never wavering from Carlos's face. "You have to face it, you can't keep running from what you've done and the pain it's caused," she said, her voice laced with steel. "If you end up destroyed in the process, it'll be because of your own choices."

"Face it?" Carlos laughed bitterly, his grip on his emotions slipping like wet sand. "I've faced more than you could ever imagine."

"Then help us understand," Emma pleaded, her body trembling with fear and desperation. "Help us fix this before it destroys us all."

Carlos's eyes flashed with anger, mirroring the raging tempest outside. "Fix this? How do we fix something that's been shattered for so long?"

"By starting with the truth," Emma said, her voice gaining strength from deep within her. "By being honest with each other and ourselves. By recommitting to each other, by being faithful."

"Truth and honesty," Carlos scoffed, his lips twisting into a cruel smile. "Such simple concepts for such a complicated mess."

"Maybe," Emma conceded, her determination hardening like unbreakable metal. "But they're all we have left now to save ourselves."

The room fell silent except for the relentless rain against the glass—a staccato rhythm to their fractured harmony. Emma stood there, the embodiment of vulnerability and strength, her heart openly bleeding yet somehow refusing to yield. It was a dance of shadows and light, and as the storm raged on, so too did the battle within the confines of their home—each person clinging to their own version of love and loyalty, each one searching for a peace that seemed just beyond reach.

# Chapter 12

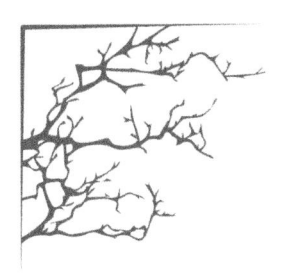

Jaxon's hands clenched into fists at his sides, the knuckles whitening as he stood with his back pressed against the cool wall of the hallway. He had become a shadow in his own home—the silent observer of a slow-burning fuse that threatened to ignite at any moment. His hazel eyes, sharp and unyielding, followed every tremble that shuddered through his mother's frame. It was like watching a fragile bird trapped in an ever-tightening snare, and something primal within him stirred—a fierce protectiveness that had lain dormant until now.

"Hey, that's enough." Martha's voice sliced through the tension like a blade, her words steady but laced with a simmering anger. She stepped between Emma and Carlos, her slim figure deceptively strong as she faced the man who had brought chaos into their midst. The steely glint in her gaze held a warning that could not be ignored.

"Carlos, you will not stand here and watch while you tear this family apart," she declared, her red hair seeming to flame in the muted light of the room.

Jaxon's resentment towards Carlos swelled, cresting like a wave as he listened to Martha's defense of Emma. He could see the fight in his grandmother's stance, the determined set of her shoulders as she became the bulwark against the storm that was Carlos.

"Martha, your daughter needs—" Carlos began, but was cut off swiftly.

"Needs what, Carlos? More of your lies? More nights wondering where you are or what secrets you're keeping?" Martha's voice was a whip-crack, leaving no room for excuses or half-truths. "I've watched my daughter fade because of you."

In that moment, Jaxon felt the weight of his own silence bearing down on him. He wanted to step forward, to lend his voice to the chorus of accusation and to shield his mother from the pain that seemed to radiate from Carlos like a malignant force. Yet, his feet remained rooted, as if the very floorboards conspired to hold him back.

"Ma, please," Emma's gentle plea reached out, a lifeline in the swelling darkness. Her green eyes found Jaxon's, and it was as though he could hear her unspoken words: 'Be strong for me.'

"Jaxon?" Carlos whipped around, desperation lining his voice and seeping through his pores. His eyes searched for a glimmer of understanding or support but found only a cold mirror reflecting back all of his failings, magnified and unsympathetic. "You see what's happening here, don't you?"

"See?" Jaxon's voice was quiet, but it reverberated with the intensity of a ticking time bomb. "I see everything, Carlos. I see the pain you've inflicted, the lies you've told that are suffocating this family like poison —rotting away all that used to be good."

"Jaxon!" Emma's voice rang out like a warning bell, her maternal instincts urging her to shield her child from the storm brewing within their home.

"Emma, let the boy speak," Martha commanded, her gaze never faltering as it bore into Carlos with unyielding force. "He's been silent for far too long."

"Speak?" Carlos scoffed, barely able to contain his boiling rage. "What could he possibly know about—"

"More than you know," Jaxon interrupted sharply, stepping away from the wall with purposeful strides. "I understand that family is supposed to be safe. That trust is not given freely but earned. You have destroyed both, and I refuse to stand by and watch you destroy anything else."

The room pulsed with a tangible energy, a current that ebbed and flowed with the raw emotions laid bare. Jaxon stood, a young man pushed to the brink, his loyalty to his mother casting a stark light on the shadows Carlos had drawn over them all. And Martha, the matriarch, stood unyielding, ready to confront whatever came next. They were united, each in their own way, fighting for a peace that seemed just beyond reach.

Carlos's dark eyes flickered with a dangerous spark, his stance widening as though he were bracing against an unseen force. His lips curved into a cold smile, one that failed to reach the increasingly turbulent depths of his gaze. "So this is it, then? A little rebellion in my own home?"

Emma drew a sharp breath, her trembling hands now balled into fists at her sides. Her voice, when she spoke, carried a strength that seemed to surprise even her. "No, Carlos. This isn't rebellion. It's realization. We see you for who you truly are."

"Careful, Emma," Carlos warned, the menace in his voice slicing through the thickening air. His posture shifted, a predator poised to strike, and Jaxon felt his own muscles coil in response.

Martha's voice boomed through the room, her eyes blazing with determination. She stood tall and unyielding; her hands planted firmly on her hips as she stared down Carlos.

"Carlos, that's enough!" she commanded, her words cutting through the tension. Carlos shrank back, cowed by her unwavering strength. "You don't get to intimidate us anymore," she continued, her gaze flickering between him and her daughter. "Not me, not my daughter, and certainly not Jaxon." Her hands clenched into fists at her sides, ready to defend against any further attacks from this man who had caused them so much pain. "I think it's time you left this house. Pack your things and get out, now."

The silence that followed was fraught with unspoken ultimatums, each heartbeat stretching into eternity. Jaxon's hazel eyes locked onto Carlos's, a silent vow passing between them—an assurance that there would be no backing down.

"Is that so? You think you can just push me out? What do you think you are going to do about it, eh?" Carlos's voice was barely above a whisper, yet it boomed in the charged stillness. He took a step forward, and without hesitation, Jaxon mirrored him, stepping in front of Emma as a shield.

"Jaxon, please," Emma reached out, her touch feather-light on his shoulder, but Jaxon remained steadfast, a young sentinel in defense of all he held dear.

"Let him come, Emma," Martha said softly, her gaze never leaving Carlos's face. "He needs to know we're not afraid."

"Shouldn't I be the one you're afraid of?" Carlos taunted, his eyes glinting with cruel amusement. But beneath the bravado, a flicker of uncertainty betrayed him.

"Go ahead," Jaxon dared, his voice steady as bedrock. "Show us if there's anything left to fear."

The standoff was palpable, each participant acutely aware of the delicately balanced scales before them. In that moment, the Dawson household became an arena where the slightest misstep could tip the balance irrevocably.

Emma swallowed hard, her resolve battling the instinctive dread that clawed at her insides. She knew they stood on a precipice, the outcome of their collective courage uncertain. Yet in facing the abyss, something within her began to crystallize—a determination to reclaim the life that had been slowly eroded away by fear and manipulation.

Carlos's chuckle broke the spell, a sound devoid of humor. "You think you've won something today?" he asked, his voice low and dangerous. "This isn't over. Not by a long shot."

"Then we'll be waiting," Martha replied, her tone unwavering. The matriarch's words hung in the room like a gauntlet thrown.

As Carlos retreated, his back receding from the living room, the tension did not dissipate but instead morphed into a silent promise of storms on the horizon. The small family stood together, yet apart—united in their resolve but divided by the chaos that lingered in the wake of Carlos's exit.

Emma watched as Carlos packed a bag and shoved past her in the doorway of their room. He tossed his bag in the back seat of his car and peeled out as he pulled away from the house.

Jaxon glanced at his mother, her green eyes reflecting the storied bravery of warriors past, and at his grandmother, the fierce guardian of their lineage. They were ready for whatever came next. And as the front door clicked shut after Carlos' departure, the echo seemed to whisper that the battle had only just begun.

# Chapter 13

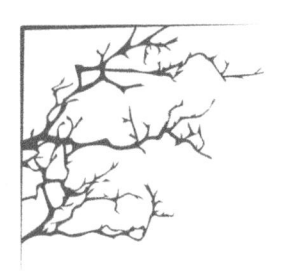

The morning light filtered through the kitchen blinds, casting a soft glow over the modest room. Emma moved with practiced ease, the rhythm of her routine a comforting melody against the chaotic symphony that was her life. The sizzle of eggs in the pan harmonized with the gentle scrape of toast being buttered, creating an ambiance of domestic tranquility that belied the underlying dissonance of her marriage.

"Jax, breakfast is ready!" she called out, her voice carrying the warmth that came so naturally to her. She plated the food with a nurse's precision, ensuring each portion was balanced and nurturing.

Jaxon, emerged with sleep still clinging to his hazel eyes, his lanky frame sliding into a chair at the table. They exchanged a silent glance, a momentary connection that spoke volumes of shared experiences and unspoken worries. He smiled weakly, a gesture that tugged at her heartstrings as she set his plate before him.

"Thanks, mom," he mumbled, his words muffled by a yawn. "Where's Nana?"

"Of course, Jax. Nana ran to her house to get some clean clothes, she'll be back in a bit." she replied, tousling his curly brown hair affectionately before sitting down to join him. The familiar clink of cutlery on porcelain filled the air, punctuated by the occasional chime of a spoon against a coffee mug.

With breakfast coming to a close, Emma collected the dishes, her movements automatic as she piled them into the sink. That's when she noticed it—a sliver of black plastic peeking out from beneath a crumpled napkin. Carlos's phone. Unattended again. A rare occurrence that piqued her curiosity and sent a flutter of unease through her. Had he come back in the night? Where had he slept? She didn't hear him return, so why was his phone here?

Glancing over her shoulder to ensure Jaxon was absorbed in his thoughts, she reached out and slid the device towards herself. It felt heavier than she expected, as if weighted by the secrets it might hold. Her thumb hovered over the screen, hesitating, before pressing down and awakening the display.

One new message flashed across the screen, an unknown number with no name attached. Emma's pulse quickened, her green eyes scanning the preview of the text that seemed innocuous at first—until the implications of the words twisted inside her like a knife.

"Can't wait for our next trip together," the message read, its brevity doing nothing to mask the illicit promise within.

A sour taste of betrayal flooded Emma's mouth, the breakfast she had lovingly prepared now a lump in her stomach. The room seemed to tilt, her grip on the phone tightening as she fought against the swell of emotions threatening to capsize her composed exterior.

Emma's heart pounded in her chest as she stared at the text on the phone, the words taunting her with their blatant betrayal. She could feel a fire building inside her, fueled by anger and hurt.

She knew she should look away, hide the evidence and pretend she hadn't seen anything. But the text was like a magnet, drawing her in with promises of answers and revelations that would only bring more pain.

In that moment, Emma saw herself through Carlos's eyes - a predictable and convenient presence, easily taken advantage of. Her own empathy had been her downfall. But no longer.

With a steely determination, Emma gripped the phone tighter, her insides churning with insecurities but also a newfound resolve. This was not the time to crumble. She steeled herself for the inevitable confrontation that lay ahead, ready to face whatever chaos and turmoil came her way.

Emma's thumb hovered over the screen, a hesitant sentry guarding against the floodgates of truth. With a trembling touch, she tapped the message open, and as the words cascaded before her eyes, her pulse quickened into a frantic rhythm. The sentences were laced with intimacy, a stark contrast to the cool indifference that had become Carlos's signature at home.

"Miss you already," it began, a whisper through the digital void. "Last night was..." A string of suggestive emojis followed their colorful levity mocking the gravity of their implication.

Her heart thudded in her chest, a discordant drumbeat to the silent symphony of betrayal. She read on, each word a serrated edge sawing at the delicate threads of trust they had woven together over years. There were mentions of secret meetings, stolen moments and promises of discretion that unearthed a raw, aching wound in Emma's chest.

Disbelief curdled into cold clarity within her. This was no mistake, no benign text from a wrong number. It was evidence of Carlos's infidelity as tangible as the phone burning in her grasp.

The air around her thickened, heavy with the scent of treachery, as she clutched the device—now a grenade with its pin steadily being worked loose by every heaving breath she took.

"Mom, are you okay?" Jaxon's voice, tinged with concern, cut through the fog of her shock. But she couldn't afford the luxury of falling apart—not now, not with her son's eyes upon her.

"Everything's fine, sweetheart," she managed, her voice a fragile veil over the tremors of her heart. The lie tasted bitter, but necessary.

With Jaxon appeased for the moment, Emma redirected her focus. She needed answers, deserved them. Standing there amidst the remnants of what she once believed to be a wholesome family breakfast, Emma straightened her spine, channeling every ounce of strength she possessed as a nurse who had faced countless crises.

"Carlos will have to answer for this," she murmured to herself, the words bolstering her resolve.

She forwarded the text's to herself and deleted them from his screen, then glanced down at the phone one last time before setting it back beneath the napkin, a temporary shroud for the truth that would be unveiled.

Taking a deep breath that did little to quell the storm inside, Emma paused, picked up the phone and made her way toward the bedroom. Each step was measured, a countdown to the inevitable confrontation. She could hear the muffled sounds of Carlos moving around, the hum of normalcy that now seemed a grotesque performance.

Outside the spare bedroom door, her hand lingered on the knob, the cool metal grounding her swirling emotions. Her green eyes closed momentarily, and she summoned an image of herself—not as the overlooked wife, but as a woman of valor who could weather any storm.

"Here I come, Carlos," she whispered to herself, steeling her nerves. It was time to shed the light on the shadows that had infiltrated their marriage. Emma turned the handle, pushed open the door, and stepped inside, ready to face whatever lay beyond.

## Chapter 14

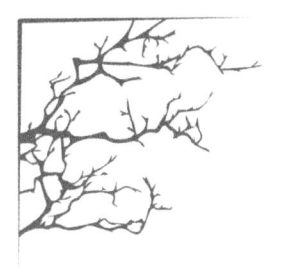

He wasn't in the spare room. The sounds were coming from their bedroom, she rushed to the door. The morning light spilled across the bedroom, throwing shadows that danced with Carlos's movements as he knotted his tie in the reflection of the dresser mirror. Emma's silhouette filled the doorway, her presence a silent accusation. Her heart thrummed a chaotic rhythm, but her voice, when it came, was a fragile shard of glass lodged in her throat.

The phone flew past Carlos' head as Emma poised herself for the impending fight that was sure to come like a violent storm.

With a twisted smile, Carlos turned to face his wife, his eyes meeting hers in the mirror before he pivoted to confront her fully. His charming facade now cracked, revealing the true deceit that lurked beneath.

"Who is she, Carlos?" Her tone was laced with fire and betrayal.

Emma's voice was a raging inferno, her words slicing through Carlos' lies like a sharp blade. Her eyes blazed with unyielding determination as she repeated the number etched into her mind, the one that shattered the façade of their perfect life together.

But he only laughed mockingly, attempting to brush off her accusations with a dismissive wave of his hand. His expression feigned confusion, but Emma saw through his manipulative tactics. As a nurse, she was skilled at deciphering truth from deception. Now, she turned those skills inward, studying the man she had thought she knew so well. She saw the cracks in his façade and the darkness lurking behind his eyes, and she knew she could never trust him again.

"I saw your phone, the new messages," She persisted, unwilling to let him diminish her suspicions. "Don't lie to me. You are still fucking her? You fucker, I saw her messages."

But like a predator cornering its prey, Carlos closed in on her with an outstretched arm, aiming to smother her doubts with a false embrace. Emma stepped back, her hands clenching at her sides as she refused to be swayed by his manipulations.

"Don't you see it, Emma? You're stressed, overworked. Your mind is playing tricks on you," Carlos' voice dripped with condescension and pity, as if he were dealing with a delusional patient rather than his own wife.

But Emma had found her footing, her voice firm and unwavering as she fought against his gaslighting.

"I am not crazy. I'm not imagining this." Her words cut through his attempts like a sharp scalpel, revealing the ugly truth that lay beneath his carefully constructed façade.

"Em, listen to yourself," Carlos countered, his veneer of concern slipping as his tactic failed to yield its accustomed result. He stepped closer again, his gaze attempting to dominate, to regain control.

"That's fucking enough!" Emma's exclamation reverberated off the walls, a clarion call of her reclaimed power. "No more lies, no more manipulation. I deserve the truth."

Carlos's face tightened, the charm dissolving into the hardness she had glimpsed only in fleeting moments before. They stood locked in a tableau of tension, the balance of power shifting palpably as Emma held his gaze, unflinching.

"Tell me about her," she demanded, her voice steady now, the shaking gone. She was the eye of the storm, and she would not be moved. "Is she prettier than me? Does she fuck better than me? Does she suck your dick because I won't? Tell me, Carlos. Tell me."

Carlos's eyes, once a deep well of feigned innocence, now sparked with the fire of his temper. His fists clenched at his sides, and the air seemed to crackle with the fury emanating from him. Emma, though her heart pounded like a caged bird against her ribs, met his anger with an unwavering stance.

"Well? Who the fuck is she, Carlos?" The words left her lips, a steel thread weaving through them.

He took a menacing step forward, his voice a low growl. "You want to know so bad? Jealous, are we?"

"Jealous?" Emma's laugh, sharp and bitter, cut through the tension. "No, not jealous. Betrayed. Hurt."

Her hands trembled, but she wouldn't let them betray her. She couldn't. Not when every fiber of her being was stretched taut, ready for whatever lash might come from the man she once believed she knew.

"Look at you," Carlos sneered, "playing the victim as always."

Emma could feel the walls of the room closing in, the very air thick with the toxicity of his contempt. This wasn't just about infidelity; it was the unveiling of a charade that had been her life.

"Playing?" she countered, her voice a whisper, but her resolve loud and clear. "You think this pain is a game?"

The façade crumbled, and a torrent of emotions surged forth—years of unspoken doubts and swallowed pride. "I've given you everything. My love, my trust. And you... you've been living a lie."

Her green eyes blazed with a fire he had never seen, a tempest of hurt that refused to be quelled by his manipulations. She stood there, a woman who healed others for a living, yet remained unable to mend the fissures within herself.

"Living a lie?" Carlos echoed, mockery lacing his tone. "You don't know what living a lie is, Emma. You have no idea."

"Then enlighten me!" Her plea was both a challenge and a cry from a soul pushed to its limit.

"Fine!" He threw his hands up, the affable mask gone, revealing the scorn beneath. "You want the truth? I needed someone who didn't make me feel like less of a man. Someone who didn't pity me! Someone who would think of me as a god, as the center of her world. Someone who would worship me."

The words were a physical blow, leaving a stinging trail across Emma's heart. Each syllable confirmed her deepest fears—that she was never enough, that her nurturing nature was, in his eyes, nothing but condescension.

"Is that what you think this is about? Your pride?" Emma's voice rose, raw and laden with years of suppressed emotion. "What about me, Carlos? What about my pride? How do you think I feel, knowing that my husband..." The sentence hung unfinished, too painful to complete.

"Knowing that your husband what?" Carlos's challenge was a goad, pushing her toward a precipice she had long avoided.

"Chose some bitch over his own family," Emma finished, her voice breaking on the last word. The admission shattered the last vestige of pretense between them. Her vulnerability lay bare, exposed to the harsh light of his betrayal.

"She's no bitch, believe me. And family?" he sneered. "Please. Don't play saint with me."

"Saint?" A bitter laugh escaped her, the sound foreign even to her own ears. "No, not a saint. Just a fool who thought she married a good man."

The silence that followed was deafening—a chasm into which their fractured marriage tumbled. Emma closed her eyes briefly, gathering the shattered pieces of her composure. When she opened them again, they were clear, resolute.

"Get the fuck out," she snarled, her voice laced with a quiet but unmistakable intensity that sent shivers down Carlos' spine.

## Chapter 15

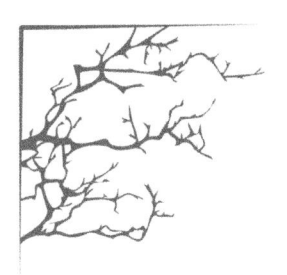

"Em—"

"Don't you dare 'Em' me," she spat, her words dripping with venom. "Pack the rest of your shit and get the hell out of my house, right now Carlos. And don't you dare come back. I won't repeat myself."

The fire in her eyes burned hotter than ever before. Her words were like daggers, cutting through the years of blurred boundaries and broken promises.

Carlos glared at her, his anger melting away to reveal a mix of fear and begrudging respect. He stood his ground, determined to stay in the house despite her commanding presence.

The doorbell rang. Emma could hear Jaxon greeting her mom.

The door creaked open; Jaxon's silhouette filled the frame, his lean figure casting a long shadow that sliced through the tension. Emma felt a surge of warmth at the sight of her son, her protector in the guise of a teenager. Jaxon said nothing, but his presence was a wordless bastion against the chaos. His hazel eyes, so much like hers, met Emma's with an intensity that spoke volumes of his silent vow: he would not let her stand alone.

"Mom?" His voice, barely above a whisper, cut through the heavy air—a lifeline amidst the storm.

Emma nodded, unable to form words, her heart throbbing with a cocktail of fear and gratitude. Jaxon took a step closer, his stance resolute, an unspoken promise hanging between them in the charged atmosphere.

Thundering footsteps echoed down the hallway, each one a heavy hammer striking against the walls. With a fiery mane of red hair flowing behind her like a war banner, Martha burst into the room with unrelenting urgency. Her eyes snapped to Carlos like daggers, her lips twisted into a snarl that could strike fear into the bravest of men.

"Carlos," she hissed, her voice reverberating with raw fury. "What have you done to my daughter?" Her words dripped with potent venom; each syllable punctuated by a surge of rage that threatened to consume her.

Caught off guard by her ferocity, Carlos stumbled back until his back hit the wall with a resounding thud. Emma's heart raced as she watched her mother stand tall and unwavering beside her, forming an unbreakable barrier between her and the man who had caused her so much pain.

"Martha, you stay out of this," Carlos growled, attempting to regain some semblance of control.

"Stay out? Fuck you, Carlos. I will not stand idly by while you tear apart my family with your selfishness!" Martha's voice was sharp as a razor blade coated in velvet, her southern accent thickening with raw emotion. She took another step forward, her small frame suddenly towering over him with an intimidating presence.

"You thought you could break my daughter's heart, and we would just sit back and watch? Well think again."

Jaxon moved closer to Emma, his body language exuding a fierce protectiveness that defied his young age. With her son and mother by her side, Emma felt a change occurring within her—the fragile façade of her former self breaking, making room for a newfound strength.

"Jaxon, take your mother out of here," Carlos tried to command, but his voice wavered, betraying him.

"Nobody is going anywhere," Martha declared, her stance as immovable as the earth itself. "Not until you understand the damage you've done and answer for your sins."

In the sudden stillness, the only sound was the ragged breaths of four people caught in a moment of reckoning. Emma, bolstered by the love that flanked her, met Carlos's gaze with newfound determination. She was no longer just a woman scorned; she was a force, a maelstrom of hurt and resolve, ready to reclaim her life.

Emma's gaze pierced through Carlos, her green eyes a stormy sea reflecting the turmoil within. She could feel the walls of their bedroom closing in, each photograph on the wall chronicling a lie that had burrowed deep into her soul. The air was thick with tension, and it pressed down on her chest like a physical weight. Her marriage—this life she had built with meticulous care—lay in shards at her feet.

"Carlos," Emma's voice quivered, yet it held an edge of clarity that surprised even her. "How long?" There was a desperation in her question, a plea for something salvageable amidst the wreckage.

"Em, you're misunderstanding—" he started, but Emma cut him off with a blood curdling scream that came from deep within her, loud and feral.

"Stop lying to me!" The exclamation came from deep within, a guttural release of years of suppressed doubt and self-deprecation. She was tired of questioning herself, scrutinizing her worth through the distorted lens of his deceit. In this moment of raw exposure, the veil lifted, and she saw the truth Carlos had masked for so long.

"How fucking long?" She insisted as he stood, unmoving in the center of the room.

Her mind raced, tracing back through countless small moments—a hastily ended phone call, a faint trace of perfume, an unexplained late night—that now seemed as glaring as neon signs.

Yet, there was also a rising tide of fury. How dare he make her feel less than? How dare he tarnish their family with his selfishness?

The nurturing woman who thrived on caring for others, the empathetic nurse who healed wounds daily, now needed to mend her own fractured spirit. Emma felt the ground shift beneath her, an internal earthquake toppling long-standing insecurities. The pieces of her old self lay scattered, clearing space for a reconstruction, one where she was the architect of her own worth.

Jaxon's voice pierced through the chaotic atmosphere like a siren, filled with concern and fear. Emma's heart clenched at the sound, her protective instincts kicking in. She turned to him, seeing her own terror reflected in his eyes.

In that moment, a primal force ignited within her, fueled by a fierce need to shield her son from the storm raging around them. With unwavering determination, she became the sanctuary he had always sought, a pillar of strength amidst the chaos.

"Jaxon, honey, go to your room for now," she commanded, her voice soft but firm, a mother's unwavering authority.

He hesitated, torn between his loyalty to his mother and his desire to stay and protect her. But Martha's presence beside him gave him courage and he stood his ground, a silent vow of allegiance.

With Martha by her side, Emma drew upon the lineage of strong women before her, finding strength in their resilience. It was time to break free from the chains of abuse and forge a new path of self-respect and independence.

"You bastard," Emma hissed, her voice low but seething with fury. "How long have you been with her? How long have you lied to my face?" Her eyes, ablaze with determination, locked onto Carlos, who stood there, silent and stone-faced. "I won't let you break me again," she said, her tone fierce, yet steady.

The pain still lingered, a deep, raw ache in her chest, but it was no longer paralyzing. Instead, it fueled something new inside her—an unshakable resolve to rise from the ashes and carve out a future free of deceit. She knew the road ahead would be hard, the fractures in her heart still fresh. But as she looked around the room, at the remains of a love she'd once believed in, Emma understood that the first step forward was hers to take.

For Jaxon. For herself. For the future they both deserved—one untainted by betrayal.

"Ma," she called, turning away from Carlos as if he no longer existed. "Can you take Jaxon out of the house for a while today?" Her words were steady, purposeful.

"Of course, baby girl," Martha replied, her voice filled with a mix of love and fierce protectiveness. She sensed the shift in Emma, the warrior emerging from the ashes of her broken marriage.

"Thank you," Emma whispered, though her voice held no weakness—only resolve. She inhaled deeply, grounding herself in the moment. It was time to plan, to act, to rebuild—not just her life, but her very self. The woman she was meant to be, the one who had been smothered by years of lies, was stirring awake.

She squared her shoulders, a silent vow passing through her: she wouldn't just survive this—she would come out stronger.

Turning back to Carlos, her voice rang with finality. "It's over. I'm taking back my life."

Without waiting for his response, Emma strode into their bedroom and began pulling his clothes from drawers, emptying the closet, tossing everything onto the front lawn. Carlos stood in the doorway for a moment, watching her with a detached indifference, as if this was beneath him. Then, without a word, he left, driving off without a glance at the pile of belongings scattered across the yard.

The silence that followed was different now. It wasn't heavy with grief or regret. It was filled with the quiet hum of possibility.

In the stillness of that moment, Emma Dawson began to weave the threads of a new beginning. Her heartbeat, once weighed down by doubt and despair, now drummed with a steady rhythm, a promise to herself—a future reclaimed, on her terms.

## Chapter 16

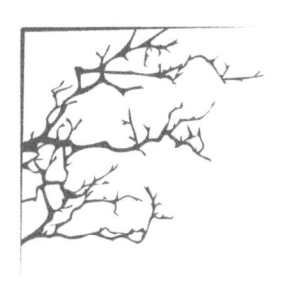

Jaxon's bedroom at Martha's house was cloaked in shadows, except for the ominous glow of a single lamp that cast angular patterns across the table where Jaxon and Martha sat. Their faces were etched with lines of resolve, both sets of eyes mirroring the gravity of their silent pact.

"Nana," Jaxon's voice was a whisper, yet it carried the weight of steel. "We can't let him control our lives any longer."

Martha nodded, her red hair like a flame in the dim light, her gaze never wavering from her grandson's. "I know, Jax. I know."

With deliberate slowness, Jaxon reached into his backpack, producing a stack of research papers that rustled like dry leaves as he placed them on the table. They fanned out, a mosaic of data and potential strategies, each one a calculated step towards their deliverance from Carlos's tyranny.

Jaxon gestured to the stack of papers on the desk. Martha grabbed them, her fingers leaving smudges on the crisp white pages as she scanned each one with laser focus.

"Jaxon, what is all of this?" Martha asked, thumbing through the pages.

"These are some of the methods I've gathered," Jaxon explained, his voice low and urgent. "Each one has the potential to expose him, to drag him into the light and hold him accountable for his actions. Maybe even to undo some of the damage he has caused to our family."

Martha leaned in closer, her sharp eyes skimming over every word as if searching for a hidden weapon. "Are you absolutely certain these are accurate?" Her tone was cool and calculated, revealing years of experience in the art of manipulation.

"Positive," Jaxon replied firmly, his hazel eyes hardening with determination. "I've double-checked every single detail."

Martha's finger traced a particular paragraph, her lips parting slightly as she absorbed the information. "This...this could work," she murmured, a glimmer of excitement dancing in her eyes. "If we play it right, Carlos won't know what hit him until it's too late."

"Exactly," Jaxon agreed with a fierce grin. "He may think he's untouchable, but everyone has a weakness. We just need to exploit it."

"But we have to be careful," Martha reminded him, her expression serious once more. "We can't risk getting caught up in any backlash."

"Of course," Jaxon nodded solemnly. "We always have to consider Emma's safety first." The mention of their shared loved one was like a sacred vow between them, solidifying their alliance and driving their motivation forward.

"Then we proceed carefully," Martha stated, her steely gaze meeting his. "We gather what we need and make our move. No hesitation, no second-guessing."

"Agreed," Jaxon replied. His fingers brushed over the research papers, the tangible evidence of their commitment to action. He felt the surge of adrenaline at the thought of finally facing down the man who had brought nothing but chaos into their lives.

"Let's start here," he said, tapping a section of the paper. "If we can prove this, it'll be the beginning of the end for Carlos Martinez."

The two of them huddled closer, conspirators in the dim light, crafting a plan from whispers and willpower. There would be no turning back now. With every word they spoke, every detail they pored over, Jaxon and Martha Dawson were setting in motion the downfall of a tyrant.

Martha leaned forward, her elbows resting on the scarred wooden table that bore the weight of their daunting strategy. In the dim light, her vibrant red hair seemed to smolder like the coals of a subdued fire, a vivid contrast against the shadows that cloaked the room.

"Each plan has its own set of teeth," Jaxon said, his voice a steady murmur as his finger traced down the column of text. "And they bite back in different ways."

"Tell me more." Martha urged, her gaze sharp and piercing through the semi-darkness. Her mind was a fortress, prepared for the onslaught of grim possibilities Jaxon's words would unleash.

"Wiretaps could expose him, but if we're caught, it's us against the law," Jaxon explained, his hazel eyes locking onto hers, ensuring she understood every implication. "Anonymous tips could backfire, leading to investigations... on everyone involved."

"Emma..." Martha whispered, the name falling from her lips like a protective spell.

"Exactly." Jaxon nodded, acknowledging the unspoken vow to shield his sister at all costs. "We can't let her become collateral damage."

His hand stopped moving across the paper, fingers drumming a silent rhythm.

"But there's one thing we haven't taken into account—his unfaithfulness. The thought of his dicking around, the shitty way he treats mom, it fills me with so much anger. It has started lighting a fire in me that makes me mad enough to kill him. How could I have let him do this to my mom for so long?" A cold edge crept into Jaxon's tone, hinting at the bitterness that had taken root in his heart.

"Unfaithfulness?" Martha asked, her voice laced with skepticism yet intrigued by the thread he was pulling at.

"Picture it—photos, messages, proof of Carlos's bitches. It's ammunition that hits where it hurts, in the ego and the wallet," Jaxon elaborated, his mind already calculating angles and outcomes. "It's personal, devastating, and most importantly, legal. I can post them online from an anonymous account that I can create with a program that blocks my IP address. Out him to the world, and to his women, show that he is still with mom, show that he always comes home to her no matter what he says to them."

"Blackmail." The word hung between them, heavy with implication. Martha's lips pressed into a thin line and one eyebrow raised as she weighed the moral cost against the potential gain.

"No, it's leverage," Jaxon countered, his expression unreadable in the half-light. "A way to push him out without dirtying our hands more than necessary."

Martha sat back; the creak of the chair lost in the silence that followed. She pondered the paths laid bare before them, each fraught with peril, yet undeniably leading toward liberation. Emma's safety, their peace, it hinged on the cunning with which they played this treacherous game.

Martha's voice rang through the room like a battle cry, her steel resolve filling every corner. "We have to do it," she declared with unwavering determination. "It's time to gather the evidence of his betrayal and rid ourselves of Carlos once and for all."

# Chapter 17

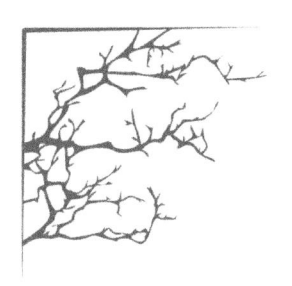

Jaxon's response was quick and sharp, mirroring his fierce determination. They stood united, driven by the burning desire to purge their lives of Carlos' toxic presence. In the quiet intensity of the dimly lit room, mother and son shared a moment of solemn understanding. They knew the risks, but the stakes were too high to ignore. For Emma, for their shattered semblance of family, they would risk everything.

"Then let's not waste another second," Martha concluded with an undertone of steel in her voice, echoing Jaxon's hidden ferocity. Together, they would unravel the tyrant's hold on them, piece by painstaking piece.

Martha's hand hovered above the stack of research papers, casting a shadow in the dim light. Her fingers trembled with uncertainty as she contemplated the dangerous path ahead.

"Jaxon," she began, her voice steady but laced with emotion, "we have to think about your mother in this. Not just her safety, but the emotional aftermath. This could shatter what little mental stability she has left."

Jaxon's usually sharp eyes flickered with a hint of doubt. He leaned forward, elbows on the table, his face a mask of concentration. "I know," he conceded with a heavy sigh, "but can we really let Carlos continue to hurt mom?"

"And tear our family apart?" Martha finished his thought with a heavy weight in her words. She closed her eyes briefly, picturing

Emma's tired and worn face trying to find normalcy in their shattered world.

"Maybe..." Jaxon hesitated before continuing slowly and thoughtfully. "Maybe we should talk to a lawyer. Find out our options if we take this evidence to court."

Martha considered the suggestion, weighing the gravity of involving the authorities. "It's not without risks. Carlos, he has connections, doesn't he? The kind that slither through the cracks of the system." Her words hung heavy, a grim reminder of the man's reach.

"True," Jaxon acquiesced, "but staying silent might be riskier. We need to know our options—what's legal, what's not. And mom... she would want us to do things the right way, wouldn't she?"

"Emma," Martha echoed, allowing herself a brief moment to envision her daughter's green eyes, bright but so easily clouded with doubt. "Yes, she would."

"Then it's settled," Jaxon said, a new layer of determination lining his words. "We find a lawyer—one we can trust. Someone outside Carlos's poisoned well."

"Discreetly," Martha added, nodding in agreement. "We can't afford any slip-ups. Not when it comes to Emma's well-being or our own safety."

"Discreetly," Jaxon repeated, a silent vow etched between them. The decision was made, the die cast. Now, they needed only to tread carefully, one calculated step after another, into the labyrinth that promised to either be their salvation or their undoing.

Jaxon traced the edge of a paper, its contents a testament to Carlos's duplicity. The room felt colder than before, each shadow pregnant with unspoken fears and the ghosts of choices yet to be made. He lifted his eyes to Martha's, finding in them a reflection of his own turmoil.

"Nana," he began, the word hanging heavy between them, "we're not just stepping over a line here—we're blowing it away. What if we become the very thing we're trying to protect mama from?"

Martha exhaled, her breath a slow release of pent-up anxiety. She leaned forward, the soft glow of the single lamp casting deep lines across her face that spoke of sleepless nights and hardened resolve.

"Justice is never black and white, Jaxon," she replied, her voice a whisper against the thick silence. "We're not dealing in absolutes. It's about survival—Emma's... and ours."

He nodded, but his hands betrayed a tremor as he stacked the papers into an orderly pile. "But there's harm in this path, too. The fallout—it isn't just Carlos who will suffer. There are others, innocents maybe, caught in the crossfire of our actions."

"Every war has its casualties," Martha said, her words edged with a sadness that mirrored the shadows around them. "Our focus must be on minimizing the collateral damage while still achieving our objective. It's a delicate balance, one we must handle with care."

"Like threading a needle with trembling hands," Jaxon murmured, the metaphor painting a stark picture of their precarious situation.

"Exactly." Martha reached across the table, her fingers brushing his for a brief moment, a silent pact formed in the dim light. "We thread that needle together."

They paused, allowing the weight of their conversation to settle like dust upon the air, thick with consequence. Jaxon then drew a slow, deliberate breath, grounding himself in the reality of their shared commitment.

"My mom," he said softly, the name a lifeline amidst the storm of their plotting. "She's the reason we're doing all of this. To give her freedom, to let her live without fear or manipulation."

Martha's expression softened, the fierceness in her eyes giving way to a tender, maternal light. "She's our heart, Jaxon. Our brave, beautiful girl trapped in a nightmare not of her making. We'll do whatever it takes to see her safe."

"Even if it costs us everything?" Jaxon asked, though in his heart he knew the answer.

"Especially then," Martha affirmed, her gaze unwavering. "She is our everything. Besides, I won't let you go down, I will take the fall if we get caught. You have to be protected too."

Jaxon's hand hovered above the stack of papers, his fingers drumming a silent cadence on the wooden table. The room was a cocoon of shadows and secrecy, its walls holding the gravity of their impending decision. He knew there was no turning back now, not when the specter of Carlos's malevolence loomed so large over their lives.

"For Emma," Martha echoed, the words a solemn vow spoken into the hush of the night, sealing their resolve as they stood together on the precipice of action.

Hours passed as the pair reviewed each page of information, tactics, plans. Jaxon reached for the stack of research papers; their corners dog-eared from frequent consultations. The room's dim light cast long shadows over his features as he began to shuffle through the pages with precise movements.

"We've got a mountain of information here," he said, hazel eyes scanning the documents before him. "Different methods, different approaches... but none without risk."

"Then we should blend them," Martha responded, her voice steady despite the gravity of their conversation. Her fingers traced the rim of her coffee mug, the ceramic cool against her skin. "We take pieces of each—only the safest, most effective parts—and stitch them into something new. Something covert and foolproof."

"Exactly." Jaxon's nod was curt, decisive. He pulled out a pen, the click echoing in the tense air. Scribbling notes on the topmost sheet, he continued, "We'll need a plan that's discreet, one that keeps mom out of the crossfire."

Martha leaned forward, the red strands of her hair catching the faint light as she peered at the papers. She didn't need to be told twice. Her life had been a testament to the power of details, each one a thread in the fabric of survival.

"Precision is key," she murmured. "Every step has to be invisible, untraceable back to us or to her."

"Understood." Jaxon's voice was low, carrying the weight of their shared resolve. They were venturing into dangerous waters, but the thought of freeing Emma from Carlos's toxic influence fueled him. His mother had endured enough.

"Good. We'll move carefully," Martha insisted, her gaze meeting his with an intensity that only years of hardship could forge. "Neither you nor Emma won't suffer for this—not if I have anything to say about it."

"Are we agreed then?" he asked, his voice barely more than a whisper but laden with an unshakable determination.

Martha nodded; her eyes fixed on Jaxon with a steely resolve that matched his own. "Yes. We've considered every angle, every risk. It's time to act."

"Once we start, we can't stop until it's done," Jaxon cautioned, the edges of the words sharp with the reality of their situation. His thumb brushed the edge of a paper, the tactile sensation grounding him amidst the swirling anxiety that threatened to rise within.

"Emma deserves a life free from fear," Martha said, her lips pressed into a thin line. "We'll give her that. I'm ready."

"Then let's plan this out." Jaxon pulled out a pen, its click echoing in the tense silence. Together, they leaned over the documents, their hands moving with precision as they annotated their intricate plan. Each note was a step toward liberation, each line drawn a pathway away from Carlos's shadow.

## Chapter 18

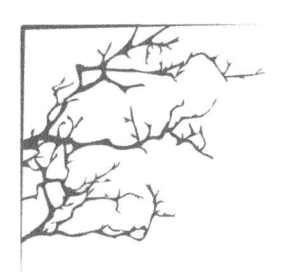

The morning came quickly. The heavy door to Martha's study creaked open, a sliver of the hallway light piercing the dimness within. Jaxon stepped inside the cave like room. It was his grandfather's study before he died last year. So many life-altering decisions had been made at this desk, inside of these walls. It was only fitting that this, too, would be handled here in the sanctity of these walls.

Jaxon's silhouette tall and menacing against the soft glow. The air crackled with anticipation as he closed the distance between himself and Martha, who sat behind the aged mahogany desk, her red hair a fiery crown in the lamp's amber light, still pouring over the paperwork of ideas.

Martha looked up from the papers scattered across her desk, her eyes sharp and piercing. She took a deep breath, steeling herself for the conversation she had known would come. "Good morning my sweet boy. I believe now is the time to start. This plan needs to deal with him—for good."

Jaxon's hazel eyes flashed with suppressed rage, mirroring the resolve in Martha's gaze. "He can't hurt Mom anymore. We've got to make sure of that."

"Yes, but whatever we decide," Martha cautioned, her voice laced with the gravity of their situation, "we must consider the risks. We're wading into dangerous territory, Jax. Once we make our move, there's no turning back."

"I know," Jaxon replied through gritted teeth, his determination solidifying with each passing second. "And that's why we have to be ruthless. We need to research...find the best way. Ways to make sure Carlos leaves no trace behind."

Martha nodded grimly, her mind already racing through sinister possibilities. Each one darker than the last. "You're right. It has to be meticulous, thorough. We can't leave anything to chance." She clutched a pen tightly in her hand, its presence a small comfort amid the growing chaos in her thoughts.

"Leave that to me," With a chilling smirk, Jaxon reassured her, his young age concealing the calculated intention in his voice.

"I'll find out everything we need to know. I'll dig into the deepest, darkest corners if I have to." Jaxon said.

"Good," Martha acknowledged, the word a sharp exhale. "But remember, Jax, you're not just looking for options. You're searching for the best one, the perfect one—the method that will erase him without a whisper of doubt left behind."

"Understood," he said, a silent promise etched in the firm set of his jaw. He turned toward the door, feeling the heavy curtain of conspiracy drape around them, a fabric woven with threads of fear and fortitude.

"Be careful," Martha called after him, her voice a mix of maternal concern and command. "We're playing a dangerous game."

"We don't have a choice," Jaxon responded without looking back. The door clicked shut behind him, sealing their pact in the quiet of Martha's study.

JAXON'S FINGERS FLEW across the keyboard with a frantic urgency, sweat beading on his furrowed brow as he delved deeper into the dark corners of the internet. The sickly blue light of the computer screen cast disturbing shadows over his strong features, accentuating the emptiness in his eyes. With each click, he descended further down the rabbit hole, uncovering more sinister secrets and damning evidence that would make even the strongest stomach turn.

Time became irrelevant as hours turned to days, his only focus on exposing Carlos's vile truths hidden behind encrypted forums and shadowed web pages. And with each post, he reveled in the chaos and destruction he exposed, leaving behind a trail of nothing but his stepfather's incriminating photos and screenshots that would haunt their victims forever.

His hazel eyes, normally brimming with youthful curiosity, now reflected a darker purpose as they scanned lines of text detailing the macabre. He bookmarked pages with clinical detachment, his mind assembling a morbid mosaic of potential methods for Carlos's removal. The cursor blinked in rhythm with Jaxon's racing heart, a silent metronome to the sinister symphony of information flowing onto his notepad.

"Acid baths, animal scavengers, burial at sea..." he murmured, the words a whispered litany of death's artistry. Each option was weighed against an invisible scale of risk and efficacy, and with each passing hour, Jaxon's resolve solidified like concrete setting in his chest.

In another part of the house, Martha hunched over a stack of aged books and yellowing papers, her red hair falling like a fiery curtain around her face. The study was her command center, a place where she could marshal her considerable intellect against the forces threatening her family's peace.

She read about infamous deceptions and criminal cunning, absorbing tales of misdirection that had left law enforcement befuddled and chasing phantoms. Every false lead, every planted clue was a lesson she intended to apply with meticulous care. Her pen scratched against paper, noting down strategies that would sow confusion and cast doubt on any investigation—should it come to that.

"Throw them off at the start," she whispered to herself, "and they'll follow the wrong scent." Martha knew that even the cleverest of predators could be undone by an unexpected turn, and she was determined to be the one leading the dance.

The hours waned, and the house grew silent save for the occasional creak of wood or rustle of paper. Two kindred spirits, bound by blood and dire intent, worked in isolation, their thoughts intertwining unseen like roots beneath the soil. They were forging a plan born of desperation and dark necessity, and as dawn crept over the horizon, the first faint rays of light found Jaxon and Martha closer to their grim resolution.

A week passed; the thick silence of Martha's study quivered as the grandfather clock marked the passing seconds with unyielding regularity. Jaxon stood by the mahogany desk, his long, wavy hair casting shadows over his intent hazel eyes. He straightened a stack of papers, each page a testament to the grim task he had undertaken.

"Nana," Jaxon began, his voice as steady as the ticking clock, "I've sifted through enough dark tales to know that bodies leave tales of their own. We need something...untraceable. We also have to burn everything we have charted out; no trace can be left behind."

Martha, her red hair a stark contrast against the pale morning light filtering through the curtains, nodded in agreement. She laid down the notes she'd been poring over, her gaze never wavering from her grandson's.

"Tell me what you've found," she said, her tone suggesting an eagerness to piece together the final, morbid mosaic.

Jaxon unfolded a paper, lines and bullets marching down in orderly fashion.

"Dismemberment, acid, burial at sea..." Each option fell from his lips, clinical and cold, "...they all carry substantial risks of discovery."

"And the psychological toll on Emma," Martha interjected sharply. "We can't have her world crumbling more than it already has."

"Agreed." Jaxon paused, tracing a line with his finger, before landing on the last item on his list. "There's one that could work—poisoning, followed by suffocation. It's cleaner, less violent."

"Poison leaves traces," Martha countered, her mind racing through scenarios where they might slip up, leaving breadcrumbs for the hounds of justice.

"Most do," Jaxon admitted, locking his gaze with hers. "But some are harder to detect. And if we follow with suffocation, it might just obscure the cause of death enough to mislead an autopsy."

"Harder to detect, I like it." she repeated, the words hanging between them like a sinister promise. "It's not just about being untraceable though, Jaxon. It's about creating a narrative that points away from us."

"Exactly," he replied, a shadow of relief crossing his features. "We control the story from start to finish."

Martha leaned back in her chair, considering the full weight of their decision. The act they pondered was monstrous, yet the monster they faced left them little choice. Carlos, with his charming veneer and venomous core, had pushed them here.

"Then it's settled," Martha declared, the decision carving itself into the room's stillness. "We proceed with the poison and suffocation. But we must be meticulous. I can't say it enough, there is no room for error or second thoughts."

"None," Jaxon affirmed, feeling the fabric of his morality stretch thin under the strain of necessity. "When do we do it?"

"Soon," Martha whispered, her eyes reflecting a storm of resolve and regret. "Before our nerve fails us, or Carlos tightens his grip any further."

"Then we need to get prepared," Jaxon said, folding his notes and tucking them away. "Every step planned; every action rehearsed."

"Every consequence accepted," Martha added softly, standing up to face her son. Together, they were a fortress against the darkness, but inside, each chamber of their hearts echoed with the cost of their looming deed.

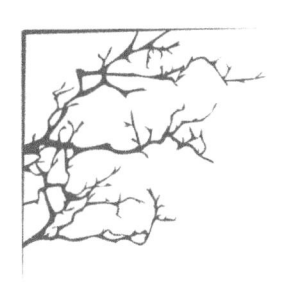

# Chapter 19

Martha's fingers flew over the keys with a staccato rhythm, each tap piercing the quiet of the study. Jaxon hovered over her shoulder, his hazel eyes scanning the growing list of substances on the screen. They had entered a world where words like "toxicity" and "lethality" were weighed with the same consideration as one might give to the choice of coffee or tea.

"Ricin is too traceable," Martha murmured, dismissing an entry with a click. "And cyanide... too dramatic."

"Digitalis?" Jaxon suggested. His voice was calm, belying the macabre nature of their task. "It's heart medicine — could be explained away if discovered."

"Good." Martha's red hair caught the light as she nodded, jotting down the name. "But let's consider something even more insidious. Something that dissipates quickly, leaves no markers."

"Dimethylmercury?" he said, noting its potency.

"Too risky for us to handle," Martha countered, her mind meticulously cataloging the dangers. "We need something silent but manageable."

"Ah, here it is—tetrodotoxin." Jaxon's finger paused on an article detailing the poison derived from puffer fish. "Difficult to detect after death because it's naturally occurring in some marine life. It's perfect."

"Perfect," Martha repeated, her lips forming a thin line. She reviewed the information, her brain ticking through their network of contacts. Someone would know how to get it; they just needed to approach this with discretion.

"Leave this part to me, Jax." Her voice was steel wrapped in velvet. "I'll secure what we need."

"Nana, the risk—" Jaxon began, concern etching lines in his young face.

"Is mine to take," Martha interjected firmly. "You've done enough. This requires... a delicate touch."

"Your connections," Jaxon acknowledged, knowing her web of allies and favors was vast and intricate. "But be careful."

"Always am." Martha pushed back from the computer, and her gaze was flinty as she looked up at him. "Remember, not a word of this to anyone. We're in waters deep enough to drown us both."

Jaxon nodded, feeling the gravity of her words settle upon him like a leaden shroud. He watched as she reached for her phone, her movements precise, betraying no hint of the darkness they were orchestrating. He knew then that his Nana was a force unto herself, capable of moving mountains or, in this case, eradicating them.

"Before we do anything else, I need you to go get us a new laptop. This one has to be destroyed." Martha said.

Jaxon nodded and twisted the pen in his hand, tapping an irregular rhythm onto the mahogany surface of Martha's study desk. The clock overhead ticked ominously, slicing through the silence as they both stared at the calendar.

"We need to think about when he'll be most vulnerable," Jaxon said, his hazel eyes scanning the weeks laid out before them.

"Carlos likes his routines," Martha replied, her voice low and even. "Wednesdays, he works late—says he's catching up on paperwork. We know that's not true. Your mother works a twelve-hour shift on Monday, Tuesday and Wednesday, right?"

"Yeah, so Wednesday?" Jaxon murmured, pressing the pen into the date two weeks from now. "That gives us time to prepare, and the house will be quiet."

"Late enough for the neighborhood to be asleep, early enough for us to deal with...the aftermath." Martha's fingers hovered over the calendar as she spoke, her touch almost reverent. "I will ask my contact at the hospital to put your mom on for an extra late shift, that will get her out of the house and keep us out of the way."

"Mark it," Jaxon said, a sense of grim determination settling upon him. Martha drew a small 'x' through the date. They each felt the weight of the simple act, a silent pact sealed in ink.

"Let's go through the steps," Martha said, pushing away from the desk. She stood by the fireplace, her silhouette casting long shadows across the room.

"Right," Jaxon agreed, standing to join her. His mind was clear, focused solely on the task ahead. "He comes in, asks about mom, I tell him she had to work late, offer to get him a drink, then I'll serve him the drink. Something strong, to mask any odd taste."

"Good. And I'll be here, just in case he suspects anything. I can distract him," Martha added, her eyes fierce with resolve.

"Once he's passed out, we'll have to move fast," Jaxon continued, his voice steady despite the tremor he felt within. "We can't afford any mistakes."

"Then the suffocation," Martha interjected, her tone clinical. "It has to look natural. No signs of a struggle."

They moved together, rehearsing each motion with meticulous care. Jaxon mimed handing over a glass, watching as Martha pretended to engage an invisible Carlos in conversation. They practiced how they would support his body, how to apply pressure without leaving marks.

"Like this," Jaxon said, demonstrating the technique they had read about online. His hands hovered in the air, shaping the ghostly outline of their victim.

"Exactly," Martha confirmed, nodding her approval. "And we can't forget—we'll need to wear gloves and clean up immediately after. Every surface, every potential fingerprint."

"Understood," Jaxon replied, his jaw set. They repeated the motions, refining their movements, until each step flowed into the next with eerie precision.

The rehearsal ended and they stepped back, surveying the empty space that had become their stage for murder. Their plan was set, their roles etched into their beings, and the night of execution loomed ominously ahead.

"Are you ready for this?" Jaxon asked, though it was more a confirmation than a question.

Martha met his gaze, her expression hard as granite. "I've never been more ready for anything in my life."

They left the study without another word, their minds replaying the scene they would soon enact in grim reality. Their hearts may have been heavy, but their resolve was unbreakable. For family, for retribution, for an end to the nightmare Carlos had wrought—they were prepared to do whatever it took.

Jaxon's fingers danced across the keys of his laptop, tapping into a digital list that grew longer with each entry. Beside him, Martha leaned over the kitchen table, her red hair cascading over a stack of papers as she cross-referenced their online findings with a printed manual of forensic countermeasures. "Latex gloves," she murmured, her voice low and even.

"Check," Jaxon replied without looking up, adding it to their virtual inventory.

"Full-face masks?"

"Got them on the list."

"Plastic sheeting, duct tape, bleach..."

"Already in the basket."

The room was silent save for the staccato rhythm of Jaxon's typing and the subtle scratch of Martha's pen checking off items on her list. They worked methodically, with the precision of a well-oiled machine, both aware that any oversight could unravel their meticulously woven plan.

Martha stood abruptly, her chair scraping against the wooden floor. She walked to the window, peering out into the darkening sky, her eyes tracing the silhouettes of trees swaying in the wind. "We'll need a strong alibi. Something ironclad."

"Leave that to me," Jaxon assured her, his voice a mixture of confidence and cold determination. "I've got a few ideas."

"Good." Martha turned back to face him, her gaze locking onto his. "We're doing the right thing, Jaxon. Remember that. Let's not forget to get rid of the lists on both of our computers. Delete what's there and insert other things, homework, work that kind of thing. Then we need to get rid of the papers full of research too, we can burn those on the grill."

Jaxon nodded, though his hazel eyes betrayed the storm brewing within—a tempest of emotions he dared not unleash. He saved the document and closed his laptop, signaling the end of their preparations for the night.

Together, they gathered the physical materials they had already acquired, handling each item with care. They placed them in a heavy-duty black duffel bag, which Jaxon zipped closed with a firm tug. He lifted the bag and carried it to a hidden compartment in the wall behind a false panel, an old trick Martha had insisted on installing years ago. With a soft click, the panel sealed shut, concealing their arsenal from prying eyes.

"Out of sight, out of mind," Martha said, though the edge in her voice suggested that the gravity of their actions would never truly leave their thoughts.

After ensuring everything was in place, they made their way to the study. The room was steeped in shadows, the only light emanating from a single desk lamp that cast long, angular shapes upon the walls. Jaxon and Martha stood side by side, their profiles etched against the backdrop of darkness.

Their faces were resolute, carved from stone, and yet beneath the surface, a current of trepidation ran deep. It was a moment suspended in time, where the past and future collided, leaving them at the precipice of a decision from which there was no return.

Martha reached out, her hand finding Jaxon's. Their fingers interlocked, a silent pact between them—a vow that bound their fates together. Jaxon met her gaze, and in the depths of her steel-blue eyes, he found an echo of his own resolve.

They shared a knowing glance, an unspoken conversation that traversed the chasm of what ifs and maybes. In that look, they acknowledged the path they had chosen, the consequences that awaited, and the singular truth that propelled them forward: they would protect their family, no matter the cost.

The day closed on their united front; their hearts heavy but their will unwavering. As the clock ticked towards the hour of reckoning, Jaxon and Martha Dawson were ready to embrace the darkness that beckoned them forth.

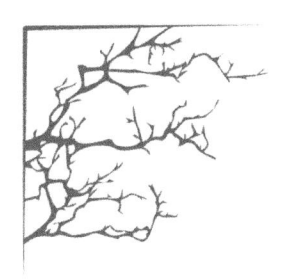

## Chapter 20

Emma stood in the kitchen, her hands trembling ever so slightly as she reached for the bottle of bourbon on the counter. She could hear Carlos in the dining room, the low hum of the TV in the background as he flicked through channels, waiting for his dinner. The house felt too quiet, like the air itself was holding its breath, anticipating something neither of them wanted to face.

"Emma!" Carlos's voice cut through the silence, sharp and impatient. "What the hell is taking so damn long? I don't have all fucking night."

She tightened her grip on the bottle, forcing herself to take slow, deliberate steps as she entered the dining room. Carlos was lounging at the head of the table, his legs stretched out in front of him, looking every bit as arrogant as he always did in their home. The flickering light from the TV cast an eerie glow across his face.

Without a word, she placed the glass in front of him and poured the bourbon, the rich amber liquid swirling as it filled the tumbler. Her stomach churned with the familiar unease that had settled in ever since things had begun to unravel between them.

"Here you go," she said softly, setting the bottle down next to him. She didn't look at his face, but she could feel his eyes on her, the way he always studied her like he was looking for something to criticize.

Carlos picked up the glass, swirled the bourbon, and took a slow sip, savoring it. He glanced at the plate of food she had prepared, lifting the corner of his lip in disdain.

"Same old fucking thing, huh? You really don't know how to change it up, do you, Emma?"

Her jaw tightened, but she forced herself to remain calm. She had heard this before. The little digs. The small ways he tried to cut her down, to remind her that in his eyes, she was never quite enough.

"I—I cooked exactly what you asked for," she said, her voice barely above a whisper.

Carlos snorted, taking another sip. "That's the problem with you, Emma. Always doing exactly what's asked of you. Never more. No creativity, no initiative. You ever wonder why nothing in your life is exciting? It's because you're boring, Emma, you're fucking boring. You always have been and always will be. I don't know what I ever saw in you."

Her chest tightened, the weight of his words pressing down on her like a stone. She stared at him, trying to remember the man she had once loved, the man she had thought she knew. But all she could see now was the cold, cruel figure in front of her.

"I have to get back to work. My break is almost over," she muttered, turning to leave.

"That's right, just walk the fuck away," Carlos called after her, his voice dripping with mockery. "You're real good at that, aren't you? You lazy fucking bitch. You are good for nothing but an argument."

She didn't turn around, didn't give him the satisfaction of a reaction. Instead, she walked back into the kitchen, her heart pounding in her chest. The sound of the silverware clinking against his plate echoed through the walls as he began to eat alone, just like he always did now.

She stood by the sink, staring out the window at the darkening sky, her thoughts swirling like a storm. Carlos had always had a temper, but lately, something had shifted. The man she had married was gone, replaced by someone bitter, angry, and unpredictable.

Emma swallowed hard, her hands gripping the edge of the counter as she tried to steady herself. She didn't know how much more she could take. The years of belittling, the constant insults—they had worn her down, hollowed her out until she barely recognized the woman she had once been.

She poured herself a glass of water, trying to calm the rising tide of anxiety inside her. As she stood there, staring into the sink, she made a decision. One that had been brewing for weeks, maybe months.

Tonight would be different.

She wasn't going to fight with him anymore. She wasn't going to let him tear her down. Not tonight. Not ever again.

The plan she had thought about in the darkest corners of her mind—one that she never thought she'd go through with—now felt like her only way out.

Emma glanced back at the dining room, hearing Carlos's muffled grumbles through the wall as he ate. Slowly, her eyes drifted to the small vial she had hidden in the pocket of her scrubs. The vial she had never imagined she'd use.

Her hand hovered for a moment, hesitation flickering through her like a last warning. Then, with steady resolve, she shoved it deeper into the pocket, feeling the cold glass against her fingers.

She took a deep breath, steadying herself for what she knew came next.

Emma slid into the driver's seat, her heart still pounding from the confrontation with Carlos. Her hands gripped the steering wheel tightly, knuckles white as she tried to steady her breathing. The familiar weight of dread sat heavy in her chest, but something felt different tonight—like a dam had finally broken inside her.

As the car engine rumbled to life, she glanced in the rear-view mirror, her own eyes staring back at her, wide and full of something she hadn't seen in a long time—resolve. She shifted the car into gear, her mind racing as she pulled out of the driveway. The vial she had taken was now tucked safely into her pocket, hidden away, just like the thoughts that had been buried inside her for so long.

The streetlights blurred as she drove, her mind wandering back to the house she had just left. Carlos, sitting at the table, drinking the bourbon she had poured for him, completely unaware. The thought made her stomach turn, but it also filled her with a strange sense of calm. This was her last chance to turn back—to undo what she had started.

But she didn't turn back.

Instead, she focused on the road ahead, the hum of the car's engine drowning out the storm in her mind. Her break at work was over, and she needed to return to the hospital. The night shift was waiting for her, the mundane routine that had become her escape from the chaos at home.

As she drove, the rain began to fall, light at first, then harder, tapping against the windshield in a steady rhythm. The sound was soothing, almost hypnotic, and for a moment, Emma allowed herself to breathe. The weight of what she had done—what she was about to do—hovered in the back of her mind, but for now, she pushed it away.

She pulled into the hospital parking lot, the large building looming in front of her like a beacon in the night. The bright lights flickered through the rain, casting long shadows across the wet pavement. Emma turned off the car and sat there for a moment, staring out at the empty lot, her fingers still gripping the steering wheel.

She could feel the ticking of time, the countdown she had set into motion. Inside, Carlos would finish his drink, the poison slowly working its way through his system. By the time she got home, it would be done.

Emma took a deep breath, her chest tight. She had done what she needed to do. What she had told herself she had to do. But as she sat there, in the stillness of the car, the enormity of her actions washed over her.

Her phone buzzed in her lap, jolting her back to reality. It was a message from the hospital. They needed her inside.

She stuffed the phone into her purse, next to the empty vial, and stepped out into the rain. Each step toward the hospital felt heavy, like she was wading through water. The familiar smell of antiseptic and fresh linens greeted her as she pushed through the doors.

For now, life had to go on as usual.

But when she went home, everything would be different.

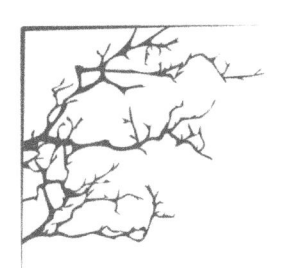

# Chapter 21

"Tonight," Jaxon repeated, his voice low but unwavering. "We have to start tonight."

Martha's gaze hardened, her resolve evident in the sharp lines of her face.

"We won't let him destroy her any longer," she said, her voice thick with the weight of years spent watching her daughter suffer. "This ends now."

Their movements mirrored one another, efficient and methodical. Every action was deliberate, the culmination of countless sleepless nights spent strategizing. Carlos had underestimated them, mistaking their patience for passivity, their silence for submission. But that was his fatal flaw—his arrogance. It had blinded him to the quiet strength growing within them, the kind that could only come from love.

As they stepped into the night, the world seemed to pause, the air heavy with anticipation. The cool breeze whispered through the trees, carrying with it a sense of inevitability. The moon hung low in the sky, casting long, skeletal shadows that stretched across the yard like ghostly fingers. Some of Carlos's belongings, left behind from having been carelessly thrown across the lawn the week before, were illuminated in the silver light, a stark reminder of the life he had shattered.

Jaxon paused for a moment, his eyes drifting toward the house. He thought of how this house had been happy before, filled with love and laughter, now just an empty shell of sadness. His mama had fought for so long—silently, endlessly, enduring the slow unraveling of a life she had once cherished. But tonight, that battle would no longer be hers to fight alone. Jaxon's heart clenched with the fierce love of a son determined to shield his mother from further harm.

"She won't be home until after eleven," Jaxon murmured, more to himself than to Martha. "She'll never suspect we had anything to do with this, right?"

Martha nodded. "She doesn't need to know anything, not now, not ever. This is about freeing her, not burdening her further."

They exchanged a look, the kind of look shared only by those who have lived through the fire together, who know the depths of the other's resolve.

"This is for her," Martha said, her voice steady. "For the life she deserves. For Emma."

Jaxon's jaw tightened, his fingers curling into fists. "For Mama."

Their silent pact solidified, they moved forward, their steps synchronized, their mission clear. There was no turning back now. The plan was set in motion, and Carlos—blind to the rising tide—would soon face the consequences of his cruelty. Whatever risks lay ahead, they were willing to face them, because they knew that by morning, the world would look different.

THE QUIET HUM OF THE night engulfed them as they approached the car. The weight of what they were about to do settled between them, not as a burden, but as a shared responsibility. Jaxon's hand hovered over the door handle for a moment before pulling it open with a soft click. As they slid into the house, the atmosphere felt charged, as if the very air around them could sense the impending shift.

Martha glanced over at her grandson, a look of quiet pride in her eyes. "No matter what happens next, we did the right thing," she whispered. "Carlos won't take anything more from this family."

Jaxon stared ahead, his face a mask of calm, but inside his mind raced, calculating every move. The plan had to work—failure wasn't an option. They'd been careful, every step planned with ruthless precision. Now, all that remained was one final push to topple the fragile house of cards Carlos had so carelessly built.

As they entered the house, the air seemed to thicken, pregnant with the weight of what had to be done. Each footfall felt heavy with purpose. Jaxon's grip on the surgical gloves tightened, his pulse a steady, hammering beat in his chest. It wasn't fear that gripped him, but raw adrenaline. He and Martha had crossed the line—there was no turning back. And Jaxon was ready to see this through, no matter what.

The night stretched before them, dark and impenetrable, but with it came a strange sense of freedom. After tonight, there would be no more waiting, no more helplessly watching as Carlos tore their family apart, piece by agonizing piece. This was their moment. Their chance to take back control, to reclaim what had been ripped from them.

In the suffocating silence of the room, Martha's hand found Jaxon's. Her grip was firm, a grounding force amidst the storm of emotions swirling within him.

"We'll be okay," she whispered, her voice steady, though laced with an undercurrent of steel. "Emma will be okay."

Jaxon turned to look at her, his Nana's face bathed in the soft, eerie glow of the night light's faint illumination. Her eyes held a fierceness he hadn't seen in years, a mother's resolve, hardened by the years of watching Emma suffer. For the first time in a long time, Jaxon felt the flicker of belief. They had to be okay. They *would* be okay. For

Emma. For Jaxon. For every day spent in silent torment, leading to this very moment.

They slipped into the den, pulling their gloves snugly onto their hands, their movements deliberate, synchronized. With each step down the narrow hallway, they moved deeper into the unknown, yet for the first time in months, it didn't feel suffocating. Instead, it felt like possibility—like the door to a new beginning was slowly creaking open.

In the silence of the back room, the night cloaked them in darkness. They waited, their breaths shallow, the tension in the air thick as it pressed against their skin. Every second that passed unfurled their plan further, winding tighter around Carlos's fate like a noose. They didn't speak, didn't need to. The unspoken understanding between them was enough — tonight was the night that everything changed.

By the time the sun broke over the horizon, their family would be free. Carlos would never see it coming.

And when it was all over, there would be nothing left for him to take.

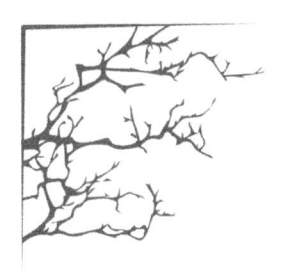

# Chapter 22

The early morning sun streamed through the kitchen windows, casting a warm glow across the breakfast table. Emma sat with her mother, Martha, sipping coffee in a quiet moment of peace. Jaxon, with his lanky frame still growing into itself, leaned against the counter, munching on a piece of toast. The air was thick with the kind of unspoken tension that had become all too familiar in their household, but for now, they clung to the semblance of normalcy.

The calm was shattered by the sharp, insistent ring of the doorbell. Emma frowned, exchanging a glance with Martha. "Who could that be this early?" she muttered, pushing back her chair and heading for the door.

When she opened it, the woman standing on the doorstep was the last person Emma expected to see. The woman in the pictures from Carlos's texts. Beatriz—stunning even in her disheveled state, with dark curls framing a face that held a beauty marred by the stormy expression she wore. Her eyes, sharp and unforgiving, locked onto Emma's.

"Are you Emma Dawson, Carlos Martinez's wife?" Beatriz's voice was low, controlled, but beneath it simmered a rage that threatened to spill over.

Emma's heart sank as she recognized the name from the credit card statements and the text messages she had found. The woman before her wasn't just a headless dirty picture in a text, not just the initial B anymore—she was a living, breathing reality.

"Yes, how can I help you?" Emma replied, her voice wavering despite her attempt to remain composed.

"We needs to talk," Beatriz said, pushing past Emma into the house without waiting for an invitation. Emma followed her, heart pounding in her chest. Martha and Jaxon looked up in surprise as Beatriz entered the kitchen, her presence immediately changing the atmosphere.

"Who the hell are you?" Jaxon asked, his teenage bravado faltering as he took in the tension radiating from the stranger.

"I'm Beatriz. Beatriz Alvarez," she said, her eyes darting between the three of them, her Spanish accent thick and forceful. "I am here because I am pregnant with Carlos's baby."

The words hung in the air like a bomb that had just exploded, shattering the fragile peace of the morning. Emma felt the ground shift beneath her, her knees threatening to give way as the full weight of Beatriz's declaration hit her. She reached out, gripping the back of a chair for support.

Martha's face hardened; her jaw set in a way that Emma recognized all too well—the same expression she wore when preparing to fight for what was hers. But before she could speak, Jaxon stepped forward, his voice cutting through the heavy silence.

"What did you just say?" he demanded; his tone incredulous. The toast forgotten in his hand, his eyes were wide with a mix of disbelief and anger.

"You heard me," Beatriz replied, her voice steady. "I'm pregnant with Carlos's baby. And I'm not going to be kept in the shadows any longer."

Emma felt a wave of nausea roll through her. This was too much, too fast. She had been struggling to come to terms with Carlos's infidelity, but this—this was something she hadn't been prepared for. The room seemed to tilt, the walls closing in as the enormity of the situation crushed her.

"How... how do we even know it's true?" Martha finally spoke, her voice trembling with barely contained fury. "How do we know you're not just trying to tear this family apart?"

Beatriz's eyes flashed with a mix of anger and defiance. "I have nothing to gain by lying, Mrs. Dawson. Believe me, this isn't how I wanted things to go. But I am not going to hide anymore. Carlos has responsibilities, to me and to this baby, besides you all deserve to know the truth. Since he has not come by to see me in a few days, I think he is hiding, so I came to you, so he won't be able to hide me anymore."

Jaxon's fists clenched at his sides, his knuckles white. "You're lying, Carlos wouldn't do this to my mom," he said, his voice breaking slightly. "He wouldn't betray any of us like this."

Beatriz softened for a moment, her gaze shifting to Jaxon. "Oh mihijo, I'm sorry," she said, and for the first time, her voice held a hint of sorrow. "I never wanted to hurt you. But the truth is, your step father and I have been involved for a long while. This is not something that just happened. And now... now there is a baby involved. My baby."

Jaxon stood up to his whole height to become larger, "Do not call me that, I am not your anything, you whore."

Beatriz's face flushed with anger, "I am not a whore, I am the love of Carlos's life. He told me so." She crossed her arms over her chest in a move of false bravado.

Emma's mind raced, trying to make sense of it all. The evidence had been there, but she had clung to the hope that it wasn't as bad as she feared. Now, faced with the stark reality, there was no denying it. She looked at Beatriz, seeing the desperation in her eyes, the way she held herself as if she were bracing for impact. This woman wasn't a villain in a story—she was as trapped as Emma was, a pawn in a game neither of them had wanted to play.

"He's not here, I haven't seen him in a few days. I kicked him out last week, but he wouldn't go, but..." Emma paused, "What, exactly, do you want from me?" Emma's voice was barely above a whisper, but it carried the weight of her shattered world.

Beatriz took a deep breath, her hand unconsciously drifting to her stomach. "I only want Carlos to take responsibility," she said simply. "And I want to make sure that my child—his child—does not grow up hiding in the shadows."

Martha opened her mouth to argue, but Emma raised a hand to stop her. "Ma, stop. This isn't the time or place for this," Emma said, her voice firmer now. "Jaxon, go to your room."

"Mom, I—"

"Go. Now." The steel in Emma's voice left no room for argument. Jaxon hesitated, anger and confusion warring on his face, before he stormed out of the kitchen, his footsteps echoing through the house.

When he was gone, Emma turned back to Beatriz.

"Like I said, Carlos hasn't been home in days. I thought he was with you. Anyway, you've said what you came to say," she continued, her voice calmer than she felt. "Now leave, leave and don't come back here, not to my home."

Beatriz looked like she wanted to argue, but after a moment, her shoulders fell, and she nodded. "You know about me? Well, that is good that he finally tell you. I'll go, for now. But I'll be back. You tell Carlos that he cannot ignore me and our baby, not anymore." she said, a promise rather than a threat. "This is not over, not over at all."

As the door closed behind Beatriz, Emma sank into a chair, her strength finally giving out. Martha rushed to her side, wrapping her arms around her daughter as the first sobs tore from Emma's throat. The illusion of control she had so desperately tried to maintain was shattered, and all that was left was the broken pieces of the life she thought she knew.

Outside, the sun continued to rise, its light falling on a world that would never be the same again.

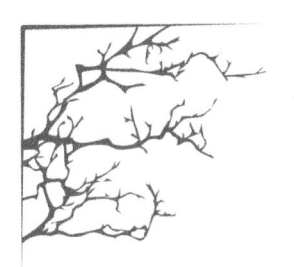

# Chapter 23

The front door of the Dawson residence swung open, and Detective Michael Ross stepped over the threshold. His muscular build filled the doorway, and his piercing blue eyes surveyed the room. A silver badge clipped to his belt gleamed under the hallway's light, echoing the streaks of gray in his otherwise dark hair. The lines on his face were like etchings on a map, each one charting a case, a confrontation, a story that demanded justice.

"Detective Ross," he introduced himself, extending a firm hand to the unshaken woman who must have been Emma Dawson's mother, Martha.

Detective Ross extended a firm hand to Mrs. Martha Dawson. Mrs. Dawson responded with a firm handshake of her own. Detective Ross was impressed by the woman's firm handshake and strong aura. It conveyed her strength and resolve to the detective.

Martha was a strong-willed woman, and she didn't mince words.

"How can I help you, Detective?" she asked firmly, her gaze holding steady as she locked eyes with the detective with a tight smile.

Detective Ross knew he had to take charge of the situation. He was good at reading people, and he could tell that the family was in a state of shock.

"I am here about Carlos Martinez. He has been reported missing." Detective Ross said as he surveyed the foyer.

"Carlos? Missing? I hadn't heard. I just assumed he was on another of his business trips. Who reported him missing, if I might ask?" Martha asked, holding her position in the hallway.

Detective Ross suggested that they move to the living room, where they could talk more privately. As they walked to the living room, he noticed the family portraits on the wall. They showed the family at various stages of happiness, but the edges of the frames were frayed, as if they had been damaged by time and neglect. He also noticed a figure retreating up the stairs.

"Who was that?" He asked nodding to the top of the stairs.

"My daughter, Emma. Carlos's wife. Surely she would know if her husband was missing." Martha said.

"I'd like to speak with her." Said Detective Ross.

"She really isn't up to company right now; she has been working long shifts and..." Martha started.

"Mrs. Dawson, it's important that I get this investigation started, if in fact, he is missing. The sooner the better, I'd like to get this matter resolved quickly. Could you call her please?" He insisted.

A palpable tension hung in the air, dense enough to slice through. The mother hesitated, then nodded reluctantly.

"Emma!" she called out with a voice that tried to sound calm but carried an edge of distress. There was a pause, a moment of uncertainty where the household held its breath.

Footsteps echoed down the staircase, and Ross turned, allowing himself a brief assessment as Emma Dawson appeared. His sharp eyes noted her guarded posture, the way her shoulders tensed with each step she took. Her expression was carefully neutral, but the detective didn't miss the fleeting shadows that danced behind her green eyes—fear? Resignation?

"Ms. Dawson, I am Detective Ross with Oakdale Police, missing person's department." Ross greeted her, standing to offer a respectful nod.

"Detective," she replied, her voice barely above a whisper.

"Would you mind if we spoke for a few minutes?" Ross asked, his demeanor softening slightly to put her at ease.

"Sure, okay," she consented, though her lips pressed into a thin line as if bracing herself.

"What's this about Detective?"

"Your husband, Carlos Martinez, he has been reported missing." Detective Ross said, trying to read her reaction.

"Missing? Are you sure? Who reported him missing?" She asked with genuine concern lacing her voice.

"A Ms. Beatriz Alvarez, she states in the report that she is his girlfriend?" Detective Ross reads from his notes and watches Emma over the top of his notebook. "I'm sorry, I don't know why she would do that, Detective. My husband is away on business." Emma said, her brows furrowing with confusion.

"Well, according to the report, he was supposed to visit this Ms. Alvarez, and he has not been there or called in a few days, which she states is very out of character for him." Detective Ross says softly.

"I don't know anything about that Detective. My husband travels for work, he is out of town now, in fact." Emma said softly.

As they sat, Ross's acute senses picked up on the discordant notes of a family symphony in disarray. The room felt too still, the kind of quiet that screamed louder than any shout. Emma's fingers twisted together in her lap, betraying a nervous energy that belied her composed exterior.

"Can you tell me about Carlos," Ross began, leaning in just so, his tone inviting confidence. "When did you notice something was wrong?"

Her breath hitched, almost imperceptible, and Ross filed away every detail, every flinch and falter. In the game of truths and lies, he was a master at discerning which notes were played false. Here, in this living room with its worn carpet and the scent of unease,

Detective Michael Ross could feel the melody of mystery beginning to unfold. And he was determined to hear every note. "As I said, Detective, he is out of town, not missing. There is nothing to notice that is out of the ordinary. He travels all the time." Emma said.

Detective Michael Ross leaned forward, elbows resting on his knees, a posture that belied the coiled intensity within. The case file of Carlos Dawson's disappearance lay open before him, its contents spilling out like the fragmented pieces of a jigsaw too complex for any ordinary mind to solve. But Ross was far from ordinary.

"Mrs. Dawson," Ross said, keeping his voice even, "I need to understand Carlos's movements on the day he vanished. Can you recall any unusual behavior, any deviation from his regular routine?"

Emma Dawson, seated across from him, seemed almost to fold into herself, her slender frame shrouded in the oversized sweater that hung off her shoulders. The gentle sway of her shoulder-length brown hair couldn't soften the hard lines of fatigue etched around her eyes—a palette of sorrow and sleepless nights. Her green eyes, once vibrant, now resembled glass marbles clouded by the storms of her psyche.

"Carlos is not missing, he was his usual self the morning he left on another work trip," she murmured, the words seeming to cost her more than they should. "He kissed me goodbye...and then..." She trailed off, her gaze flickering to a corner of the room as if expecting to find him there, hidden in the shadows.

Ross noted the pause, the way her fingers ceased their endless dance and clung to each other, knuckles whitening. He recognized the signs of someone who had weathered many storms and yet still stood—barely. Emma Dawson was a survivor, but survival came at a price.

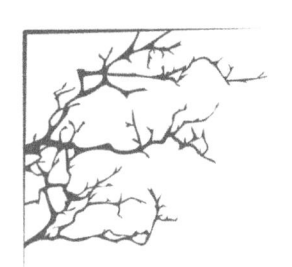

# Chapter 24

"Mrs. Dawson," he continued, "it's crucial that we establish a timeline. Anything out of place could be the key we're looking for."

Her eyes locked onto his with a silent plea, but Ross's own gaze was unwavering, his blue eyes reflecting a determination as immovable as bedrock. Here was a man who had stared down the darkest alleys of human nature, yet never blinked. His graying temples spoke of years spent chasing specters through the fog of crime, while the subtle creak of his leather jacket whispered tales of pursuit and capture.

"Emma, I'm here to help," Ross reassured, softening his delivery, keenly aware of the delicate strands of trust he wove with each word. "But I can only do that if you're completely honest with me. Did Carlos have any enemies? Anyone who might want to harm him?"

She took in a deep breath, her chest rising and falling with the effort. "I don't know," she admitted, her voice frail. "He had secrets, you know? We all do. But Carlos...he was good at burying them."

"Secrets have a way of surfacing, Mrs. Dawson," Ross replied, his tone laced with experience. "And I intend to dig all of them up."

The silence that followed was thick, filled with the unspoken truths that hung between them. Ross watched Emma closely, observant as ever, piecing together the fragments she unwittingly dropped into the void between them. Every hesitation, every glance away was a note in the symphony of deception that surrounded Carlos's disappearance.

"Detective Ross," Emma said finally, her voice stronger than before, as if the act of speaking gave her strength. "If you find out what happened to Carlos...will it change anything?"

Ross's answer was immediate, resolute. "It will bring the truth into the light. And sometimes, that's all we can hope for."

Emma nodded, a gesture that conveyed both resignation and relief. As Ross prepared to delve deeper into the shadows of the Dawson family history, he made a silent vow to unearth every lie, every secret, until the truth lay bare, glaring and undeniable. For Detective Michael Ross, justice was not just a duty; it was an oath, a promise to the lost and the searching, that he would fight for answers until the very end.

Detective Michael Ross leaned forward, placing his hands deliberately upon the weathered wood of the kitchen table. His eyes, a penetrating blue, met Emma Dawson's with an intensity that managed to be both commanding and gentle.

"Mrs. Dawson," he began, his voice a low timbre that carried empathy as clearly as it did authority, "I know this is difficult for you. But I need to understand what happened to Carlos to help you find peace."

The room seemed to shrink around them, every creak of the old house punctuating the silence that followed. Emma sat across from him, her fingers entwined tightly in her lap. The subtle tremble in her hands betrayed an inner turmoil that Ross recognized all too well—the mark of secrets held too close for too long.

"Detective, please call me Emma. His girlfriend came here yesterday, she made some wild accusations and threatened me, not directly but she did threaten me. " Emma whispered, her voice barely carrying over the distance. Her expressive green eyes were clouded with apprehension, a wariness that spoke volumes of the battles she's fought within herself. "I—I don't know what's going on. I can tell you that he's an illegal. He's here working for cash. I knew he had girls, I... I just want this to be over."

"Understood. What does he do for work?" he replied, nodding slowly, respecting the fortress of her hesitation. Yet he remained seated, patient as the evening shadows stretching across the threadbare rug.

"I don't really know; he was very secretive about it all. He told me not to worry about it, as long as the bills were paid, I didn't need to know anything more." Emma said, lowering her eyes.

"I can tell that you've been through so much, Emma. I'm here to listen, to help you through this."

There was something about his presence—calm, unyielding—that began to coax the walls around Emma's resolve to crumble. In him, she saw not the harbinger of painful truths but instead a sentinel against the ghosts that haunted her.

"Carlos has his demons," Emma said after a long pause, each word seeming to cost her something. She looked up at Ross with an earnestness that made her look suddenly younger, more vulnerable. "But he loves us. He wouldn't just leave..."

"Sometimes love is complicated," Ross offered softly, acknowledging the complexity of human emotions. "People do things out of love that are hard to understand. My job is to make sense of those actions when they lead down darker paths."

Emma drew in a shaky breath, the first signs of trust blooming in her eyes. "He would stay up late, working on his laptop, always worried about keeping everything safe." A sliver of a memory found its way into her voice, a note of confusion. "But safe from what, I never knew."

"Whatever he was protecting, we'll find out together," Ross assured her, his words not just a statement but a commitment. There was a silent promise in his gaze, an oath that transcended the badge he wore—a vow to stand beside her amidst the chaos that threatened to engulf her world.

"Thank you," Emma murmured, a fragile smile touching her lips for the first time. It was faint, but it was there—a glimmer of hope reignited by the understanding offered by the man before her.

Ross gave a slight nod, allowing himself a moment to share in the light of her gratitude before the gravity of their situation pulled him back. "Let's take this one step at a time, Emma. Together, we'll bring this to light."

As the evening sun dipped below the horizon, casting long shadows through the kitchen window, Detective Michael Ross sensed the shift within Emma Dawson. The flicker of hope, once smothered by fear and uncertainty, now found fuel in the solidarity of their newfound alliance. And in the heart of that quiet kitchen, a partnership was forged—one born of mutual determination to uncover the truth, whatever it might reveal.

The kitchen clock ticked an ominous rhythm as Emma wrapped her arms around herself, a subconscious shield against the memories that lingered like cold drafts in a once-warm room. Detective Ross leaned back against the worn counter top, his eyes steady on her face, reading every flicker of emotion with the precision of a seasoned investigator.

"Emma," he began, his voice gentle but firm, "I need you to tell me about Carlos on the days leading up to his disappearance."

She bit her lip, the question stirring the sediment of her thoughts. Her green eyes wandered past Ross, settling on the darkness outside the window. "He was... unsettled," she admitted, the words emerging from a place of vulnerability. "We had a really bad fight, I kicked him out. Lately, it was like walking on eggshells. One wrong step, and—"

"Everything shatters," Ross finished for her, his internal monologue acknowledging the fragility of her situation. He observed the tremble in her hands, the way her gaze darted away when she spoke of Carlos. He needed her trust to peel back the layers of fear that Carlos had so meticulously wrapped around her life.

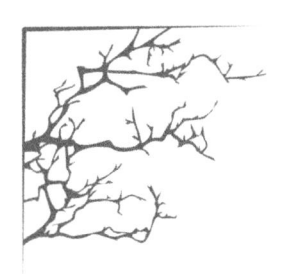

## Chapter 25

"Did he say anything that might indicate where he was going?" Ross pressed gently, making sure his tone carried more concern than interrogation.

"No, nothing specific," Emma sighed, finally meeting his gaze again. "He'd rant about being trapped, needing space. I thought it was just the stress talking." She paused, her throat constricting with the effort of keeping composure. "I never imagined he'd actually leave." Emma paused, her brow furrowed, "Could Immigration have picked him up? He only had his high school identification to prove who he is."

Detective Ross nodded, "It's possible, I will look into that." He was giving her the space to breathe, to compose herself in the silence that followed. His experience told him that patience was key; the human heart opened at its own pace.

"Carlos's need for 'space,'" Ross mused aloud, carefully choosing his words, "do you think it could relate to his... activities outside your marriage?"

Emma's protective arms tightened around her frame, a barrier crumbling within her. A tear betrayed her stoicism, tracing a path down her cheek. "I suspected there were others, then I found some texts, some filthy pictures that someone sent him..." she confessed, the admission pulling her into the undertow of her own fears. "But confrontation only led to arguments, to more fighting."

"Emma, look at me," Ross urged, bridging the physical gap between them with a step forward. His blue eyes held hers with an intensity that left no room for doubt in his sincerity. "You're not alone in this. Not anymore."

Her lips parted; a silent acknowledgment of the solace found in his presence. For years, she had navigated the treacherous waters of her marriage to Carlos, each day another exercise in survival. Now, here was Ross, offering her a lifeline—a chance to reclaim the truth of her own story.

"Thank you, Detective," she whispered, allowing herself to lean into the strength of his resolve. In Ross's unwavering gaze, she saw not just a promise of justice, but the possibility of a future unmarred by the shadow of Carlos Martinez.

"Call me Michael," he said, a soft smile touching the corners of his mouth. The intimacy of first names marked a turning point, a shared commitment to unraveling the enigma that was Carlos's disappearance—and perhaps, in doing so, restoring the fragments of Emma Dawson's world.

Emma's fingers toyed with the frayed edge of the throw blanket that rested upon her knees, a physical manifestation of the unraveling nerves within her. The room was silent save for the soft ticking of the grandfather clock—an inherited piece that stood like a stoic guardian against the wall. She exhaled a shaky breath, her heartbeat slowing as she glanced up at Michael Ross.

"Detective—Michael," she corrected herself, her voice barely above a whisper, "I can't begin to express my gratitude for all you've done. I've felt so lost." Her eyes shimmered with unshed tears, but there was a fire behind them—a fire that had been kindled by his unwavering support.

"Emma," Ross began, his tone even and reassuring, the timbre grounding her in the present moment, "it's my job to find the truth, but it's more than that. I care about what happens to you and your family." He leaned forward, elbows resting on his knees, his gaze never wavering from hers. His presence was like a beacon in the storm, steady and sure.

"Sometimes I feel like I'm drowning in all this uncertainty," Emma confessed, the words tumbling out of her. "But when you're here, I feel like I can breathe again. Like I can face whatever comes next."

Ross's hand reached out, enveloping her own, a tangible connection that bridged the gap between detective and confidante. "You will get through this," he assured her, his grip firm yet gentle. "I'll see to it personally. No one should have to endure what you've been through. And I promise you, Emma, I won't rest until we have answers."

The sincerity in his voice wrapped around her like a protective shroud, and for a heartbeat, she allowed herself to believe in the possibility of a life free from the haunting questions that plagued her nights.

"Thank you," she said again, the words weighted with the heaviness of her heart. "For believing in me, for fighting for me...for him."

"Justice doesn't pick sides, Emma. It simply seeks to balance the scales," Ross said, his conviction strong as steel. "And I intend to balance them."

He rose to his feet, the movement pulling back the veil of intimacy they'd woven around themselves. Yet, the strength he exuded filled the room, leaving no corner untouched by his resolve. Emma watched him, seeing not just the seasoned investigator he was, but also the man who had unexpectedly become her anchor in the turbulent sea of her life.

"Rest now," he said with a nod, the simple command laced with an empathy that reached deep into her weary soul. "I'll be working on this until we uncover every last secret. You have my word."

As he stepped toward the door, Emma clung to the lifeline he had thrown her, the gratitude and newfound hope swirling together to form a silent vow within her. This was the turning point—the moment when the tide began to turn, and the shadows that lurked in the depths started to retreat before the relentless pursuit of Detective Michael Ross.

"Please, wait. There's something you need to see." Emma said to the Detective. Leading him to the kitchen, she pulled out the small box of things she had collected. She spread them on the table in front of him, watching his expression as he realized what he was looking at.

Emma sat across from Detective Ross, the kitchen table between them a landscape of scattered photographs and documents. The overhead light cast shadows that seemed to press in on her, but his presence was a beacon in the dim room.

"Carlos had a way of... unraveling me," she said, voice faltering as she picked up a photograph from their last vacation, fingers tracing the outline of Carlos's face. "He made me feel seen, understood—and then it was like he could see too much."

Ross leaned forward, folding his hands atop the table, his eyes never leaving hers. He nodded for her to continue, an unspoken assurance that he was there to listen, not judge.

"Sometimes, I'd catch glimpses of someone else behind his eyes. Like he was fighting his own demons." Her green eyes flickered with pain. "That last night, there was this intensity about him, a fear that I couldn't soothe."

"Emma, what you're describing—it takes strength to admit these things," Ross said softly. His voice held the warmth of a seasoned detective who had seen humanity at its most vulnerable. "Fear can be a powerful motivator—for both love and hate."

She swallowed hard, the knot in her throat tight with years of untold secrets. "He just kept repeating that he needed to protect us, that there were things I didn't understand. It was like he knew something was coming."

"Did he ever say what it was?" Ross asked, his tone carefully neutral, inviting confidence without pressing too hard.

"Only that it was bigger than us—that it would change everything." Emma's gaze fell to her hands, wringing together in her lap.

"Whatever Carlos was involved in, whatever he feared, it's imperative we uncover the truth," Ross stated, his determination etched into the lines of his weathered face. "You're not alone in this anymore."

"Thank you," she whispered, her eyes meeting his with an earnestness that conveyed the depth of her trust. "I want to understand, no matter how frightening the truth might be."

Ross gave her a reassuring nod, then stood, collecting the papers with practiced efficiency. "We will get to the bottom of this, Emma. Rest assured, I have resources and methods at my disposal that aren't common knowledge."

Her heart quickened at the implication of hidden depths in his investigation, a tangle of hope and dread knitting within her.

"Be careful, Detective Ross," she cautioned, her intuition sensing the gravity of what lay ahead. "There are shadows in this family...shadows that have teeth."

"Shadows don't bother me," he replied, the hint of a wry smile playing at his lips. "It's my job to bring things to light."

With that, he stepped out into the chill of the evening, leaving behind a charged silence that spoke volumes. Emma wrapped her arms around herself, contemplating the enigmatic man whose quest for justice had become intertwined with her own search for peace.

As the door clicked shut, the weight of unsaid words hung heavily in the air, the charged atmosphere rich with the promise of revelations yet to come. Emma gazed out the window where Ross's silhouette merged with the darkening sky, and she knew that the road ahead would unearth more than just the fate of Carlos—it would challenge everything she thought she knew about the man she loved, about her family, and about herself.

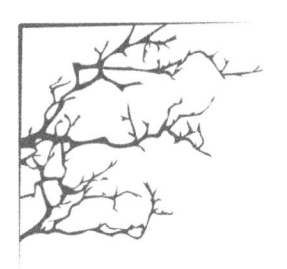

## Chapter 26

The next day, Monday, Emma's hands shook as she fastened her nurse's badge to her scrubs. The crisp, white fabric felt too clean against the mess of emotions swirling inside her. She took a deep breath, trying to steady herself for her first day back at Oakdale General Hospital. Everything had fallen apart, but now, she needed to pull it together. The familiar scent of antiseptic filled her lungs as the automatic doors slid open, welcoming her into the busy ICU. The hum of monitors, the calls of nurses and doctors, the bustle—it was all so familiar, a comforting noise that helped push back the chaos in her mind.

"Hey, Emma! Good to see you. Were you sick yesterday?" A colleague called out, smiling warmly as he passed.

Emma forced a small smile, the weight of everything still hanging heavy on her. "No, I had an appointment. But I'm good now, thanks."

She walked over to the nurses' station, her smile fading as she picked up a clipboard. Her green eyes, once filled with passion for her work, now showed signs of weariness. Still, she scanned through the patient charts, letting herself focus on something other than the mess her life had become. Vitals, medications, treatment plans—it was all routine, familiar, and safe. With each room she entered, each patient she checked on, she found herself slipping back into the version of herself that knew what to do, that had a purpose.

As the hours ticked by, Emma felt a small sense of relief. In the ICU, she wasn't just a woman whose marriage was crumbling, or a mother trying to hold it together. Here, she was a nurse—competent, focused, and needed. The patients didn't care about her personal life. They needed her to be strong, to know what to do, and that was something she could give, even if she couldn't quite figure out her own life.

Her heart still ached with the weight of everything she'd been through, but as the shift wore on, the ache dulled, replaced by the familiar rhythm of her work. Each patient brought a small sense of normalcy, a reminder that she was still capable of something, even when everything else felt so uncertain.

Emma, wrapped in the sanctity of her vocation, moved between the sterile walls of the hospital, oblivious to the dark currents moving just beyond her view. She adjusted IV lines with a gentle touch, murmured words of comfort to those fighting pain, and found solace in the gratitude that shone from her patients' eyes. It was here, in the trenches of human frailty, that Emma rediscovered shards of her strength, piecing them together with each life she touched.

The clink of porcelain on porcelain punctuated the air as Emma set down her coffee cup, a soft chime that seemed to resonate with the newfound clarity in her green eyes. Across from her, Rachel's laughter spilled out like warm honey, sweetening the bitter remnants of past turmoil.

"Remember that time we snuck out to see that band play at The Rusty Nail?" Rachel's grin was infectious, her own cup cradled in hands that had offered solace more times than Emma could count.

"Snuck out? I recall it being more of a tactical operation," Emma quipped, the corners of her mouth lifting in genuine amusement for the first time in months. "You were always the mastermind."

Their shared memories unfurled between them, a tapestry woven from years of friendship and resilience. Emma felt the comforting embrace of normalcy, the laughter and stories serving as balm to wounds that were slowly healing.

"Look at you, Emma," Rachel said, her voice taking on a tender note. "I am so freaking proud of you. You're finding yourself again."

"Thanks to you," Emma replied, reaching across the table to squeeze Rachel's hand. "You've been my rock."

As they lingered over lunch, the café around them buzzed with the energy of lives in motion, yet for a brief moment, Emma's world seemed to stand still, bathed in the glow of recovery and rebirth.

Back at the café, as the final notes of laughter faded, Emma checked her watch and sighed. It was time to return to reality, to the hospital, to the patients who depended on her. She stood, feeling the strength that had returned to her limbs, a testament to her own resilience and the support she'd found in others.

"Same time next week?" Rachel asked, already gathering her belongings.

"Wouldn't miss it," Emma said, smiling. As she stepped out into the afternoon sun, a gentle breeze stirred, whispering promises of hope and new beginnings. But in the distance, where shadows crept and plans lay hidden, the winds carried a different tale—one of vengeance and retribution waiting to unfold under the cover of night.

The ticking of the wall clock in Dr. Amelia Thompson's office was a metronome to Emma Dawson's fractured thoughts, each tick resonating with a heartbeat of apprehension and hope. Sitting across from the therapist, whose calm blue eyes offered a harbor in the storm of her past, Emma folded her hands tightly in her lap, knuckles whitening with the grip.

"Your progress is remarkable, Emma," Dr. Thompson said, her voice a soothing balm against the cacophony of memories that often plagued Emma's mind. "Given all you've been through, it's inspiring to see how much strength you've found."

Emma looked up, her green eyes flickering with a fragile light. "Sometimes I feel like I'm just one step away from falling apart again. But then I think of Jaxon... and I find a way to keep moving forward."

"Remember, healing isn't linear. It's okay to have moments of doubt," Dr. Thompson reminded her, leaning forward slightly. "It's what you do with those moments that defines your journey."

"Speaking of journeys," Emma ventured, her voice betraying a hint of newfound determination, "I was thinking about starting a support group at work for others who've been through similar experiences."

"An excellent idea," Dr. Thompson affirmed with an encouraging nod. "Helping others can be a powerful part of your own healing process."

As they continued to discuss strategies for maintaining emotional balance, Emma felt a sense of purpose crystallize within her, a beacon to guide her through the fog of her past.

Emma, oblivious to the dark currents swirling around her, exited Dr. Thompson's office with a tentative smile curving her lips. As she stepped into the cool night air, her breath formed clouds before her, dissipating like the remnants of her former life. She walked with her head held high, unaware that the path she trod was shadowed by secrets yet to surface, secrets that would test the very fabric of her being.

Emma's hands moved with a precision and care that belied her inner turmoil. As she sorted through the donations at the Oakdale Community Center, her green eyes flickered with purpose, finding solace in the simple act of folding children's clothes and organizing them by size. The charity event was a mosaic of goodwill, each volunteer a piece crucial to the whole.

"Hey, Emma," called out one of the volunteers, "this box is full of toys. Where should it go?"

"Over there, by the book stand," Emma replied, her voice steady despite the weariness that clung to her like a second skin. She watched as people from all walks of life united for a common cause, their collective energy igniting something within her, something that had been dimmed by years of emotional strife.

The community center buzzed with activity, echoing with laughter and conversation. Emma couldn't help but smile as she saw the impact of their work; this was healing, a way to rebuild not just her own shattered pieces, but those of others too.

Her satisfaction, however, was a fragile bubble, unbeknownst to her, moments away from being burst by the sharp needle of reality.

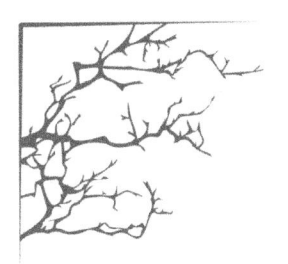

# Chapter 27

The warm glow of the television painted fleeting shadows across Emma's living room as she nestled into the corner of the couch. Beside her, Jaxon sat wrapped in a comforting silence that only a shared history could weave. They were engrossed in the classic thriller flickering before them, a story of suspense and redemption—an ironic choice, given the night's unseen drama.

"Mom," Jaxon said during a lull in the action, his voice betraying none of his inner turmoil, "you remember when we first watched this?"

Emma glanced at her son, noting the way his hazel eyes caught the screen's light, flickering with memories. "Of course," she replied, the corners of her green eyes crinkling with affection. "You hid behind the pillow every time the music got scary."

A soft chuckle escaped him, a sound that resonated with an imperceptible dissonance. "I was six. Give me a break."

They shared a moment of laughter, one bright and untainted by the darkness that encroached just beyond their sanctuary. For Emma, these instances of levity were precious, a balm to the wounds left from a life too often marred by shadows.

"Thanks for tonight, Jax," she said, reaching out to squeeze his hand. "It means more than you know."

He returned the pressure, his fingers trembling slightly against hers—a tremor she mistook for the chill in the air. "Anything for you, Mom."

THAT EVENING, JAXON arrived at Martha's. They gathered some tools and set about finishing the last part of their plan.

Outside, beneath the cathedral of stars, Martha's breaths came out in ragged puffs as she and Jaxon maneuvered Carlos's body through the back door. The once vibrant man, reduced now to a vessel of secrets, lay between them, a silent testimony to their resolve.

"Deep enough," Martha whispered, her voice a tight thread in the tapestry of the night. Her hands, though quivering, were steady as they dug into the earth—a grave for the man who had brought nothing but desolation to her daughter.

"Here." Jaxon reached into his pocket, producing a small urn, the surface cold and unyielding against his warm skin. With a solemnity that belied his years, he scattered the ashes over Carlos's shrouded form, watching as they melded with the soil.

"Goodbye, dad," he murmured, not to the man in the ground, but to the spirit of the one they honored with this act.

Martha placed a comforting arm around Jaxon as they filled the hole, the dirt muffling any trace of the man who had been their tormentor. She thought of Emma, innocent and laughing within the house, and felt a surge of fierce determination.

"Let's finish this," she said, her voice firm. "For Emma."

Together, they worked under the cloak of night, each shovelful of earth a barrier between the past and Emma's future. When the deed was done, they stood back, their faces ghostly pale in the moonlight, the garden now holding more than just the promise of new life. It held the secret of death, neatly tucked away beneath the unsuspecting beauty of nature's hand.

EMMA STEPPED OUT INTO the cool night, the moon weaving its silver light through the leaves of her beloved garden. The jasmine was in bloom, its scent heavy and intoxicating, mingling with the earthy aroma of freshly turned soil. She let out a breath she hadn't realized she'd been holding, the tension from her shoulders unraveling like a knotted string.

"Em," she whispered to herself, a self-imposed reminder to take this rare moment of peace for herself, to just be.

She wandered along the stone path, tracing the same route she had walked countless times before, each step an echo of routine and memory. Yet tonight there was something different, an undercurrent that made her heart thrum gently—a whisper of something amiss that she couldn't quite grasp.

"Probably just the stress," she reasoned, trying to shake off the vague unease.

Meanwhile, back at the house, Jaxon closed the door with a soft click, his movements deliberate and noiseless. He leaned against the solid wood for a moment, closing his eyes as if to will away the images that clung to his mind's eye. Beside him, Martha stood silent, her gaze fixed on the window that framed the silhouette of her daughter in the garden.

"Did we do right, Nana?" Jaxon's voice was almost lost in the stillness of the room, a mere whisper against the enormity of their act.

Martha didn't turn to meet his eyes; she didn't need to see the conflict written across his face—she felt it mirrored in her own soul.

"For Emma," she replied, her voice steady but laced with an unspoken question that clawed at her insides.

In the garden, Emma paused by the rose bushes, where the ground seemed oddly uneven under the moon's pale scrutiny. A frown creased her forehead as she crouched down, her hands hovering over the spot. It was as though the earth had been disturbed, but the thought slipped away as quickly as it came, rationalized by a tired mind that sought no more drama.

"Rabbits," she murmured, the explanation sitting uneasily in the pit of her stomach.

"Emma, you coming in? It's late," called Martha from the open doorway, her voice carrying a strange urgency that tugged at Emma's senses.

"Coming, Mama," Emma replied, standing up and brushing her hands against her nightgown. She cast one last glance at the roses, an inexplicable shiver running down her spine despite the warmth of the night.

As Emma retreated towards the house, Jaxon watched her retreating figure, his hazel eyes reflecting the turmoil within. With every step she took away from the secret they had buried, he felt both a crushing weight lift and a new burden settle—one that would forever alter the fabric of their existence.

"Are you alright, Jax?" Emma asked when she reached him, her green eyes searching his face for signs of the boy who had laughed with her just hours ago.

"Fine, mom," he said, swallowing the truth that threatened to spill out. "Just tired."

"Me too," she sighed, unaware of how close she stood to the precipice of revelation.

Together, mother and son watched Emma climb the stairs, her shadow flickering against the walls as if in a dance with the secrets they kept. When she vanished from view, Jaxon and Martha exchanged a glance, a silent communion of two souls forever bound by the dark deed done in the name of love and protection.

"Sleep well," Martha whispered, not to the empty space where Emma had been, but to the part of themselves they feared might never rest again.

Emma perched on the edge of her bed, the soft glow of the bedside lamp casting a warm aura around the room. Her fingertips traced the stitching of the quilt—a quilt she had wrapped around herself countless nights when sleep eluded her, gripped by the specter of her unraveling marriage.

Now, in the solitude of her refuge, she allowed herself a moment to breathe in the silence that enveloped her—a silence not of emptiness, but of peace. She had fought through the tempest of doubt and despair, and here she was, still standing, still breathing.

She closed her eyes, envisioning the faces of her patients from the day. The gratitude in their eyes nourished her soul, reinforcing her belief in her chosen path. Emma Dawson, once lost in the shadows of another's design, was rediscovering the light within herself. A smile teased the corners of her lips as she considered the possibilities that lay ahead. She could almost taste the sweetness of a life reclaimed, a future crafted by her own hands.

In the stillness of her room, Emma's spirit swelled with newfound fortitude, oblivious to the undercurrents that churned just beyond the confines of her sanctuary.

Meanwhile, down the hallway, hushed tones wove through the air as Jaxon and Martha stood close, their voices barely above a whisper. They were cloaked in the dimness of the kitchen, where only the faint blue light of the refrigerator guided their clandestine meeting.

"Are we doing the right thing, Nana?" Jaxon's question was a barbed wire coiled tight with fear and resolve.

Martha's eyes, fierce embers in the dark, met his gaze unwaveringly. "We're protecting Emma," she affirmed, her voice a low thrum of conviction. "That man would've destroyed her, bit by bit. We did what we had to do."

"Even if it means living with this...forever?" His words were a ghostly exhale, the weight of their deed an anchor threatening to drag him into depths unknown.

"Forever," Martha echoed solemnly, reaching out to clasp his hand—her fingers cold yet reassuring. "We carry this burden to keep her safe, to give her the chance at happiness she deserves. That's our penance, our sacrifice."

"Mom can never know," Jaxon whispered, the 'never' lingering like a specter between them.

"Never." Martha's reply was a shroud sealing away their secret.

Their pact forged in the quiet dread of night; they stood sentinel over a truth so harrowing it could fracture the very essence of the woman they loved beyond measure.

Unseen by Emma, whose heart dared to hope, the conspirators retreated from their whispered colloquy. In the shadowed corridor, Jaxon's silhouette paused, his hazel eyes reflecting a turmoil that mirrored the storm he and Martha had weathered together—a storm that had only just begun.

Moonlight bathed Oakdale in an ethereal glow, casting elongated shadows over Emma Dawson's contemplative figure as she wandered into the garden. Her feet, encased in soft slippers, moved silently across the dew-kissed grass, her mind aswirl with fragments of memories and the tranquil solitude of night.

The air held a faint chill that whispered through the leaves in hushed secrets, teasing strands of her shoulder-length hair loose from their confines. She wrapped her arms around herself, seeking warmth, not just from the cool night but also from the lingering chill of her past.

Emma paused, drawn to a particular spot near the old oak tree, where the earth seemed to have been recently disturbed. It was nothing more than an intuition, a nurse's sense of when something was amiss. The darkness concealed much, yet the moonlight revealed enough for her green eyes to catch the subtle unevenness underfoot.

A stray breeze carried the scent of freshly turned soil mixed with something else—something acrid, almost metallic. Emma knelt, her fingers brushing the ground, feeling the raw grittiness of the dirt. The sensation sent an inexplicable shiver up her spine, as if the earth itself held a heartbeat, an echo of life that once pulsed but now lay still.

"Carlos," she whispered, not knowing why his name came to her lips. Her marriage to him had been a tapestry of light and dark threads, woven tightly until it was impossible to distinguish one from another. She stood up quickly, shaking off the odd feeling as just remnants of the day's exhaustion.

Yet, as she stood there, the truth of the garden hung heavy around her—a secret macabre and sinister, veiled by the serene visage of nature. Emma was oblivious to the grave beneath her feet, to the betrayal that seeped into the roots of the very flowers she had planted with such care.

She closed her eyes, inhaling deeply, trying to purge the sudden onset of unease, attributing the disquiet to her imagination working overtime. Opening her eyes, she looked towards the heavens, the stars appearing as distant beacons of hope amidst the vast uncertainty of her life.

Unbeknownst to Emma, the ground on which she stood was a false guardian of peace, harboring a deed so vile it could unravel the very fabric of her existence. As the chapter drew to a close, the image of Emma, framed by the spectral light, remained etched in the reader's mind—a portrait of innocence perched upon the precipice of a chilling revelation.

The garden, once a sanctuary for her troubled thoughts, now cradled a grim secret that would soon claw its way to the surface. And the reader, bearing witness to the silent drama, waited with bated breath for the moment Emma would come face to face with the horrifying truth.

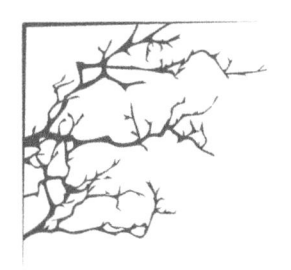

# Chapter 28

Emma clasped her hands in her lap, the tremor in her fingers betraying the calm she struggled to project. Around the circle of metal folding chairs, faces etched with varying degrees of pain and resilience turned towards her—a silent prompt for her contribution. She drew in a deep breath, steadying herself against the tide of memories that threatened to overwhelm her.

"Carlos never left marks where people could see them," Emma began, her voice threading through the hush of the room. "He said it was his way of showing mercy. He said that if he was only emotionally abusive, no one could prove he did anything to me." The confession hung heavy in the air, a stark contrast to the sterile scent of antiseptic that pervaded the community center.

As others shared, Emma listened, their stories weaving a tapestry of sorrow and survival that mirrored her own. Each word spoken by these women, these survivors, stitched a little more strength into the frayed edges of her resolve.

The session ended with embraces and murmured words of encouragement, but as Emma exited the building, the comfort of solidarity quickly faded under the shadow of an approaching figure. Detective Michael Ross's silhouette cut a sharp line against the waning daylight.

"Ms. Dawson," he greeted, his tone carrying the familiar blend of professional courtesy and underlying scrutiny. "May we talk?"

"Of course," Emma replied, her heart rate ticking up like a metronome set to allegro.

They settled on a nearby bench, the metal cool beneath her, the sounds of the city a distant hum compared to the thrumming in her ears.

"Any new developments about Carlos?" Emma asked, folding her hands to conceal their shaking.

"Nothing concrete," Ross admitted, his gaze fixed on her with a piercing clarity. "But I need to ask you some questions. It's important we go over the details again."

"Details that don't change, Detective," Emma responded, her voice firmer now, edged with the steel she had honed within the therapy sessions. "I haven't seen Carlos since the night he disappeared. I told you everything."

Ross leaned forward, elbows resting on his knees, his expression unreadable. "Sometimes, even the smallest detail can make all the difference."

Emma met his gaze, holding it, letting him see the well of pain and defiance in her green eyes. "I wish I could help you find Carlos; I do. He chose to leave me; he chose not to tell me he was going. But there's nothing more to tell. I need to move on from this...from him."

The detective studied her a moment longer before nodding slowly. "Alright. If you remember anything else, you have my number."

"Thank you, Detective," she said, though gratitude was the last thing she felt. Standing, she wrapped her arms around herself, a self-embrace that fortified her for the journey ahead.

As Detective Ross walked away, his steps heavy and deliberate, Emma felt a strange hollowness settle in her chest. Each question he asked seemed to chip away at the defenses she'd worked so hard to build. Her life was already unraveling, piece by piece, and his probing only reminded her how fragile everything had become.

She stood still, watching him leave, her mind racing through everything she'd tried to lock away. Carlos had disappeared weeks ago, without a trace, and no one seemed to know what happened. The silence surrounding his absence was deafening, but Emma had convinced herself it was for the best. After everything he'd put her through, maybe this was just the universe finally giving her the break she needed. Yet, the mystery of it all clung to her, an uneasy weight she couldn't quite shake.

Detective Ross's words echoed in her mind. "If you remember anything, give me a call." The look in his eyes had been careful, but there was suspicion there, even if it was faint. Emma knew the type—he'd keep digging, and eventually, he'd find something, whether she wanted him to or not.

She inhaled deeply, trying to steady herself, forcing her thoughts back to the present. The sterile smell of the hospital, the hum of activity around her—it was all so familiar, comforting in its routine. But even here, in the place where she used to feel in control, everything seemed different. She wasn't the same woman who had walked these halls just a week ago.

Taking a shaky breath, she pushed her way back into the ICU. Her patients needed her focus, her care. Whatever had happened to Carlos would remain outside these walls, at least for now. But as the hours ticked by and the day wore on, the unanswered questions gnawed at the edges of her mind. How does a man like Carlos just vanish?

Her shift ended, the usual exhaustion creeping in, but something else lingered—an undercurrent of dread. Emma pulled her jacket tighter around her as she stepped outside into the cold evening air. Glancing up at the darkening sky, she couldn't shake the feeling that Carlos's disappearance wasn't the end. It was the beginning of something she wasn't sure she was ready for.

And for all the peace she tried to convince herself she deserved; one truth remained: things were far from over.

Under the veil of dusk, Jaxon's shadow melded with the darkening trunks of oak trees as he made his way to the weathered garden shed, now a silent conspirator in their clandestine meetings. Inside, Martha waited, her silhouette sharpened against the faint glow of a single lantern.

"Is he gone?" she whispered, the urgency in her voice belying her calm exterior.

Jaxon nodded, his eyes reflecting the flickering light like shards of amber. "The detective left again with nothing. Mom's holding up."

"Good." Martha's lips drew a tight line. "We need to stay vigilant. Emma's been through enough; we can't let our guard down."

"Nana, I know," Jaxon replied, an edge of frustration creeping into his tone. He was tired of the reassurances, the endless cycle of planning and paranoia. But he knew they were necessary—their family's future hinged on the success of their plan.

"Emma can't suspect we're involved," Martha continued, her gaze piercing through the darkness. "She needs to believe things will settle, that she can heal from this."

"Of course," Jaxon agreed quietly. He understood the stakes all too well. Protecting his mother had always been his driving force, even when it led him down paths darker than he ever imagined.

They sat in silence for a moment longer, the weight of their shared secret hanging between them like a tangible specter before Martha finally broke the stillness. "Go back to the house, keep an eye on her. I'll be in soon."

Jaxon slipped away, leaving Martha alone with her thoughts and the ghosts of decisions past.

A GENTLE BREEZE STIRRED the fallen leaves around Emma as she knelt by the small headstone beneath the old oak tree, the spot where they had scattered her father's ashes. The smooth marble felt cool under her fingers, a stark contrast to the flood of warmth and memories filling her heart. Her dad had been her rock when life felt too overwhelming, always there to steady her when the world felt like it was spinning out of control.

"Hey, Daddy," she whispered, running her fingertips over the engraved letters of his name. Her voice barely broke the silence, as if she were afraid to disturb the stillness of the evening.

Emma closed her eyes, letting the quiet surround her. The yard, normally so full of life and sound, felt like a sanctuary, a place where she could still feel close to her father. He had taught her so much—how to be strong, how to protect the ones she loved. Now, she clung to those lessons, more than ever.

"I'm trying, Daddy. I'm trying to stay strong like you taught me," she said, her voice trembling slightly. "I have to keep our family safe... no matter what."

Her eyes flickered open, and as she gazed down at the ground around the tree, something caught her attention. The earth looked different, disturbed in a way she hadn't noticed before. The soil seemed looser, as if it had been recently deeply weeded, moved or shifted. A knot of unease formed in her stomach. She reached out and brushed the dirt gently, frowning at the subtle changes. She couldn't shake the strange feeling that something wasn't right.

Emma's chest tightened as her thoughts turned to the secret she carried—heavy and unrelenting, always lingering just below the surface of her carefully constructed facade. The weight of it threatened to crush her at times, and tonight was no different. The need to protect Jaxon, to keep him safe, had driven her to make choices she never thought she'd face.

"Please," she whispered, her words barely audible, "if you can hear me, Daddy, help me carry this. Help me keep Jaxon safe."

She stayed there a moment longer, her fingers still tracing the dirt as her mind raced. The ground had changed—she was sure of it now. But why? And what did it mean? Emma's heart pounded in her chest, her father's tree now feeling like both a place of comfort and of unease. Something was different. And whatever it was, she would have to face it—just like everything else.

A gentle breeze stirred the leaves around her, and for a second, Emma let herself believe it was her dad sending her a sign—a soft, wordless way of telling her she wasn't alone. Maybe it was just her imagination, but the thought gave her a tiny bit of comfort, like he was still watching over her.

She slowly got to her feet, brushing the dirt from her jeans. Before heading back to the house, she glanced once more at the small headstone. Her face, though tired, showed a new sense of determination. Everything she'd been through had made her stronger, and she knew that strength would be put to the test soon enough.

As she walked back toward the house, Emma's steps were steady, even though her mind was still racing. Each step felt like a small victory—proof that, no matter how tough things got, she could keep moving forward. Whatever challenges were ahead, she was ready. Or at least, she had to be.

DETECTIVE MICHAEL ROSS'S phone buzzed urgently on the corner of his cluttered desk, piercing the silence of the precinct with its insistent vibration. His seasoned fingers snatched it up, eyes scanning the text message that could be the lead he had been doggedly chasing for weeks.

"Possible sighting of Martinez in Willow Creek," the message read, sent anonymously, yet Ross's gut told him there might be truth to it. He stood abruptly, urgency etching itself into the lines of his face as he grabbed his coat and keys. If Carlos was alive, if he was out there, this could change everything.

"Ross! Where you headed?" a colleague called out as he strode past the rows of desks.

"Got a lead on Martinez. I'm following it up," Ross replied without breaking his stride. In his line of work, time was a luxury one couldn't afford to waste.

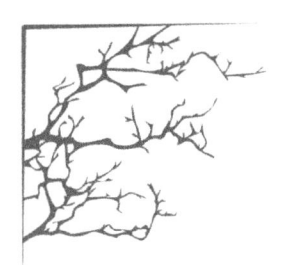

## Chapter 29

At the small café on Oakdale's main street, Emma sat across from Rachel Jenkins, her best friend since their grade school days. They met here often, and what used to be carefree catch-ups had turned into heavier conversations, the kind that left their coffee cups half-empty and the air between them filled with unspoken words.

"Thanks for meeting me again," Rachel said, giving Emma a small smile that didn't quite reach her eyes. "Feels like last week was a lifetime ago."

"Of course," Emma replied, trying to return the smile. "We've both been through a lot."

They talked, as they usually did, sharing pieces of their lives. Rachel opened up about her divorce, the loneliness that had crept in even when she was surrounded by people. Emma listened, nodding, fully understanding that feeling all too well. She shared some of her own struggles, but as usual, she left out the darkest parts. Still, Rachel could sense the weight Emma carried.

"Looks like we've both been fighting battles, haven't we?" Rachel said quietly, her hands wrapped around her coffee cup, fingers trembling just a little.

"Yeah," Emma agreed softly, her eyes drifting to the window. "Warriors with battle scars. But we're still here, Rachel. We're survivors."

"Survivors," Rachel echoed, the word a solemn oath between them.

Their conversation flowed from heartache to hope, from loss to the painstaking process of rebuilding what had been shattered. Emma felt a kindred spirit in Rachel, a reminder that she was not alone in her fight to reclaim her life.

The cafe door chimed, drawing Emma's attention momentarily. Detective Ross entered, his gaze sweeping the room before landing on her. Even from a distance, she could see the resolve that marked his features. He was a man on a mission, and something in the pit of her stomach told her that his presence was no mere coincidence.

"Excuse me, Rachel, I think Detective Ross wants a word with me," Emma said, rising from the table with an apologetic glance.

"Is everything alright, Em?" Rachel asked, concern creasing her forehead.

"Everything's fine, just police business," Emma assured her quickly, though her heartbeat thrummed a warning against her chest.

"Emma," Ross greeted, his voice low and measured when she approached. "I need to ask you a few questions. There's been a development."

"Development?" The word hung in the air between them, fraught with implications Emma wasn't sure she was ready to face.

"Let's step outside," Ross suggested, and Emma nodded, casting a reassuring smile back at Rachel before following the detective into the bright light of day, where unknown truths waited to be unearthed.

LATER THAT EVENING, under the pale glow of the moon, the house lay silent except for the creaks and shivers of its old bones settling into the night. Emma's sleep had been light, a mother's instinct tuned to the faintest disruptions in her home's nocturnal symphony. It was Jaxon's voice that pierced the silence, a plaintive wail cutting through the veil of her dreams. She bolted upright, heart racing as if trying to escape the confines of her chest.

"Jax?" she whispered into the darkness before her feet found the cold floor. The hallway seemed to stretch endlessly before her as she made her way to his room. The door was ajar, an eerie sliver of light creeping out to meet her.

"Jaxon!" she called out louder this time, pushing the door open with a tremble in her hand. He was thrashing in his bed, ensnared by some invisible foe only he could see. Emma rushed to his side, her hands reaching out to gently shake him awake.

"Mom... no, please, I didn't mean it," Jaxon murmured between gasps, still caught in the clutches of his nightmare.

"Jaxon! Wake up, sweetheart. It's just a dream," Emma coaxed, her voice imbued with a firmness fortified by countless nights of similar vigil.

His hazel eyes snapped open, wild and unfocused. Emma watched as recognition slowly fought its way back into his gaze. A shared silence enveloped them, heavy with words unspoken, the air thick with the residue of a past they both wished they could erase.

"Another nightmare?" she asked softly, brushing away the damp curls from his forehead.

He nodded, sitting up and wrapping his arms around himself as if to hold together the pieces of his fragile psyche.

"Want to talk about it?" Emma probed, though she knew the answer before it even left his lips.

"It's always the same..." His voice trailed off, lost in the labyrinth of his guilt.

Emma reached out, her touch a balm to the turmoil that churned within him. They sat together until the first hints of dawn began to seep into the room.

"Come on, let's get some breakfast," Emma said, trying to inject normalcy into the moment. But as they descended the stairs, she couldn't shake the image of Jaxon, haunted and alone, fighting demons only he could see.

Later that day, Emma found herself standing in a nondescript gym, the smell of sweat and determination hanging in the air. She had signed up for a self-defense class, driven by a newfound resolve to never feel powerless again. Her eyes scanned the room, taking in the faces of those around her. Some were there for fitness, others for confidence. For Emma, it was a lifeline.

"Alright, everyone, let's get started." The instructor, a woman with the build of a fighter and the eyes of a compassionate teacher, began to demonstrate a series of moves. "We're not just training our bodies here; we're training our minds to stay calm and react under pressure."

Emma felt the weight of every word. Each pivot, strike, and block was more than a technique—it was a step towards reclaiming her agency, a dance of defiance against the shadows that sought to engulf her world.

"Good, Emma! That's it, use your body weight to drive the punch," the instructor commended as Emma executed a move with more force than she thought she possessed.

"Thanks," Emma panted, feeling a rush of adrenaline and pride. With each jab and kick, the image of Carlos's menacing face flashed in her mind, fueling her resolve. She imagined herself as a shield, a guardian capable of protecting Jaxon from the horrors that stalked their lives.

As the class drew to a close, Emma felt something she hadn't felt in a long time—a sense of control. She was no longer the victim of her circumstances but the architect of her future. And she would do whatever it took to ensure that future was one where she and Jaxon could heal, free from the specters that haunted them.

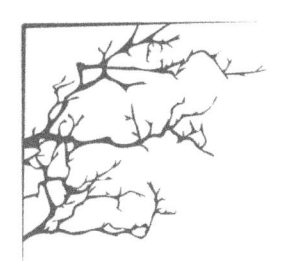

# Chapter 30

Detective Ross parked his car in front of the small, worn-down apartment building. The sun beat down hard, making the pavement almost too hot to stand on. He glanced in the rear-view mirror, adjusted his collar, and stepped out into the heat.

Inside the apartment, it was cool and dark. Thick curtains blocked out the sunlight, casting shadows across the room. Beatriz Alvarez sat on a big, old sofa, her dark hair falling around her face. Her eyes were wary as she watched Ross sit down in the chair across from her.

"Ms. Alvarez," Ross began, his voice calm, "I'm trying to understand Carlos better. Anything you can tell me might help."

Beatriz hesitated, nervously playing with a strand of her hair. "Carlos... he wasn't easy. Not easy to love," she said slowly, looking down. "He had this temper... it came fast, like a storm. You never knew when."

Ross leaned in a little. "Did he ever physically hurt you?"

Beatriz's eyes darted around the room before she answered. "Carlos... he wanted control. Everything. Where I went, who I talked to. He said it was because he cared, but it didn't feel that way. It was too much."

"Was there something that made him angry, something that set him off?" Ross asked, keeping his voice gentle.

"Jealousy," she said, her voice dropping. Her face grew tight as she remembered. "Always jealousy. If he thought another man even looked at me, he changed. He wasn't Carlos anymore. He was scary."

Ross nodded, taking mental notes.

"He wouldn't just leave me and the baby, I am pregnant, you know. He wouldn't leave his baby Detective. He just wouldn't." She said, tears flowed down her cheeks.

"Thank you for telling me this. What you've shared is important."

As Ross left the apartment, Beatriz leaned back into the sofa, tears still falling and her heart racing. She couldn't shake the feeling that talking about Carlos might bring trouble she wasn't ready for.

Meanwhile, Jaxon stood in the doorway of his step father's study, a room that felt more like a tomb now, laden with the ghosts of unspoken truths. The shadows seemed to cling to the edges, reluctant to let go of their secrets. His eyes fell upon the desk that had once been his step father's command center, where secrets were kept, where decisions were made without concern for the consequences.

He approached the desk, the floorboards creaking under his weight, and ran his fingers along the smooth surface. A loose panel caught his attention, a subtle inconsistency in the wood grain. With a tentative tug, the compartment revealed itself, and inside lay a box—a Pandora's chest of memories.

Jaxon's heart pounded as he lifted the old, creaky lid. Inside, yellowed photos stacked inside became visible — snapshots of a younger Carlos, smiling in a way Jaxon had never seen. His face, back then, was free from the anger and bitterness that had twisted him over the years. Letters, messily scrawled, painted a darker picture: unpaid debts, threats that hung in the air like a noose. The letters spoke of survival, of doing what had to be done in a world where the weak were crushed.

A cold shiver ran through Jaxon as he shuffled through the pile. He was beginning to see the puzzle pieces fitting together—Carlos's past, full of violence and fear, shaped the man he had become. The photos and letters told a story of a desperate man, one who had been pushed too far and who, in turn, pushed others past their limits. The Carlos Jaxon had known wasn't born a monster—he had become one, forged in chaos and danger.

"Damn you, Carlos," Jaxon muttered, barely loud enough to hear. He finally understood the weight of the past that had haunted their lives. Carlos had been trapped in a cycle of control and fear, and now Jaxon and his family were caught in that same storm.

Jaxon put the box back in its place, but the secrets it held pressed down on him like a heavy weight. He felt the walls of the study closing in, the air thick with the legacy of a man who had used power to survive. But somewhere in the darkness, a new sense of purpose flickered inside him. Jaxon wasn't going to let the past keep hurting them. He wasn't going to let Carlos's shadow destroy everything.

Walking out of the study, Jaxon knew what he had to do. He had to protect his mother, keep her safe from the dark truth they had uncovered. His mind raced, thinking about the photos, the letters—how could he use them? How could he throw the detective off their trail, make sure he and Martha stayed out of it? The truth could ruin them, but maybe it could also be their escape, if Jaxon played his cards right.

EMMA'S HANDS TREMBLED as she unfolded the crumpled envelope that had been wedged into her mailbox, an unassuming messenger of chaos. She withdrew a single photograph, its edges frayed with age, and a slip of paper that fluttered to the ground like a fallen leaf in autumn. Her green eyes, usually a soft haven of warmth, now mirrored the storm brewing within her as they settled on the image of Carlos, his gaze captured in a moment of deceptive calm.

The paper bore a message, each letter meticulously scribed to form words that constricted around Emma's heart like a vice: "How serene looks can deceive." No signature, no further explanation—just enough to send her thoughts spiraling into paranoia. The cryptic hint tore through the veil of normalcy she had draped over her life, exposing the raw vulnerability beneath.

"Mom?" Jaxon's voice cut through the silence, pulling Emma back from the precipice of her fears. She hastily tucked the photograph into her pocket, hiding her distress with a practiced smile that had fooled many but never her son.

"Everything's fine, Jax," she lied, her voice betraying a quiver that did not go unnoticed.

"Mom, I know better, what is it?" Jaxon insisted. "I—I don't know, it's just..." Emma handed the photo to her son, watching his brow furrow and his face twist into concerned confusion.

"Who sent this?" Jaxon asked. "It was just in the mailbox, no name, nothing. It had to have been left over night." Emma said.

He flipped the photograph over, examined the note. His eyes flashed with anger. "Who would do this? Why?" Jaxon asked loudly so if someone was listening, they could hear what he was saying. "I don't know. I just wish he would call me or let me know he's ok. Something so I can... So the police..." Emma's voice trailed off with notes of concern heavy in her tone.

Jaxon observed her with piercing hazel eyes that seemed to see through the facade. He reached out, placing a comforting hand on her shoulder, a silent promise of solidarity. Together, they would face whatever storm lay ahead, with heads held high and hearts full of courage. Nothing could stop them now. They were warriors, and they were ready for whatever came their way.

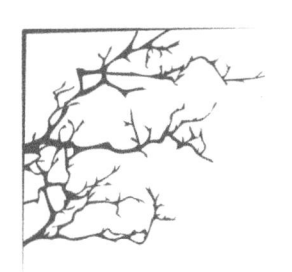

# Chapter 31

Jaxon woke up with a jolt, his whole body tangled in the bed sheets like he was trapped. His t-shirt was drenched in sweat, and he struggled to catch his breath, trying to shake off the scary dream that still lingered in his mind. His heart raced in his chest, pounding like a drum as fear coursed through him.

He paused, taking deep breaths to calm himself down, while the silence of the room surrounded him. The only sound was the beating of his heart, thumping loudly in his ears. He took a moment to gather himself, listening to the quietness of his room and feeling the fear slowly subside. But the darkness seemed to creep closer, making shapes and shadows that played tricks on his eyes. He knew they were just illusions from his dream, but it didn't stop him from getting spooked.

Jaxon slowly rolled out of bed, his throat scratchy and dry from the cold. The floor was freezing on his bare feet as he cautiously stood up, careful not to make any noise and wake up his mom. The room was pitch black, the only source of light peeking through the closed curtains, casting a dim glow on the worn rug. Jaxon tiptoed through the dark room, using his hands to guide him along the walls. Every sense was on high alert, as he didn't want to disturb his mom's already troubled sleep. He knew she was going through a tough time, but she always seemed to handle it with grace that he couldn't comprehend.

He paused at the threshold of his room, listening for the telltale signs of his mother's slumber. The quiet house yielded no sound of disturbance, and he allowed himself the faintest sigh of relief before continuing on.

The hallway stretched before him; a narrow corridor bathed in the pale glow of the moonlight that filtered through the curtains. It was a path he had traversed countless times, yet each step felt laden with a gravity that pulled at him, an invisible force that made his limbs heavy and his resolve waver.

Jaxon cautiously made his way to the kitchen, trying not to make any noise or attract attention. The cold tiles under his feet caused a chill to run up his legs. He carefully approached the sink as if it were a sacred place where he could leave behind the remnants of his terrifying nightmare.

He grabbed a simple, clear glass and turned on the faucet, feeling the cool metal against his hand. The water flowed into the glass, mocking the chaos in his mind with its clarity. Jaxon took a sip, hoping for a moment of relief from the turmoil inside him, but even the peacefulness of the night couldn't soothe his troubled thoughts completely.

The tremor in Jaxon's hands was slight, but it was there—a physical testament to the turmoil that churned within him. Droplets of water quivered and danced as they fell from the lip of the glass, each one a tiny echo of his unsettled thoughts. He tried to steady his grip, focusing on the coolness of the glass, the simple act of filling it, but the water's gentle sound seemed to amplify in the silence of the kitchen, resonating with the erratic beat of his heart.

He picked up the glass, the drink shining in the moonlight, and took another sip. The water was refreshing, but it didn't make him feel any better after the scary dream he had just had. He couldn't stop worrying, his mind filled with bad thoughts and fears that wouldn't go away no matter how much he drank.

In the other room, Emma lay awake in the dark, her eyes searching for sleep that wouldn't come. She felt uneasy for reasons she couldn't explain. She thought of Jaxon and noticed he had been acting differently lately, always seeming sad even when the sun was out.

Quietly, she slipped out of bed and stood on the cold floor, her instincts as a nurse guiding her in the dark. With careful steps, she made her way to the kitchen, listening for any signs of what woke her up. Something felt wrong, throwing off the peaceful balance of their home, and her first thought was for her son's safety.

Emma moved with caution down the hallway covered in soft carpet, almost like a ghost gliding through. She had learned to move silently from her years working in hospitals during late nights when every noise mattered. Her usually warm and welcoming green eyes were now sharp and watchful as she approached the kitchen.

The house was eerily silent, as if it held its breath in anticipation of what would happen next. Emma stumbled along the wall for support, her fingers grazing the bumpy wallpaper before she let go. As a mother, her instincts were heightened, and she could sense that something was wrong with her child. Every step she took was fueled by the urge to protect him and make him feel better.

The dull kitchen light barely illuminated the room, casting Jaxon's shadow on the floor like a strange ghostly figure. Emma moved closer, suddenly overcome by the quietness of the room. She stopped at the doorway, taking in her son's tense posture and his tight grip on a glass as if he were holding onto it for dear life.

"Jax?" Her voice, though barely above a whisper, cut through the silence with the precision of a scalpel.

He jumped, making a loud noise as the glass he was holding hit the counter. He turned quickly, the light coming through the window showing his face—a mix of trying to look calm but really feeling very upset.

"Mom," he said with strain in his voice, "I...I didn't mean to wake you up."

Emma's heart lurched seeing her son obviously trying not to show how much he was struggling. She instinctively moved closer to him, wanting to comfort him and make things better.

She reached out towards his arm but stopped hesitantly. She wanted to help, but she didn't want to make things worse for him. Her worry deepened as she looked at his face, which seemed changed from his usual energetic self. It was like something heavy was weighing him down.

"Is everything okay, Jax?" Her voice was soft, a tender note that sought to wrap him in comfort without smothering.

Jaxon's eyes briefly flicked towards her; hesitation evident in the way they darted away. He fell silent, grappling with the vulnerability of his own thoughts. Emma, patient from years of experience as a nurse and mother, held back the urgency that gnawed at her insides.

"I've been having nightmares," he finally confessed, the words scraping against his throat as he spoke. His once guarded posture now sagged with the weight of his admission. "And... it's more than that. It's like I'm drowning in everything - the days blur together and something just feels... off."

Emma encouraged him softly, conscious of the delicate tightrope she was walking while trying to uncover the truth from a person lost in shadows.

Jaxon's lips parted, then closed, his inner turmoil evident in the slight tension around his mouth. He shifted his gaze past her, searching for answers in the cold light of the refrigerator or the monotonous pattern of the linoleum floor. He picked up the glass, the drink shining in the moonlight, and took another sip. The water was refreshing, but it didn't make him feel any better after the scary dream he had just had. He couldn't stop worrying, his mind filled with bad thoughts and fears that wouldn't go away no matter how much he drank.

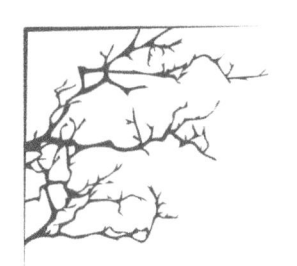

## Chapter 32

Emma listened, her heart sinking. She could feel the distance growing between them, even as he opened up. She leaned in, her voice soft, trying not to push too hard.

"It's okay, Jaxon," she said, her tone steady but gentle. "I'm here. We'll figure it out together. What's bothering you?"

Jaxon's eyes flicked away, avoiding hers. He stared at the floor, his jaw tight, fingers fidgeting with his shirt. Emma could see it—there was something he wasn't telling her. Something important.

"It feels like something's missing," he mumbled, more to himself than her. "Like there's a piece we don't have. Something we're not seeing, and without it, we'll never understand everything."

Emma put a hand on his shoulder, trying to steady him. "What do you mean, Jax? What piece? I don't understand what you are talking about. Maybe I can help if you tell me."

Jaxon swallowed hard, his thoughts swirling. The secret he and his grandmother shared was hanging between them, thick and suffocating. If his mom knew, it would change everything. She wouldn't forgive them. He was sure of it.

He stayed quiet. The silence between them grew heavier, but Emma didn't push. She could feel it—something was deeply wrong, but she knew better than to force it out of him.

"We're in this together, Jax," she said, gently rubbing his back. "Whatever it is, we'll figure it out. You don't have to carry it alone."

Jaxon tensed under her hand, but didn't pull away. "It's not just nightmares, Mom. It's Carlos... him being gone, and all this stuff with his girlfriend and the baby. It's too much. I can't handle it anymore."

Emma's chest tightened hearing his pain. She kept her hand on his back, hoping it would help, but there was something else—something big—that he was holding back. She could feel it.

"Jax, you can always tell me," she said quietly, her voice full of love. But deep down, she knew whatever he was hiding wasn't going to come out tonight.

The kitchen fell into silence, broken only by the hum of the fridge. Emma's eyes stayed on him, steady and full of quiet strength. Jaxon felt her concern like a weight pressing down on him, but he couldn't tell her—not now, maybe not ever.

Finally, Jaxon nodded, his eyes catching the faint light of the kitchen. He knew this wasn't over. What he was keeping inside would follow him, creeping into every part of his life, haunting him every night.

As dawn broke through the window, a new day waited for them. Slowly, they both stood from the table. The simple act felt heavy, like they were stepping into something far deeper. Their bond, once strong, would be tested.

Emma reached for his hand, holding it firmly but gently. She didn't need to say anything—her touch promised that no matter what, she wouldn't let go. They would face it together, whatever it was.

Together, they stepped into the pale light of morning. The secrets they kept, the truths they couldn't speak, would shape the path ahead. They weren't ready, but they had no choice.

MARTHA ARRIVED MID-morning, her usual calm demeanor in place, though Jaxon could sense a certain tension in the way she carried herself. Emma had just left for work, leaving the house quiet, almost too quiet. Jaxon had been pacing, waiting for the right moment, and now it had come.

"Nana," he said slowly, not sure how to start. "I found something... in Carlos' desk."

Martha frowned, her sharp eyes locking onto him. "What do you mean? What did you find?"

Taking a deep breath, Jaxon told her about the secret compartment he'd discovered in Carlos' desk. The box of old photos, the letters, and the other things that Carlos had hidden away for so long. He explained how the images showed a side of Carlos they'd never known, a younger man, but also someone already caught in dark, dangerous circles. And the letters—they were full of threats, debts, and warnings, painting a picture of a man who had been running from trouble his whole life.

As Jaxon spoke, Martha went still. Her face, usually so composed, seemed to drain of color. She wasn't one to show much emotion, but Jaxon could see the weight of his words hitting her, hard.

"I knew he was hiding something," she whispered, more to herself than to him. "But I didn't know it was this bad."

Her eyes, usually sharp and calculating, softened for a moment as she took in the reality of what Jaxon had uncovered. She had always suspected Carlos had skeletons in his closet, but she hadn't been prepared for just how many.

Jaxon sat down, feeling the heaviness of the situation press down on him. "What do we do now?" he asked, his voice quieter than before.

Martha stayed silent for a long time, her mind racing. She had always been the one with the answers, the one who could fix things, but this... this was bigger than she had imagined. If these letters and photos got into the wrong hands, it could ruin everything—not just for her, but for Jaxon and especially Emma. They were already walking a tightrope, trying to keep their lives together after Carlos' disappearance.

"We destroy it," Martha finally said, her voice firm despite the fear lurking in her eyes. "Every letter, every picture. We can't let anyone see this."

Jaxon's stomach twisted. "But what if someone already knows? What if—"

Martha cut him off, her voice sharper now. "No one else knows. Carlos is gone, and we have to make sure these secrets go with him. If anyone asks, we deny, deny, deny. Everything."

Jaxon stared at her, realizing just how serious she was. She wasn't just talking about hiding the truth; she was talking about burying it—forever. And if they didn't, the fallout could be worse than he ever imagined.

"Jaxon," Martha said, stepping closer. "We have no choice. If your mother finds out, if the police find this... it'll destroy us. We're the ones left to clean up Carlos' mess, and we have to be smart about it."

Jaxon nodded slowly, the reality sinking in. They were standing at the edge of a cliff, and one wrong move could send them over.

"What do we do first?" he asked, his voice steadying.

Martha took a deep breath, her resolve hardening. "We get rid of everything. Tonight. Burn it, bury it, I don't care. No one can ever know what we've found."

As she spoke, Jaxon felt a chill run down his spine. This wasn't just about hiding Carlos' secrets—it was about survival. They were in too deep now, and there was no turning back.

The fire flickered in the corner of Jaxon's mind as they planned their next steps. As the sun rose higher in the sky, they both knew that by the end of the day, Carlos' past would be nothing more than ashes.

She motions for Jaxon to sit, her hands trembling slightly as she paces the small living room. The weight of what he's uncovered presses down on her—those photos and letters could ruin everything. They were not just remnants of Carlos' past, but proof of dangerous ties and choices that they had hoped would remain buried.

"Nana," Jaxon says quietly, breaking the tense silence. "How do we do all of this though?"

Martha stops pacing, her lips pressed into a thin line. She looks at Jaxon, her grandson, the one person she's tried to protect all these years. She knows the truth will devastate him, but more than that, it will destroy Emma. And if the police got their hands on this... there was no telling what would happen.

"First," Martha finally says, her voice low and calm, though her eyes betray her panic. "You don't tell your mother. She can't know any of this. Do you understand me, Jaxon? None of it."

"But what about the detective? He's already asking questions about Carlos. And these letters—Nana, they prove he was in deep. There's no way we can just hide this."

Martha's face hardens. "We don't have a choice. If your mama finds out... if anyone finds out, it'll tear our family apart. Carlos might've been a bastard, but you and I—" She hesitates, knowing the depth of her own involvement. "We're tied to him whether we like it or not. And you've seen the kinds of people he was dealing with. They won't stop at him. They'll come for us."

Jaxon feels a wave of nausea wash over him. He hadn't thought about the wider implications, only about getting rid of the nightmare that was Carlos. Now, with Martha's words weighing on him, the situation feels even more hopeless.

"So where do we go to burn it all?" Jaxon asks, his voice barely above a whisper.

Martha's eyes narrow as her mind works quickly, calculating their next move. "We take it to my house. Out in the field where I burn my garbage," she says after a long pause. "We burn the letters. Burn the photos, all of it. Anything that ties us to Carlos and his mess, everything has to be destroyed. We can't let anyone—especially that detective—get wind of this. Not a single scrap of evidence can survive."

Jaxon sits there, his heart pounding. Destroying the evidence means wiping out any chance of justice for whatever dark things Carlos was involved in, but it also means protecting his mother, protecting his Nana—and himself.

"And what if someone else knows?" he asks, fear creeping into his voice. "Carlos had people. People who knew more than we do. They could come after us."

Martha's gaze sharpens. "Then we handle them. One way or another. We don't really know what he was involved in, not really. We can deny everything if someone should approach us."

There's a chill in her words, a darkness Jaxon hasn't seen before. He realizes then that this isn't just about covering up Carlos' past—it's about survival.

"Are you sure we can do this?" Jaxon asks, doubt gnawing at him.

"Oh sweet boy...we don't have a choice," Martha replies, her voice firm. "We bury the past, Jaxon. Or it'll bury us."

With a heavy heart, Jaxon nods. He stands and follows Martha to the desk, where they begin the grim task of erasing Carlos' shadow from their lives.

In the evening, she and Jaxon return to her home. Gathering everything they have found; they take it out with the kitchen garbage. Using a lighter fluid, the fire flickers in front of them, consuming the evidence of the life they wish they could forget; Jaxon feels the weight of the secret settle deep into his bones. It would follow him now, just as it had followed Carlos.

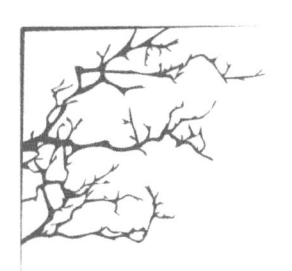

# Chapter 33

The next morning, Emma sat alone in the dimly lit room, her fingers tracing the cool edge of a photograph that laid before her. It was one of the few relics she had of Carlos; his dark eyes seemed to follow her with an intensity that made her heart race. The silence around her was heavy, laden with secrets that whispered from every corner of their shared home.

Her mind raced with the disjointed pieces of information she had painstakingly gathered over the past weeks. Receipts crumpled at the bottom of drawers, recalling the hushed phone calls she wasn't meant to hear, and Carlos's increasingly erratic behavior prior to his disappearance—all these fragments screamed foul play. Yet Emma's heart clung to a sliver of hope, a fragile thread that perhaps, just perhaps, there was another explanation.

Even as she grappled with the sharp sting of betrayal, Emma's resolve hardened. She needed answers. The need to uncover the truth about Carlos, about the man she married, consumed her. But beneath the layers of determination, fear coiled like a serpent—the fear of what those truths might unravel about the people she loved, about herself.

The shrill ring of the telephone shattered the quiet, making Emma jump. Her hand trembled slightly as she picked up the receiver.

"Hello?" she said, her voice steadier than she felt.

"Emma, it's Detective Michael Ross. I was hoping we could meet to discuss some new developments in your husband's case."

Emma's breath hitched. This was it—the moment when the veil might be lifted. The detective's voice was authoritative yet carried an undertone of empathy that offered a modicum of comfort amidst the storm of her emotions.

"Of course, Detective Ross," Emma replied, her words carefully measured. "Where would you like to meet?"

"There's a café downtown, The Roasted Bean. Can you be there at 3 PM?"

"Yes, I'll be there." She paused, gripping the phone tighter. "Thank you for keeping me updated."

"See you then, Mrs. Dawson." The line went dead.

For a fleeting second, Emma allowed herself to close her eyes, drawing a deep, steadying breath. When she reopened them, her green eyes reflected a tempest of thoughts. She stood up, straightening her blouse with a practiced hand, the photograph of Carlos left staring blankly from the table.

Determination coursed through her veins as she headed towards the door. Today, she would face Detective Ross, armed with grace and grit—a woman on the precipice of revelation, prepared to dive into the abyss for the sake of the truth.

Emma Dawson slipped through the doors of The Roasted Bean, her eyes scanning the room until they landed on the familiar figure of Detective Michael Ross. He sat in the far corner, a steaming cup before him, his gaze fixed on the entrance. Emma's heart thumped a chaotic rhythm as she approached, each step measured and deliberate.

"Detective Ross," she greeted, extending a hand that betrayed none of the tremors that fluttered like caged birds within her chest.

"Mrs. Dawson," he replied, his handshake firm, his blue eyes assessing her with an intensity that could peel back the layers of any pretense.

"Thank you for meeting me on such short notice."

She smoothed the fabric of her skirt and took the seat opposite him, her posture erect, an embodiment of composed concern. "Of course," she said, folding her hands on the table.

"There have been some developments." Detective Ross said.

Emma inclined her head, feigning the role of the anxious spouse. "News about Carlos?"

"Actually, yes," Ross began, his voice a low rumble, "we've uncovered some... inconsistencies in Mr. Martinez's behavior leading up to his disappearance."

Her pulse quickened, but she kept her expression molded into one of puzzled worry. "Inconsistencies? I don't understand."

"His routine changed," the detective explained. "Withdrawals from your joint account, unexplained absences, phone calls at odd hours."

Emma's mind raced, threading together fragmented suspicions into a tapestry of dread. These were signs she had noticed but dismissed, details her family might be entangled in. She blinked slowly, summoning shock to her features. "I—I had no idea," she lied, the words tasting like ash on her tongue.

"Did he seem different to you in the days before he vanished?" Ross watched her closely, a seasoned hunter gauging his prey.

"Carlos was, well, distant. He said he was under a lot of stress," Emma offered, skirting the edge of truth. "He kept so much to himself. I just thought he needed space."

"Understood," the detective nodded, his scrutiny unwavering. "We're trying to piece together his movements. Anything you can remember could be crucial."

"Of course," Emma assured him, her brain churning with the implications of her next words. "I have told you everything I know, but if I think of anything new, you'll be the first to know."

Detective Ross gave a satisfied nod. "Let's keep in touch, Mrs. Dawson. And please, call me if anything comes to mind."

"I will," she promised, her voice steady despite the storm brewing beneath her calm exterior.

As she left the café, the weight of her deception pressed down on her conscience. Emma knew the path ahead was fraught with peril, but she treaded it willingly—for truth, however harrowing, must be unearthed.

"Excuse me, Detective Ross," Emma interjected, the practiced tone of concern threading through her words. "I need to use the restroom. Will you excuse me for a moment?"

"Of course, Mrs. Dawson," he replied, his gaze lingering on her just a beat too long as if trying to decipher the sudden urgency in her demeanor.

Emma rose, her chair scraping softly against the floor. As she walked, her shoulders were squared with the feigned composure of someone accustomed to life's emergencies. Yet beneath her calm stride, her heart hammered against her ribs, each beat echoing the cacophony of thoughts swirling in her mind. She pushed open the door to the café's restroom, the muted click of the latch granting her a fleeting sanctuary from the probing eyes of the world outside.

In the solitude of the small, tiled room, Emma leaned against the cool sink, staring into the mirror but not truly seeing her reflection. The woman who looked back at her was a stranger—composed, serene, her green eyes betraying none of the tempest that raged within. But those same eyes had seen too much, and now they could not unsee the sinister web that entangled her family.

She reached for the faucet, letting the water run cold before splashing it on her face. It was a futile attempt to wash away the guilt that clung to her like a second skin. Her breaths came in short, controlled bursts, an exercise in maintaining the façade that was slowly crumbling with each passing second.

The chime of her phone shattered the silence, a jarring note in the quietude. She snatched it up, her fingers trembling as she read the message that flashed across the screen:

"Meet me in Willow Park. Now. - Jax"

Her heart skipped. Jaxon. His messages were always direct, imbued with an urgency that belied his years. There was no room for questions, no space for hesitation. He knew, she realized—the weight of that knowledge settled like lead in her stomach.

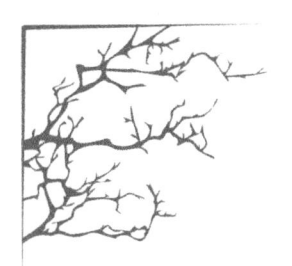

# Chapter 34

Without a word, she slipped out of the restroom, her exit from the café unnoticed by Detective Ross or the patrons lost in their own worlds. The late afternoon sun cast long shadows on the pavement as she made her way to the park, her steps quickening with each block she put behind her.

Willow Park was a haven of tranquility amidst the chaos of Oakdale—a place where children's laughter usually filled the air, where couples strolled hand in hand beneath the canopy of ancient trees. But today, it felt different to Emma. Today, it was a stage for revelations that would alter the course of her life.

She found the old oak easily, its gnarled branches a testament to the passage of time. Jaxon stood beneath it; his silhouette etched sharply against the waning light. His presence was both a comfort and a harbinger of truths she wasn't sure she was ready to confront.

"Jax," she murmured as she approached, her voice barely above a whisper.

"Mom," he acknowledged, his hazel eyes locking onto hers with an intensity that spoke volumes. In his gaze, she found the reflections of her own fears—and the resolve to face whatever storm lay ahead.

The crisp rustle of dry leaves underfoot punctuated the tense silence as Emma approached Jaxon. His back was to her, shoulders squared as if bracing against an unseen adversary. She stopped a few paces away, her heart hammering in her chest.

"Jaxon, what is it?"

He turned, and the fading light played across his face, revealing the grim set of his jaw. "They're going to find out, Mom. There's too much we didn't account for," he said, his voice threaded with urgency.

Emma's breath hitched. "We? Who do you mean? What did you do?" The question emerged as a whisper, laced with dread.

"It was never supposed to go this far," Jaxon admitted, stepping closer. "But Carlos... he was going to ruin everything—our family, our name. He had to be stopped."

"Stopped..." Emma repeated, the word splintering into fragments in her mind. Stopped equaled silenced. Silenced meant gone. And gone...

"Tell me he's alive, Jax." Her eyes searched his, desperate for a sliver of hope.

"Mom, I—I can't tell you that." Jaxon's admission was a physical blow, leaving her swaying on her feet.

"God, Jaxon!" Tears pooled, threatening to spill over. "How could you? What have you done?"

"Nana and I, we took care of it." The mention of her own mother involved in such an act was a bitter pill that wouldn't go down.

"What? What are you saying Jaxon? You... Nana... you did what?" Emma's voice faltered; she began to sway unsteadily.

"We took care of it, we had to do something to protect you!" His outburst cut through the quiet park. "We did it because we love you, we did it to protect you, understand? To protect all of us."

"Love doesn't destroy lives, Jaxon!" Emma countered, her grief morphing into anger. "You've crossed a line that can never be uncrossed."

"Mom, please. You have to understand—" Jaxon reached out, but she recoiled, wrapping her arms around herself as though to ward off the contamination of his actions.

"Understand?" she spat out, each word a shard of glass. "What is there to understand about taking someone away, Jaxon? About lying and covering it up? How do you expect me to live with this?"

"Because we're family. Because without us, you're alone." Jaxon's plea hung between them, a desperate tether.

"Alone might be better than living with this...this horror." The weight of what they'd done pressed down on her, suffocating, relentless.

"Mom, look at me." He stepped forward again, his hands gentle on her arms as he turned her to face him. "We couldn't just stand by and let him continue to destroy our family."

"Destroy our family..." Emma echoed hollowly. "Yes, it's destroying us, now there's blood on all of our hands—Carlos's blood."

"Mama, you don't have to tell anyone, no one else knows. We can—"

"Stop," she whispered, breaking free of his grasp. "Just stop."

Jaxon's face was a mask of sorrow and resolve. "We had to do whatever it takes to fix this. For us. For our family."

"Fix?" A bitter laugh escaped her. "You can't fix this. You can only hide it, bury it—and hope it never sees the light of day."

"Isn't that worth something? Keeping our family together?"

"Is it?" Emma asked, her voice a mere shadow as she backed away from him, the distance growing with every step. "I don't know if I can ever look at you, at Nana, the same way again. I don't know if I can live with this, Jaxon."

"Mama, please—" His voice cracked, reaching out for her retreating form.

But she turned away, leaving him standing beneath the oak, a solitary figure consumed by the creeping darkness. Emma walked on, each step away from Jaxon a battle between the love she held for her family and the horror of their deeds—a war raging within her soul with no end in sight.

THE CONFRONTATION WITH Martha unfolded in the living room where family photos lined the walls, their smiles a stark contrast to the tension that now crackled through the air like static.

"Mother, how could you?" Emma's question sliced through the silence, shattering it into jagged shards. Her green eyes, usually so warm, now blazed with a fury she struggled to contain.

Martha stood with her back straight, her red hair a fiery halo in the sunset light streaming through the window. "You have to understand, Emma, we did what was necessary for the family. For us."

"By what? Hurting Carlos? Making him disappear?" The words tumbled out of Emma's mouth, each one laced with incredulity and pain.

"Life is complex, baby girl. Sometimes the right choice isn't always the kindest one," Martha said, her tone unwavering. It was the voice of reason that had guided Emma all her life, but now it struck a dissonant chord.

"Is this who we are now? A family of secrets and lies?" Emma's hands trembled, and she clasped them together to keep them still.

"Sometimes love means protecting each other from harsh truths," Martha responded, her gaze unflinching.

"Even when it destroys us inside?" Emma countered, her inner turmoil spilling over. The smell of her mother's lavender perfume intermingled with the scent of betrayal, suffocating her.

"Especially then," Martha insisted, her voice soft yet steely.

They stood there, two reflections of the same bloodline, bound by love and torn by choices that would haunt them both. In the depths of Martha's eyes, Emma searched for absolution but found only the resolve of a woman who believed she had done what was necessary.

As night fell, the house enveloped them in shadows, a family united and divided by the secrets they kept. Emma grappled with the knowledge of her family's dark entanglement and the realization that some bonds, once broken, could never be fully mended.

Emma drew a deep breath, steadying her nerves as the silence stretched between them.

"Where did he... What did you do with his... Where is he?"

"We put him under the tree, the same place we put your father's ashes. He is under the headstone. I had it re-set after a 'accident' with the new riding mower." Martha said with a terrifying calmness to her voice.

"Ma," she began, her voice wavering but determined, "I won't expose us... but don't expect me to forget." The words hung heavy in the air, a vow laced with sorrow and resignation.

Martha's eyes softened ever so slightly, the first crack in her fortress of conviction. "I know, Em," she murmured, "and we'll live with that. We have to find a way to move forward, together."

A fragile understanding passed between them, as delicate as spider silk and just as likely to snap under too much strain. They stood amidst the remnants of their argument, the kitchen light casting a warm but stark glow over faces marked by an emotional skirmish. Emma felt the weight of the secret press down on her shoulders, a burden she had never asked for yet could not refuse.

She retreated into her room, closing the door on Martha's world-weary silhouette. The walls seemed to close in around her, the familiar patterns of the wallpaper now reminiscent of bars on a cage.

Emma sank onto her bed, the springs creaking under the load of her despondence.

In the quietude of her sanctuary, the magnitude of her decision settled around her like a shroud. Emma hugged herself, seeking comfort where there was none, her mind reeling from the obligation to protect a secret that gnawed at her conscience like a relentless pestilence.

The image of Carlos haunted her — his smile that once lit up her darkest days, now nothing more than a ghostly flicker in the recesses of her memory. How could she reconcile the love she held for her family with the horror of what they had done?

"Protect them," a voice whispered from within, the mantra taking root. It was a commitment etched in pain, sculpted by necessity. Emma realized that shielding her family meant a lifetime of looking over her shoulder, every knock on the door a potential downfall, every sidelong glance a seed of suspicion.

Yet, as the night pressed on, her resolve hardened like ice on a wintry pane. She would carry this secret, bury it beneath layers of smiles and mundane conversations. Emma Dawson, once a fortress of empathy and care, now fortified her heart against the onslaught of truths that could destroy the very fabric of her being.

When dawn painted the sky with hues of new beginnings, Emma emerged from her cocoon of contemplation. Her green eyes, once reflective pools of vulnerability, now shimmered with an unspoken fortitude. She made the agonizing choice to walk the tightrope strung with lies and sacrifice, to protect her family, no matter the cost.

"Whatever it takes," she whispered into the cold morning air, her breath misting before her, a spectral testament to the invisible chains she willingly clasped around her soul.

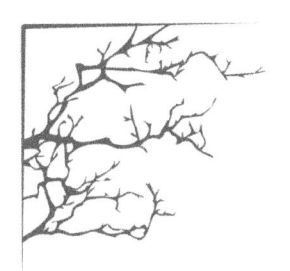

## Chapter 35

Emma sat motionless on the blue sofa, the dim glow of the table lamp casting long shadows across the room. Her hands cradled her face, fingers entwined in the rich blonde strands of her hair as if holding onto them might anchor her to reality. The fabric of the cushion beneath her was damp — testament to the silent cascade that had yet to cease. She breathed raggedly, the air shuddering through her as though it traveled across a field of thistles, stinging and cold.

The house was silent, but for her sobs that echoed against the bare walls, filling the space with the sound of heartbreak. Jaxon's school books lay abandoned on the floor, their bright colors a stark contradiction to the darkness enveloping her soul. Martha's cross-stitch frame rested on the mantelpiece, the needle mid-stitch as if frozen in time. These remnants of domestic life seemed like artifacts from another world—one where the shadow of her family's actions didn't loom over her.

With each tear that traced her cheek, Emma grappled with an internal tempest. Love for her son, Jaxon, clashed with the horror of his deeds, their bond now marred by a crimson stain that no amount of maternal affection could cleanse. And then there was Martha—her rock, her fierce protector—whose sharp tongue had whispered justifications that chilled Emma to her core.

"Is standing by them my complicity?" she murmured into the silence, the question hanging heavy in the air. "Or is abandoning them a betrayal of everything I am, everything I've taught him to be?"

Her nurturing nature, honed through years of caring for the infirm and comforting the dying, now faced its greatest trial. Could empathy extend to those who commit the unforgivable? As a nurse, she had held the hands of many, offering solace without judgment. But these were not strangers; they were her flesh and blood, their lives intertwined with hers in ways that defied simple ethics.

The green eyes that had so often been a source of comfort for others now reflected a turmoil they could not soothe. The certainties of her life had crumbled, leaving her stranded in a moral quagmire that pulled her deeper with every attempt to wrest free. Emma knew the world outside these walls would demand justice, but the sanctuary of home pleaded for loyalty.

"Where do I stand, Jax, Ma?" she whispered to the emptiness around her, seeking answers that refused to come. The weight of the decision pressed down upon her, suffocating in its gravity. To shield them was to sink into the abyss alongside them, yet to expose them was to tear out her own heart.

A solitary figure amidst the wreckage of her life, Emma's resolve flickered like the flame of the candle on the windowsill—a beacon searching for truth in the encroaching darkness. It was a choice between the love that had defined her existence and the justice that gnawed at her conscience, each as relentless and demanding as the other.

And in that moment, as the tears continued their relentless path, Emma Dawson understood the true cost of love. It was measured not in the sweetness of tender moments, but in the bitter dregs of choices that cleaved the soul in two.

Emma's knees buckled as she rose from the couch, her feet finding a rhythm on the hardwood floor that echoed the cadence of her pounding heart. She paced, each step a beat in the tumultuous symphony of her thoughts. Her mind was a maelstrom, spinning with the gravity of decisions yet unmade and truths that could shatter the very foundation of their lives.

As she moved, a gust of wind rattled the windowpanes, and the room seemed to close in on her. The walls, once adorned with the comforting hues of family life, now felt oppressive, trapping her in a prison of her own making. She paused for a moment, closing her eyes against the relentless assault of memories.

TWO WEEKS LATER.

The air around her shifted, and she was no longer in the dimly lit living room but bathed in the warm glow of a summer evening long past. Laughter spilled from the open kitchen window, carrying with it the sizzle of a barbecue and the sweet fragrance of blooming jasmine.

"Emma, come quick! Jax is about to unveil his masterpiece," Martha called out, her voice tinged with mirth.

Emma remembered stepping onto the deck, where Jaxon stood, all gangly limbs and teenage pride, gingerly flipping burgers with an oversized spatula. His hazel eyes sparkled with excitement as he presented each perfectly charred patty like a treasure unearthed from the depths of culinary adventure.

"Behold, the fruits of my labor!" he had exclaimed, and they had laughed together, a family united in joyous simplicity.

Martha, red hair glinting in the setting sun, rested her hand on Emma's shoulder—a silent message of solidarity and love that transcended words. It was a tableau of contentment, a snapshot of a life rooted in shared affection and unwavering support.

A sharp breath escaped Emma's lips as she was wrenched back to the present, the warmth of reminiscence fading into the chill of her solitary vigil. She swallowed hard, the taste of those happier times turning to ash in her mouth.

"God, what am I going to do?" she murmured to herself, resuming her restless pacing. The stakes were unimaginable; the truth had the power to unravel everything they had built, every memory they had cherished. Yet, silence was complicity, a dark stain that would spread through the fabric of her being, leaving indelible marks on her soul.

Her feet traced paths across the floorboards, worn smooth by years of Dawson footsteps. With each stride, she weighed the cost of loyalty against the price of justice. How could she betray her own flesh and blood? But how could she not, when the specter of their deeds hung over them like a guillotine blade, poised and ready?

Emma's hands clenched into fists at her sides, nails biting into her palms. The duality of her love for Jaxon and her mother warred with the stark reality of their actions. Their faces—Jaxon's intense gaze, Martha's determined set of jaw—flashed before her eyes, urging her toward silence, pleading for protection.

Yet, somewhere deep within, a part of Emma screamed for release, for the cleansing fire of truth to burn away the tangled webs of deceit. She stopped pacing, standing still as the last rays of sunlight died away, leaving the room in twilight's grasp.

In the shadows, Emma Dawson found a flicker of resolve. Tomorrow would bring its own trials, its own demands for answers, but tonight she stood at the crossroads of her own conscience, a sentinel guarding the fragile boundary between love and honor.

Emma crouched by the low coffee table, her fingers tracing the spines of books she had turned to in times of need. Self-help guides, nursing manuals—a stark contrast to the turmoil brewing within her. The quiet of the living room echoed too loudly, each tick of the grandfather clock a resounding gavel in the courtroom of her mind.

"Maybe someone else should know," she whispered into the silence, the words feeling like blasphemy on her tongue. Could she confide in Rachel, her oldest friend who shared memories of childhood but not the burden of this truth? Emma pictured Rachel's eyes widening in shock, the inevitable recoil. Trust could shatter on the harsh cliffs of judgment, and friendships once broken were hard to mend.

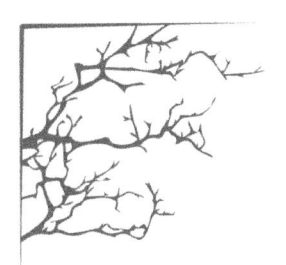

## Chapter 36

But what if she sought counsel from a stranger instead, a professional with a code of confidentiality? A therapist who could offer a detached perspective, untainted by personal connection. Yet even that thought sent spikes of panic through her veins. Would they see her as an accomplice? Would their duty to report overshadow their role as confidant?

Tears threatened to spill again, blurring the edges of the room, when her gaze landed on the frame nestled among the scattered mementos on the table. With hesitant steps, she approached, her hand reaching out with trepidation before her fingers curled around the cool metal.

The captured moment was one of pure happiness—Jaxon's laugh frozen mid-chuckle, his hazel eyes sparkling with unguarded joy. Beside him, Martha stood proud, her red hair a vivid flame against the muted backdrop, her arm slung over her grandson's shoulders in a protective embrace. Their smiles were a testament to the bond they shared, a bond that now tethered Emma to a precipice.

Her fingertips ghosted over the glass, tracing the outlines of Jaxon and Martha's faces, the gesture a silent apology for even considering betrayal. She remembered the strength in Jaxon's hug, the safety in Martha's unwavering support. How could she upend the lives of those she cherished above all else?

"Forgive me," she murmured to the smiling images. The photo trembled in her grasp, a physical manifestation of the war raging within her soul. Love, fierce and encompassing, fought against the gnawing insistence of her conscience.

Emma held the frame close, the heartbeat of her family pulsing against her chest. She was the keeper of their secrets, the guardian of their past—and now, the architect of their uncertain future.

Emma inhaled deeply, the air filling her lungs like a buoyant force, steadying the tremor of her limbs. The photograph in her hand, a relic of happier times, was placed gently back on the table as if it were made of the thinnest glass, its joy too delicate to withstand her reality. She straightened her back, each vertebra locking into place with a newfound firmness that anchored her wavering spirit.

Her eyes, once clouded with tears, cleared as she wiped the moisture from her cheeks with the back of her trembling hand. There was a decision to be made, one that would wrap her family in the armor of her resolve. Emma's posture, rigid and unyielding, now told a story of determination—a silent proclamation that she would shield Jaxon and Martha at any cost.

The silence of the room, thick with secrets and the echo of distant memories, was shattered by the piercing ring of the telephone. It cut through the stillness like a siren call, demanding attention, commanding fear. Emma's heart skipped a beat, then doubled its rhythm in a frenzied drum of anxiety.

"Mrs. Dawson?" came the gravelly voice from the other end—Detective Michael Ross. His tone was neutral, but even without seeing his piercing gaze, Emma felt it upon her, dissecting her every word, searching for truth amid the shadows.

"Detective Ross," she replied, her voice steady despite the dance of her pulse. "How can I help you?"

"Ah, just following up on a few details regarding Carlos's disappearance," he stated matter-of-factly. The casual nature of his words belied the gravity they carried, each one a potential landmine under the soil of her composure.

"Of course," Emma managed, the receiver slick against her skin. Her mind raced, thoughts scattering like leaves in a storm. What did he know? What had he uncovered?

"Are you alright, Mrs. Dawson? You sound...distressed," pressed Detective Ross, his instincts as sharp as the razors that must have trimmed the edges of his seasoned career.

"Just tired, Detective," she lied smoothly, a mask of normalcy painted over her panicked features. "It's been a long day."

"Understandable," he conceded, and Emma could almost hear the cogs turning behind his words. "We'll be in touch, Mrs. Dawson. Take care of yourself."

"Thank you, Detective," she said before the line went dead, the click echoing like a final verdict in the hollow space.

Emma remained frozen, the phone an obsolete weight in her hand. The walls of the living room seemed to press in closer, the shadows cast by the fading light morphing into menacing figures. She had navigated the treacherous waters of suspicion—for now. But the tide was unpredictable, and Emma knew she had to brace herself for the waves yet to come.

Emma's thumb hovered over the end call button, her breath a silent whisper trapped in her chest. She could almost feel the gaze of Detective Ross through the phone, his eyes sharp enough to cut through lies like a scalpel.

"Mrs. Dawson," Detective Ross began, his voice steady and deliberate, "in cases like these, we often find that people close to the situation may remember something they initially overlooked. Anything at all can be helpful."

"Oh Detective, please, not this again, I have already gone over everything with you before." Emma replied, her voice a controlled melody of concern and innocence. She felt the weight of her every word, each one a stepping stone over a chasm of suspicion. "Again, as

I said, Carlos and I... we had our difficulties, but nothing that would lead to... him leaving like this."

"Understood," he responded. The silence stretched between them like a tightrope, and Emma knew she must tread carefully. "And there hasn't been any unusual activity around your home? No unexpected visitors?"

"Nothing out of the ordinary, Detective." A lie wrapped in the blanket of truth; she had learned to play this game too well. "Although, with everything going on, I might not have noticed."

"Sometimes the smallest detail can be the key," Detective Ross said. His tone was encouraging, but Emma sensed the underlying scrutiny, the unspoken challenge.

"Believe me, Detective, as I have said before, if I think of anything, you'll be the first to know," she assured him, her fingers clutching the photo frame on the table next to her for strength.

"Thank you, Mrs. Dawson. That's all for now. We'll keep you updated on any progress." The formality in his voice was a curtain falling after a performance, signaling the end, at least for the moment.

"Thank you, Detective Ross. Goodbye." As she ended the call, the tension in her body unraveled like a tightly wound spring. Emma closed her eyes, allowing herself a single, shuddering exhale. Her heart still pounded an erratic drumbeat against her ribs, but it was slowly steadying.

She had done it. She had maintained the façade of the grieving, clueless wife. Emma opened her eyes, glancing at the faces of Jaxon and Martha, smiling back at her from the photo frame. Her resolve hardened like ice in her veins; she would protect them, no matter what storms may come.

Emma remained motionless, the silence of the living room enveloping her like a suffocating blanket. She sat there, a solitary figure dwarfed by the expanse of the empty space, her face awash with conflicting emotions. Outside, the world carried on, unaware of the storm brewing within the four walls of her home. Her gaze was fixed on the window, eyes tracing the gentle sway of the bare branches in the cool evening breeze.

The burden she now shouldered was colossal, a weight that pressed down on her chest with an almost physical force. The future—a maelstrom of uncertainty and danger—loomed large before her. How could she navigate this treacherous path? The lives of Jaxon and Martha, the two people who were her world, hung in the balance. Emma's mind was a cacophony of desperate plans and dark scenarios, each one crashing against the next with no resolution in sight.

A car passed by outside, its headlights briefly illuminating the living room, casting long shadows that danced across the walls. Emma blinked, the trance-like state breaking momentarily as she was reminded of the passage of time, of the need for action. Clarity pierced the veil of her indecision.

She rose from the couch, a newfound determination etching itself into her posture. The softness that usually graced her features had given way to a steely resolve. Her hands curled into fists at her sides, knuckles white with the force of her grip. The glint in her green eyes hardened, reflecting a resolve that had been absent before. Emma Dawson would protect her family, come what may.

Her silent vow filled the room, echoing off the walls with the unspoken promise of a warrior preparing for battle. The challenges ahead were formidable, but Emma's love was a fortress, and she would defend it with everything she had. With each steady breath, she steeled herself for the fight of her life.

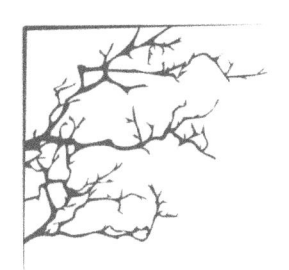

## Chapter 37

Emma sat at the small café near the hospital, her fingers drumming a nervous rhythm on the table as she stirred her untouched coffee. For days, the weight of her family's secrets had been pressing down on her, threatening to crack her carefully maintained facade.

Rachel wasn't just a colleague; she was a trusted confidante; someone Emma could turn to without fear of judgment. Today, she knew, was the day she had to unburden herself before the pressure tore her apart.

When Rachel arrived, her warm smile was a balm to Emma's frayed nerves. As she settled into the chair across from Emma, concern flickered in her eyes. "Emma, it's good to see you. Your message sounded... troubled. What's going on?"

Emma's heart raced as she took a deep breath, her voice barely above a whisper. "Well, first I need to know, can this be strictly off the record?"

"Of course, what's going on, is everything ok at home?"" Rachel asked, worry lines forming across her flawless face.

"I hardly know where to begin, Rach. It's all so tangled—my mother, Jaxon, Carlos. Everything feels like it's unraveling, and I can't seem to hold it together anymore."

Rachel leaned in, her brow furrowing. "Take your time, Emma. Let's start with Jaxon. What's happening with him?"

Emma's gaze dropped to her coffee, watching the dark liquid swirl as she spoke. "He's become so distant lately. Nightmares plague his sleep, but he won't talk to me about them. Every time I try to reach out, he just... shuts down. And then there's Carlos—ever since he disappeared, Jaxon can't stop mentioning him. It's like he's obsessed."

"And your mother?" Rachel prompted gently.

Emma's eyes flickered up, a mix of confusion and worry evident in her expression. "Ma's acting... strange. She's always been tough, but now it's like she's guarding some terrible secret. I can feel it, this undercurrent of... something. I can't quite put my finger on it, but it's there."

Rachel nodded slowly, processing the information. "It sounds like there's a lot of tension in your family right now. Have you talked with Dr. Thompson about these changes?"

Emma hesitated, her voice dropping even lower. "I have an appointment this afternoon. But Rachel, Jaxon found something in Carlos' desk. Old photos, letters—things that paint Carlos in a completely different light. I'm starting to think there's more to his disappearance than we realized. And I'm torn, Rach. Do I dig deeper, or let sleeping dogs lie?"

Rachel's expression grew serious. "Emma, this sounds like it could be quite serious. Have you considered going to the cops? If Carlos was involved in something dangerous, you might be out of your depth here."

"I can't," Emma whispered, her knuckles white as she gripped the edge of the table. "My mother... she's terrified. She says that we'll all be in danger if anyone finds out. I'm scared for Jaxon, for what this could do to him if we don't handle it carefully. But I don't even know what the right way to handle it is anymore."

Rachel reached across the table, her hand resting comfortingly on Emma's. "Emma, listen to me. Your priority has to be protecting

Jaxon. Secrets like this... they eat away at people. You're a nurse; you know the toll stress and trauma can take, not just physically but emotionally. And if Martha is insisting on silence, you need to ask yourself why. What is she so afraid of?"

A tear slipped down Emma's cheek, quickly brushed away. "I just feel so lost, so alone in all of this."

"You're not alone, Emma," her friend assured her, her voice firm but kind. "Trust your instincts. If you feel this is bigger than you can handle, don't be afraid to seek help. Talk to Jaxon again, push if you have to, but don't let this secret tear your family apart. And remember, I'm here if you need me. Don't hesitate to reach out."

As Emma left the café, a small spark of determination had ignited within her. The weight of her family's secrets still pressed heavily, but Rachel's words echoed in her mind. One way or another, she would get to the bottom of this—before it was too late.

IN THE QUIETUDE, THE clock's ticking became a countdown, each second slicing through the air, reminding Emma of the precipice upon which she stood. She tucked a loose strand of blonde hair behind her ear, a feeble attempt at composure before her world would be laid bare once more.

Her eyes fixed on the door through which Dr. Thompson would emerge—the threshold between her inner chaos and the promise of clarity. Emma leaned back, surrendering to the deceptively soft embrace of the couch, the only witness to her private struggle before the confessions began.

The door opened with a whisper, a gentle disturbance in the stagnant air of anticipation. Dr. Amelia Thompson stepped through, her presence like a balm to the charged atmosphere. Her smile was a beacon of calm, radiating understanding without uttering a word. She moved with unhurried grace, closing the door behind her with a soft click that seemed to seal away the outside world.

"Emma," she greeted, the name cradled in warmth. "I'm glad you're here today." Dr. Thompson gestured toward the couch opposite her own chair, the space between them both an invitation and an arena for the soul's battles.

"Thank you, Dr. Thompson," Emma replied, her voice a tremulous thread in the fabric of their exchange. She clutched at her own forearms as though holding herself together, her knuckles white with the effort.

"Tell me," Dr. Thompson began, settling into her chair with a practiced ease, "what thoughts have been visiting you since our last session? I can see there's something pressing on your mind."

Emma's eyes, a tumultuous sea of green, flickered with the struggle to anchor her words. "It's just..." The sentence faltered; a bird too weary to take flight. "I don't know where to start. Everything feels so tangled, like a knot that just tightens the more I try to unravel it."

"Sometimes," Dr. Thompson offered gently, "it helps to simply voice what's at the very top. The first thread that comes to mind, no matter how trivial it may seem."

"Carlos," Emma exhaled the name, and with it, the barriers began to crumble. "He's vanished, and I feel like I'm being swallowed by the silence he left behind. It's not just his absence... it's the questions, the looks, the whispers. They're everywhere, suffocating me."

"Vanished?" Dr. Thompson echoed, her tone devoid of judgment, inviting further trust. "When did you last see him?"

"Six weeks ago," Emma whispered, her gaze lowering to her lap as if the truth could be found among the folds of her skirt. "We had an argument—a terrible one—and then... nothing. He's just gone."

"Arguments can be painful, especially with those we care for deeply. What was it about, if you feel comfortable sharing?"

Emma hesitated once more; the internal battle etched across her face. "It was about his family... about secrets that are poisoning everything. And now, I'm caught in the middle, unsure of whether I'm the antidote or just another dose of the venom."

"Secrets can be heavy burdens to bear," Dr. Thompson acknowledged, her blue eyes reflecting empathy. "You're not alone in this, Emma. We'll navigate these troubled waters together."

"Thank you," Emma murmured, a fragile smile touching her lips as she met Dr. Thompson's gaze. In that small exchange, a sliver of hope glinted, a subtle but defiant light against the encroaching darkness of her fears.

Dr. Thompson settled into her chair, a quiet sentinel in the midst of Emma's storm. Her fingers tented together, and she leaned forward slightly, an anchor in the tempest of Emma's emotions.

"Emma," Dr. Thompson began, her voice a lifeline thrown across the chasm of uncertainty, "this room is a sanctuary for your thoughts and fears. No matter how dark or tangled they may appear, here you can lay them bare, safe in the knowledge that they will be met with understanding, not judgment."

Emma drew in a shuddering breath, as though inhaling the courage offered by Dr. Thompson's words. The room felt insulated from the world outside, a private universe where her truths could unfold without repercussion.

"Carlos," Emma started, her tone a tremulous thread in the still air. "He has this... this anger inside him, like a beast he can't control." Her hands twisted in her lap, knuckles whitening with the strain of her confession. "That night, the argument we had—it unleashed something in him, something I've never seen before."

"Can you tell me what sparked the argument?" Dr. Thompson's inquiry was gentle, yet it tugged at the seams of Emma's reluctance.

"His phone," Emma replied, the word a catalyst to her unraveling composure. "I saw a message from another woman. It wasn't just flirty; it was evidence of an affair—of many, I think. When I confronted him, he flew into a rage." She paused; her eyes haunted as she relived the memory. "He accused me of invading his privacy, of being paranoid and controlling."

"Paranoid and controlling are strong accusations," Dr. Thompson observed softly. "Do you believe there is truth in those words, or might they be reflections of his own guilt?"

"Perhaps both," Emma conceded, her voice barely above a whisper. "But when I threatened to leave, to expose his lies, he said things..." She trailed off, a fresh wave of fear washing over her.

"Things that frightened you?" Dr. Thompson prodded, her presence a steady beacon.

"Yes," Emma confirmed, her green eyes brimming with unshed tears. "He said if I ever tried to leave, he'd make sure I regretted it. That no one would believe the 'crazy nurse' over him." A drop escaped, tracing a glistening path down her cheek. "Then he stormed out. And now... he's gone. Vanished into thin air."

"Threats like that are meant to trap you, to keep you silent," Dr. Thompson said, her tone imbued with both gravity and compassion. "But you're speaking now, Emma. You're breaking that silence. How does it feel to share this with me?"

"Terrifying," Emma admitted, another tear making its escape. "But necessary. Like lancing a wound to let the poison out. I can't carry this alone anymore."

"Indeed, wounds must breathe to heal," Dr. Thompson affirmed. "And you are not alone, Emma. Together, we'll find the way forward."

With each word exchanged, the heavy shroud of secrecy began to lift, and within the confines of Dr. Thompson's office, Emma

Dawson found the nascent stirrings of liberation from the oppressive shadows cast by Carlos Martinez.

Emma wrung her hands, the fabric of her skirt twisting between her fingers as Dr. Thompson settled into the chair opposite her. The psychologist's eyes were attentive, a softness in their depths that beckoned Emma to continue.

"Tell me more about what's been weighing on you," Dr. Thompson urged gently, leaning slightly forward, her gaze never wavering from Emma's face.

"It's... it's not just Carlos," Emma's voice was a whisper, barely breaching the silence of the room. "It's everything that came after. The questions, the police, and then... then there's my family."

"Your family?" Dr. Thompson echoed softly, encouraging her to elaborate.

"Ever since I was a child, there have been... secrets." Emma paused, her breath hitching as she teetered on the edge of revelation. "Secrets that bind us together but also tear us apart."

"Secrets can be like chains," Dr. Thompson acknowledged with a nod. "Heavy and cold. But speaking them aloud, that's how we start to break them, Emma."

Emma swallowed hard, her gaze flickering toward the window before settling back on Dr. Thompson. "If I speak up, if I tell the truth about Carlos... It could unravel everything. My mother, my job, our reputation in Oakdale."

"Is it the truth about his disappearance or the truth about these secrets that frightens you more?" Dr. Thompson asked, her voice a beacon in the shadow of Emma's fear.

"Both," Emma admitted, her voice breaking. "The secrets are old, Dr. Thompson. Dark. They're the kind that don't just fade away; they linger, they fester. If they come out..."

"Emma," Dr. Thompson interjected, her tone firm yet filled with empathy, "you've been carrying these burdens for a long time. Have you considered the toll it's taking on you? The cost of protecting these secrets?"

"Yes, but what else can I do? If I bring them to light, I might lose everything. And yet, holding onto them..." Emma trailed off, her eyes haunted.

"Sometimes, Emma," Dr. Thompson said, her voice tinged with wisdom, "protecting ourselves and the ones we love means facing the difficult truths head-on. It may seem impossible now, but strength often comes from the most unexpected places."

"Strength," Emma repeated, tasting the word as though it were unfamiliar. Her heart raced, the internal battle raging within her laid bare in the confines of this sanctuary.

"Remember, you're not making any decisions right now," Dr. Thompson reassured her. "This is about exploring your feelings, understanding your fears, and considering your needs. Whatever path you choose, it will be with a clearer mind and a lighter heart."

A clarity began to pierce the fog of Emma's turmoil as she sat there, locked in the tender gravity of Dr. Thompson's gaze. The realization hit her swiftly; to protect or expose—the power lay trembling in her own hands.

The clock on the wall ticked in rhythm with Emma's racing heart as Dr. Thompson leaned forward, bridging the gap between doctor and patient with a gaze that pierced through defenses. "Let's consider the different outcomes," she began, her voice a calm anchor in the storm of Emma's mind. "What might happen if you choose to reveal what you've been concealing?"

Emma's fingers knitted together in her lap, a lifeline against the swell of anxiety. "If I tell... it's like pulling the pin from a grenade," she whispered, her green eyes reflecting a battlefield of emotion. "My family—what if they never forgive me?"

"Forgiveness is a complex journey, Emma," Dr. Thompson said gently, offering a new perspective like a key to an unseen lock. "But have you considered the possibility of healing? Not just for you but for everyone involved?"

Healing. The word hung in the air, a foreign concept amidst the chaos Emma had grown accustomed to. She bit her lip, pondering the path less traveled by, where truth didn't necessarily spell destruction.

"And what of the weight you carry?" Dr. Thompson pressed tenderly, urging her to look at the heavy chains of secrecy she'd bound herself with. "How might life change if you were free from it?"

"Freedom..." Emma's voice was a mere breath, laden with longing. "I could breathe again. Stop looking over my shoulder. But at what cost?" Her gaze fell to the floor, tracing the patterns in the carpet as if they held the answers she sought.

"Costs are inevitable, regardless of the choice," Dr. Thompson acknowledged, her words echoing the stark reality of Emma's situation. "But consider also the cost of silence. How does that shape your life, your relationships, your very sense of self?"

The room seemed to close in around Emma, walls lined with the specters of consequence and repercussion. Yet within her, something stirred—a flicker of courage fanned by Dr. Thompson's probing questions.

"Silence...it's suffocating," Emma admitted, her resolve hardening like ice beneath a winter sky. "It's...it's changed me, made me into someone I don't recognize. Someone who's afraid all the time."

"Is that who you want to continue to be?" Dr. Thompson asked, not as a challenge but as an invitation to explore the uncharted territories of her soul.

Emma shook her head, a movement small but seismic. "No," she said, the word a shard of glass cutting through years of accumulated darkness. "I want to be free from this fear. I want to face the truth, even if it means facing it alone."

"Remember, Emma," Dr. Thompson said, her tone imbued with the gravity of their exchange, "whatever you decide, you won't be alone. You'll have support—the kind that helps you withstand storms and navigate the path to recovery."

"Recovery..." Emma repeated, tasting the sweet possibility of a future unshackled from deceit. The notion was terrifying yet exhilarating, a paradox fitting for the labyrinthine corridors of her mind. And in that moment, as the weight of her secret bore down upon her, Emma Dawson felt the first glimmer of a strength she had yet to fully understand.

Emma clenched her fists in her lap, the fabric of her jeans bunching under her white-knuckled grip. The clock on Dr. Thompson's wall ticked with a rhythmic persistence, marking the passage of time and the urgency of her decision.

"Emma," Dr. Thompson began, her voice a soft but firm anchor in the tumultuous sea of Emma's thoughts. "Whatever path you choose to walk, know that your steps are yours alone. Your strength has carried you here, through shadows and doubt, and it will carry you forward."

Emma drew a shuddering breath, feeling the weight of Dr. Thompson's words settle over her like a protective cloak. She looked up, her green eyes meeting the steady blue gaze of her therapist.

"But what if my choice causes more pain?" she whispered, the question a fragile bird in the stillness of the room.

"Sometimes," Dr. Thompson replied, shifting slightly in her chair, "the hardest choices are the ones that lead to healing. You've been the caretaker, the nurturer, always placing others above yourself. This time, Emma, it's about what you can bear, what you can live with. Trust in your own resilience."

A tremor ran through Emma, a silent echo of the internal quake reshaping her world. Her heart pounded, drumming out the rhythm of a new resolve.

"I can't... I won't expose them," she said, her voice gaining volume and certainty with each syllable. "The truth about Carlos, his disappearance, it would destroy everything. Our family name, our history—it would all crumble."

"Protecting them is your choice, Em," Dr. Thompson acknowledged, nodding gently. "It's a heavy burden, but one you've chosen with clear eyes. Know that whatever comes, you don't have to carry it alone. There are resources, support groups, people who understand."

"Understand," Emma echoed, tasting the word, savoring its implication of shared experience, of communal strength. Her shoulders, once hunched with the weight of untold secrets, squared as she found an unfamiliar yet welcome solidity within herself.

"Thank you," she said, the two words inadequate vessels for the ocean of gratitude churning inside her. "For helping me see that I have a choice, that I'm not just a leaf caught in the whirlwind of fate."

"Always remember," Dr. Thompson offered with a smile that held both warmth and sorrow, "you are the author of your story, Emma. And no matter how dark some chapters may be, there's always room for growth, for change."

"Change," Emma mused, allowing herself a moment to envision a future where the chains of silence didn't bind her soul. "That's something I can strive for—even if the first step is acceptance."

Standing up from the couch, Emma felt the tremors in her hands subside. With each step towards the door, the specter of Carlos and the haunting secret he left behind grew fainter, overshadowed by the burgeoning dawn of her courage.

Dr. Thompson leaned forward, her hands clasped together, her gaze locked on Emma with an intensity that seemed to acknowledge the gravity of silence. "Emma," she began, her voice a tender anchor in the stormy seas of Emma's mind, "the path you've chosen isn't an easy one. But it is yours, and I honor your courage to walk it."

Emma nodded, her heart a drumbeat in her chest, rhythmic and strong. She had made her decision—a guardian of shadows, a keeper of the unspoken.

"Remember," Dr. Thompson continued, her tone imbued with the wisdom of years spent traversing the human psyche, "as heavy as this secret may feel, you're not alone. I'm here for you, now and whenever you need to talk, to share the burden."

"Thank you," Emma whispered, the simple phrase laden with the weight of unshed tears and unspoken gratitude. She drew in a deep breath, each inhalation like drawing back the curtains to let light flood into a darkened room.

"Sometimes," Dr. Thompson said softly, "protecting those we love means making tough choices. It doesn't mean you approve or condone—it means you care, deeply and complexly."

The clock on the wall ticked away moments, but within the confines of that office, time seemed to pause, allowing Emma's fractured spirit the space it needed to begin its precarious mend.

"Your strength," Dr. Thompson assured her, reaching out to squeeze Emma's hand, "is in your resolve, in your ability to face what lies ahead, no matter how daunting."

Emma felt the warmth from Dr. Thompson's hand seep into her own—a physical manifestation of the support promised. Rising from the couch, she stood taller than she had in months, maybe even years. The door that once seemed an exit now appeared as a gateway, a passage towards a future she could shape—even with the weight of secrets pressing against her.

"Dr. Thompson," Emma said, her voice no longer trembling but steady, imbued with the determination of a woman who had peered into the abyss and found within herself the power to stare it down. "I can't tell you how much this means to me. Your guidance... it's given me a strength I didn't know I had."

"Emma," Dr. Thompson replied with a smile that was both proud and poignant, "it was always there, within you. I just helped you see it."

With a final look, Emma turned the handle, stepping across the threshold into the muted light of the hallway. Her heart carried the heavy secret, but her steps were buoyant with newfound resolve. As the door clicked shut behind her, sealing off the sanctum of shared confidences, Emma Dawson moved forward—into the life she must now navigate, armed with the silent promise to protect, to endure, and to hope.

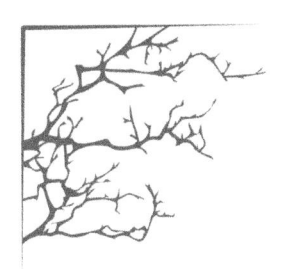

## Chapter 38

Emma drove home, her conversation with Dr. Thompson replaying in her mind. She knew she needed to confront Jaxon, but the thought made her chest tighten. She couldn't shake the feeling that whatever Jaxon and Martha were hiding could change everything.

When she pulled into the driveway, the house seemed quieter than usual. Emma stepped out of the car, her steps slow as she made her way inside. The air felt thick, heavy with the weight of unspoken words.

Jaxon was sitting at the kitchen table, his hands clenched into fists on the surface. Martha stood at the counter, her back to him, staring blankly out the window. The tension between them was palpable.

Emma hesitated in the doorway, her eyes darting between them. "We need to talk," she said softly, trying to keep her voice steady.

Jaxon looked up, his expression unreadable, but there was something in his eyes—a mix of fear and defiance. Martha didn't turn around.

"What the hell is going on, Jax?" Emma asked, stepping closer. "You've both been shutting me out, and I know something's wrong. I just talked to Dr. Thompson, and she thinks—"

"Thompson doesn't know anything," Jaxon cut her off, his voice tight. He stood abruptly, pushing the chair back with a screech. "She doesn't understand anything about what's happening here."

Emma felt her heart race. "Then help me understand. Please, Jaxon. You're scaring me."

Martha finally turned, her face pale and drawn. "Emma, baby girl, this isn't something you should be involved in," she said quietly, but there was a tremor in her voice.

Emma's eyes widened. "What are you talking about? This is my family. If there's something going on, I deserve to know."

Jaxon sighed, running a hand through his hair. "Mama, there are things... things about Carlos that we found out. Things that could ruin everything. You don't understand what kind of man he really was."

"Then enlighten me," Emma insisted, throwing her hands up in frustration. "I can't help if you don't tell me."

Martha stepped forward, her voice barely above a whisper. "Jaxon found a box in Carlos's office. But the box he found... it's not just letters and photos like you would find in anyone else's stuff. It's documented proof of the kind of life Carlos was living. Debts, threats... people he was connected to. Dangerous people."

Emma's breath caught in her throat. "What kind of people?"

Jaxon slammed his fist on the table, startling her. "People who will come looking if they find out we have that box. If they even suspect we know what Carlos was involved in, we're all in danger."

Emma's mind raced. She could feel the walls closing in around her, the weight of the situation sinking in. "What are you saying, Jax? We have to go to the police. We can't keep this secret. It's too dangerous."

"No!" Jaxon's voice a loud whisper, his face twisting in fear. "We can't. They'll kill us, Mom. You don't understand how deep this goes. If we hand this over, we're dead."

Martha grabbed Jaxon's arm, pulling him back. "Jaxon, wait." She turned to her daughter, "We have to be smart about this, Emma. We can't just rush into something that could get us all hurt."

Emma stared at them, her heart pounding. She could see the fear in Jaxon's eyes, the desperation in Martha's face. They were terrified — trapped in a nightmare she hadn't even realized they were living in.

"What do we do then?" she whispered, her voice trembling. "How do we fix this?"

Jaxon shook his head. "I don't know. But we can't go to the police. Not ever. We need to figure out who these people are, and how much they know. Then we can decide what to do."

Martha nodded in agreement. "We have to be careful. Until we know more, we're on our own. Hyper vigilance... we all need to be careful who we talk to, what we say and how it's said. We never know who's listening."

Emma felt a wave of dread wash over her. The secret they were keeping was far more dangerous than she'd imagined. But now that she knew, there was no turning back.

"Okay," she said finally, her voice barely above a whisper. "We'll do it your way. But we have to be careful. We have to protect Jaxon, no matter what."

Martha's face softened, and she gave Emma a small, sad smile. "We will. We'll protect him. Together."

As they stood in the quiet kitchen, the weight of their decision settled over them. They were in deep now, tangled in a web of lies and danger, with no clear way out. But one thing was certain—they would face it together, no matter what.

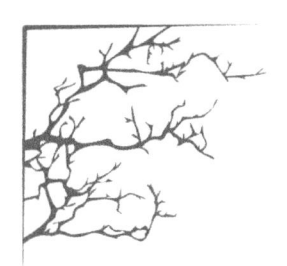

## Chapter 39

Emma's phone rang, the sudden sound breaking the tense silence that had settled over the house. She glanced at the screen and saw Detective Ross's name flashing. Her stomach twisted into knots, her fingers trembling as she swiped to answer.

"Detective?" she said, her voice a shaky whisper.

"Ms. Dawson," Ross began, his tone steady but serious, "we need to meet. It's urgent. I have some new findings, actually, it's new information about Carlos."

Emma's breath hitched, her grip tightening around the phone. She felt Jaxon and Martha's eyes on her, both of them frozen as they listened.

"I-I don't understand," Emma stammered. "What did you find?"

There was a pause on the other end. "It's complicated, I need to speak to you in person. Can we meet this morning, say, ten o'clock, at the station?"

"Of course, I will be there. Are you sure there isn't anything you can tell me over the phone, Detective? This is starting to scare me." Emma asked.

"It's best not to discuss it over the phone. I will see you shortly." Detective Ross hung up the phone, leaving Emma feeling like the bottom dropped out from under her life.

DETECTIVE ROSS WELCOMED Emma Dawson into his office and closed the door. His silence was causing the energy in the room to be thick with anticipation. "We've discovered some information, grave information Ms. Dawson." He began. "Detective, what is going on? Please just lay it out, I can take it. What I can't take is all of this suspense. Just tell me and let me ..." Her words trailed off.

Detective Ross sat with one leg hitched up over the corner of his desk as he sat on the edge. "Emma, I know you are upset, but... the man you've been married to all these years isn't Carlos Martinez. The real Carlos has been found."

Emma's world tilted, she felt faint. "Wait.... What do you mean? That doesn't make sense. Who was he, then? The man I married?"

"That's what we need to figure out," Ross said gravely. "The real Carlos Martinez... he's been missing for over a decade. We believe the man who claimed to be him, your husband, stole his identity."

Emma felt like the ground was slipping from beneath her. Everything she thought she knew about her life, her marriage, was unraveling in an instant.

"How did you find out? I mean, what does the real Carlos say about this?" Emma asked. "Does he know my husband? What does he say about this Detective?" she pushed.

"Well, the real Carlos Martinez has been dead for a number of years. We unearthed his remains in a deserted area a month ago. There was a series of studies done to confirm his identity. The usual, DNA, finger prints, dental records. I didn't reach out until the results were confirmed in case there was any discrepancy. Emma, we believe that he may have been killed by your husband." Detective Ross said.

"Oh my gosh... Then who is the man I married?" she whispered, barely able to form the words.

"That's what we're trying to find out. Emma, I have to ask. Has he ever talked about his family? His life outside of the U.S. before he came here? Where he comes from?" Detective Ross asked.

Emma swallowed hard. "Yes, of course. He told me he was from Cuba, a small town where there weren't many people. He told me his mother was a prostitute, and that she left him to come to the states when he was seven years old. He came here to look for her when he was 15. He said he never found her, so he stayed with friends and started his own life."

After saying all of that out loud, the room felt heavier, suffocating. Emma stood there, the weight of Detective Ross's words pressing down on her.

Detective Ross studied Emma carefully, his face grim. "Emma, I'm going to be honest with you. We don't know who this man is. What he told you about his past—his mother, coming here at 15—it could all be a lie. Or maybe parts of it are true. But whoever he is, he's been living under a stolen identity for a long time."

Emma's mind raced, her breath shallow. How could she have been so blind? She had spent years loving this man, trusting him, sharing her life with him. And now, everything she thought she knew was slipping away like sand through her fingers.

"Wh— what happens now?" she asked, her voice shaking. "What are you going to do?"

Detective Ross rubbed the back of his neck, his expression growing more serious. "We're trying to piece together the timeline—figure out when he took over Carlos Martinez's identity and what he's been doing ever since. We've opened up an investigation into his past, looking for anything that can give us a clue about who he really is."

Emma sat down; her legs suddenly too weak to hold her up. "You think... he killed the real Carlos?" Her voice cracked at the question.

The idea that the man she had loved for so long was capable of such a horrific act made her stomach turn.

Ross nodded slowly. "We have reason to believe he was involved, yes. We're still working through the evidence, but we know your husband has been using Carlos Martinez's identity since around the time the real Carlos disappeared. We can't say for sure yet, but it's looking more and more likely."

Emma's head was spinning. The man she thought she knew, the man she had built a life with, was a stranger—a potential murderer.

"What do I do?" she whispered, tears welling up in her eyes. "How do I live with this?"

Detective Ross leaned in, his tone softer now. "Right now, the best thing you can do is stay safe and cooperate with the investigation. We'll find out who he really is, Emma, and we'll get to the bottom of this. But I need you to stay strong. You've been through a lot, and there's more to come."

Emma wiped her eyes, her heart pounding. "What about Jaxon? He doesn't know any of this. He thinks his step father is..." She stopped herself. How could she explain this to her son?

"We'll need to talk to him too," Ross said gently. "But for now, focus on yourself. Take some time to process all of this. It's a lot, I know."

Emma nodded, but inside, her mind was reeling. The man she had loved, the father figure to her son, wasn't who she thought he was. And worse, he might have been hiding something far darker than she could have ever imagined.

As she stood to leave, Detective Ross's voice stopped her. "Emma... there's one more thing. We believe he may have had accomplices. People who helped him maintain this lie. I need you to think carefully—has anyone in your life seemed... off? Anyone close to him, anyone he confided in?"

Emma's mind flashed to Martha and Jaxon, the strange tension between them, the things left unsaid.

"No," she said quickly, but her voice betrayed her uncertainty.

Ross caught the hesitation. "Well, if you think of anything, anything at all, let me know."

Emma nodded, but as she left the office, her mind was spinning with doubts. What if the people she trusted most were also part of this dark secret? What if everything she believed in was built on lies?

"MA, CAN YOU MEET ME at the house, there have been some developments on Carlos's disappearance that I think you need to be aware of." Emma said as she drove home from the meeting with Detective Ross.

"Of course baby girl, I will meet you there. Are you ok?" Martha asked.

"No, not really. I'll explain when I see you though. Can you call Jax and make sure he's home please? He should probably know this too." Emma said.

"Emma, what is it?" Martha insisted.

"They found Carlos." Emma said, then she hung up with this revelation hanging in the emptiness of the line.

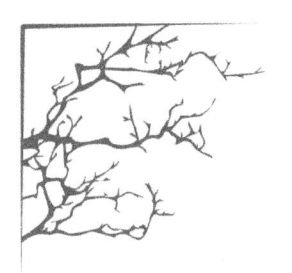

# Chapter 40

As the investigation into Carlos unfolded, Detective Ross and his team made huge breakthrough after breakthrough. Some of Carlos's associates were apprehended and after intense interviews and threats of the death penalty, they cracked under pressure. Leading the police to uncover the true identity of the man Emma had been married to all these years—Domingo Carmona, a ruthless mafia boss who had gone underground. For over two and a half decades, Domingo had evaded both law enforcement and his enemies by assuming the identity of Carlos Martinez.

With the help of his highest-ranking soldiers, Domingo Carmona had been living a double life for as long as anyone could remember, rising to power as a feared and ruthless mafia boss while keeping his true identity hidden. Carlos Martinez, the real man whose name Domingo would later steal, was just an unfortunate victim of circumstance.

Carlos Martinez had crossed paths with Domingo by accident. He was a young man from a small town in Cuba, trying to make a new life for himself in the small town of Bonita. Unlike Domingo, who thrived in the world of crime, Carlos was honest, hardworking, and naïve to the dangers lurking around him. He had no idea that his life would intersect with one of the most dangerous men in the underworld.

At first, Domingo saw Carlos as nothing more than a minor inconvenience. Carlos was dating a woman who had unknowingly been tied to one of Domingo's operations. Domingo had been watching her, tracking her movements to ensure she wasn't a threat. Carlos was just in the wrong place at the wrong time. But something about Carlos intrigued Domingo—his clean-cut appearance, his lack of criminal record, and most importantly, his complete anonymity. Carlos was the perfect candidate for Domingo to vanish into.

Domingo decided to eliminate Carlos and assume his identity. It was a meticulous plan—one that would allow him to disappear from law enforcement and from his enemies while continuing to run his criminal empire from the shadows. One night, Domingo lured Carlos out under the pretense of discussing a job offer. Carlos, eager for a new opportunity, showed up unsuspecting. Domingo, who rarely handled his own dirty work, made an exception this time.

The murder was swift and brutal. Domingo strangled Carlos, ensuring it was quiet and quick. He took Carlos's identification, personal belongings, and anything that would allow him to step into his life seamlessly. Afterward, Domingo disposed of the body in a remote location in a vacant area of the small town of Buen Visita, Cuba where he lived, ensuring it wouldn't be found for years.

Carlos was nobody to Domingo—a mere pawn in a much larger game. To Domingo, it wasn't personal; it was business. By taking Carlos's name, Domingo Carmona disappeared, and "Carlos Martinez" was born. He moved to the United States and into a quiet, suburban life, marrying Emma and slipping into the role of a loving husband while continuing to operate his criminal activities from behind the scenes.

For Domingo, Carlos was a shield, a way to evade detection and live under the radar. But for Carlos, the encounter had been a fatal twist of fate—his life stolen by a man who had no qualms about erasing his existence for the sake of self-preservation.

Once the pieces fell into place, the police shifted their focus to Domingo's criminal empire. The trail led them to several of his key lieutenants, each of whom had been involved in dangerous operations, from drug trafficking to extortion. As the authorities closed in on his inner circle, it became clear that Domingo had been running a sprawling criminal enterprise while hiding in plain sight as Emma's husband.

For Jaxon and Martha, the revelation was both a relief and a chilling reminder of just how dangerous the man they had killed truly was. Despite the tension between them, the knowledge that no one was looking at them for Domingo's death gave them a sense of safety—for now.

In the days that followed, the media was flooded with stories about Domingo Carmona's downfall, detailing the extent of his criminal network. The news painted a picture of a man who had lived two lives—one as a mafia kingpin and another as a quiet, suburban husband. Emma was thrust into the spotlight, becoming an unwitting symbol of deception. But Jaxon and Martha stayed in the shadows, knowing full well that if anyone found out about their role in Domingo's demise, everything would unravel.

Sitting at the kitchen table one night, Jaxon and Martha finally allowed themselves a moment to breathe.

"Looks like we're in the clear," Jaxon said, his voice low, though the tension in his shoulders remained. "They've got those guys pinned for everything."

Martha nodded, but her face remained serious. "We may be safe, but we can't get careless. They still don't know what really happened, and that's how it needs to stay."

Jaxon swallowed hard, the weight of their secret still pressing on him despite the relief. "Nana, what if they eventually connect the dots? What if something slips?"

Martha leaned forward; her eyes steely. "We've kept this quiet for over a year. Domingo Carmona is gone, and as far as anyone knows, he vanished because of his enemies. No one's going to connect us to him. We've got to move forward, Jaxon. We can't let fear eat us alive. He's dead, and we're safe."

Jaxon nodded, trying to convince himself that Martha was right. The danger was behind them—Domingo's men had taken the fall, and the investigation was heading in another direction entirely. But deep down, the uncertainty remained, a gnawing fear that the past might resurface someday.

For now, though, they were safe. The real Carlos Martinez's death was just another tragic footnote in a twisted tale of deception and crime. Domingo Carmona was buried along with his secrets, and no one suspected a thing.

But Jaxon couldn't help but wonder how long they could keep it that way.

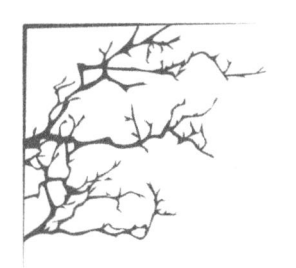

# Chapter 41

On the two-year anniversary of her husband's disappearance, Emma made a decision she had been avoiding for too long: it was time to visit her father's grave. She needed to confront the one person who might understand the weight of her secrets, even if he wasn't alive to respond.

The tree where his ashes were scattered, in her mother's back yard was eerily quiet. The kind of stillness that made every sound seem magnified. Emma's shoes sank into the soggy ground, the wet earth sucking at her soles as she approached the headstone. Each step felt heavier than the last, her legs stiff with hesitation, as if the very land was resisting her presence. She shifted her weight from one foot to the other, feeling the squelch of mud beneath her heels as she came to a stop.

Her fingers absent-mindedly traced the rough bark of the tree, its solid presence a stark contrast to the shifting moral ground beneath her feet. As twilight deepened into dusk, shadows lengthened across the cemetery, mirroring the darkness that had seeped into the very marrow of her family's legacy. Emma stood rooted to the spot, a solitary figure caught between worlds—the living and the dead, truth and deception, love and an unspeakable betrayal that threatened to consume them all.

The ancient oak that stood near her father's grave seemed to watch her, its gnarled branches twisted and reaching out, casting long shadows in the fading light. The tree had been there for as long as Emma could remember, standing sentinel over the graves of her pets long gone. Its branches stretched toward her like skeletal fingers, as if demanding something—perhaps the truth she had kept buried for so long.

Her eyes, burning with unshed tears, focused on the headstone. The words etched into the polished stone shimmered faintly in the bruised twilight. William Dawson. April 18, 1967, to December 26, 2023, Loving Father. Devoted Husband. But to Emma, the headstone didn't just mark where her father's ashes were scattered. It stood as a symbol of something much darker, the epicenter of a secret she had carried in silence—a secret that had twisted inside her like a parasite, feeding on her guilt.

She swallowed hard, her throat tight, and took a deep breath. She wasn't here to mourn. Not really. This was a confrontation, though one-sided. She was here to confess to the man who had taught her strength, integrity, and love, and yet, who had never seen the darker parts of her soul that had taken root since his death.

"Daddy," she whispered, her voice trembling. The word hung in the cool air, unanswered, swallowed by the vast silence of the cemetery. "I—I don't know where else to turn. I need you. I've done something terrible. I've kept things from Jaxon, from mama, from everyone. And now it's all closing in."

She knelt down, the dampness seeping through her jeans, but she didn't care. The cool stone was smooth under her fingers as she traced the letters of his name. The man who had always been her moral compass was now just a memory, and yet here she was, looking for guidance from a ghost.

"I need to tell you what I've done," Emma said, her voice breaking. She blinked hard, trying to push back the tears, but they fell anyway, warm trails down her cold cheeks. "You were always the one I could talk to about anything, and now... now I've done something I can't undo."

The wind picked up, rustling the branches of the oak, but Emma didn't flinch. The secret had been gnawing at her for two years, and now, standing at her father's grave, she couldn't hold it in any longer.

"I did it, Daddy. I did it." She stood with her head hanging, shaking it slowly. Memories flooded her mind—her father's stern face, his deep voice warning her to be careful, to keep her distance from Carlos. He had always been suspicious, but Emma had been too blinded by love, too desperate to hold onto the life she thought she had. Now, with Domingo's identity exposed and the walls closing in, she could feel her father's judgment as sharply as if he stood beside her.

"I should've listened daddy," Emma murmured. "I should've trusted you when you said something wasn't right. But I couldn't, I didn't want to believe it."

Tears began to spill down her cheeks, splashing onto the damp ground. The weight of her decisions, her complicity, was too much to bear. She had loved Carlos, or rather, Domingo, even when her instincts screamed against it. And now, standing at the grave of the only man who had tried to protect her, she realized she had nowhere left to turn.

The words slipped out, soft and barely audible, as though saying them aloud would give them too much power. She had rehearsed this in her head for months, but nothing could have prepared her for the feeling of actually admitting it, even if the only witness was a stone slab.

"I didn't have a choice," she continued, her voice growing stronger with each word. "He wasn't the man I thought he was. He was dangerous. And I... I couldn't let him hurt us any more than he already had. But now..." Emma paused, wiping her face with the back of her hand. "Now I don't know how to live with it. I don't know how to keep going, pretending that everything's fine."

She sat back on her heels, her eyes locked on the headstone. The weight of her confession seemed to settle in the air around her, the gravity of her actions pressing down on her chest.

"I'm sorry, Daddy," she whispered. "I'm so sorry."

The wind seemed to sigh through the trees, as if the world itself was acknowledging her words. Emma stayed there, kneeling in the wet earth, her heart pounding as she waited for a sign—some kind of forgiveness, some kind of release. But there was nothing. Only silence.

And yet, in that silence, Emma found a strange sense of clarity. Her father was gone, and nothing she could say or do would change that. But the burden she carried wasn't his to forgive. It was hers to bear.

Emma wiped her face, her gaze shifting toward the horizon where the last traces of daylight were fading. The shadows lengthened around her, and with them, the shadow of her secret loomed larger. She had come here hoping to find answers, guidance from the past, but the truth was, only she could decide what to do next.

"Daddy, I'll find a way to fix this," she whispered, as if making a vow to the ground beneath her feet. "I'll protect Jaxon, no matter what. I won't let him pay for my mistakes." She pushed her fingers into the soft dirt until she found it, a small bottle just under the edge of her father's headstone. "Good, it's still here. Daddy, keep this safe for me. If you can hear me, please keep it safe."

With one last glance at her father's headstone, Emma stood, her resolve hardening.

With a deep, shaky breath, Emma stood up, wiping the mud from her knees. She knew, now, how to move forward. For the first time in two years, she had said the words that had been haunting her. That, at least, was a start. Now, she had to take care of the rest.

As she turned to leave, the twilight sky darkening overhead, the wind rustled through the branches of the oak again, and Emma swore she heard her father's voice in the breeze, telling her it would be okay.

The evening air, thick with the scent of decaying leaves and freshly turned soil, seemed to whisper with ghostly voices. Each breath she took felt laden with unspoken truths, filling her lungs with the weight of what lay buried beneath the deceptively peaceful ground.

Emma paused again at her father's grave; the silence of the yard broken only by the rustling of leaves in the evening breeze. The anniversary of this day and everything it represented weighed heavily on her, and the secrets she had buried with her father gnawed at her conscience. She had come here not just to mourn, but to confront the truth, the tangled mess of guilt and lies she could no longer carry alone.

As she walked away, the gate in her mother's yard was creaking shut behind her, Emma knew there was no turning back. The past was close to catching up with her, and the only way out was to break through the lies she had woven and the danger still lurking in the shadows.

A whirlwind of emotions battered her from within. Maternal instinct, fierce and primal, clashed violently against a revulsion so deep it made her stomach churn. She had always been the family's touchstone—the one who stitched together wounds both seen and unseen. Now, cruel irony had cast her as the keeper of their gravest sin, a role that felt like a noose slowly tightening around her neck.

A twig snapped, and Emma's breath hitched. She didn't need to turn to know Jaxon was approaching. His presence brought a palpable shift in the air – a charge that made the hairs on her arms stand on end.

Jaxon's footsteps grew nearer, each one deliberate and heavy with a burden far too great for his young shoulders. When Emma finally turned to face him, she saw the psychological distress etched into his features. His piercing hazel eyes, usually so sharp and calculating, were now clouded with an anguish that reached into her soul. There was a tremor in his hands that he couldn't quite conceal, betraying the internal chaos he carries because of his step father's murder.

"Mom," he called softly, his voice barely carrying above the rustling leaves. "Visiting Pawpaw?"

Emma nodded, "Yes, I just need my dad some times. There are times that I feel him looking down on us from heaven, I wonder if he is disappointed in me. For my choices, for my ...." her voice trailed off.

"Grandpa wouldn't be disappointed in you. You are a great mom, and you are a great nurse. You just fell in love with a bad guy, mom. It could have happened to anyone. Carlos—er Domingo, he was a master liar."

"Jax," she replied, her own voice a tightrope of calm and fear.

For a moment, they simply stood there, mother and son, mirroring each other's torment. The tension between them crackled, an invisible barrier forged from their shared sin. They were bound together in this dreadful aftermath, yet the enormity of what had transpired seemed to push them worlds apart.

"Are you okay?" Jaxon finally asked, the question hanging between them, absurd in its normalcy.

"Am I okay?" Emma repeated internally, her heart hammering against her ribs. "How can any of us be okay after this? I was such a fool. I—I can't believe that I..."

"Never mind, honey. Let's go inside," she said, her voice steady despite the storm raging within.

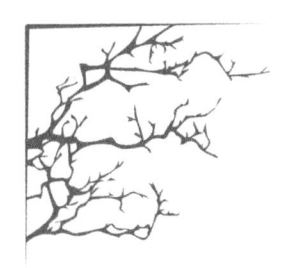

# Chapter 42

As they stepped into her mom's house, the familiar walls seemed to close in around Emma, the weight of the truth pressing down on her. Everything in her life felt like a lie now. The man she'd shared her life with, the man she'd loved and trusted for years, the man that she could never forgive.

Jaxon followed her in, his eyes darting around, unsure of what to say or do. The silence between them was unbearable, thick with the unsaid. Emma could feel the tension gnawing at her, the questions swirling in her mind. What was real? What else had been hidden from her?

She turned abruptly, facing Jaxon, her voice sharper than she intended. "Jaxon, how long have you known?"

Jaxon froze, his face pale, eyes wide. "I didn't... I didn't know, Mom. Not at first. I mean, I thought something was off, but I didn't know it was this. I swear."

Emma's eyes bore into him, searching for the truth. "Then when did you find out? When did you realize the man we've known all these years wasn't really Carlos?"

Jaxon hesitated, running a hand through his hair, the guilt and fear etched into his features. "It was... after I found the box in his desk. The letters, the photos... they didn't make sense. That's when Nana and I started putting it together."

Emma's breath caught. The box. She had no idea what it contained, but Jaxon had found the key to unraveling the mystery long before she had. And now, the burden of knowing weighed on him, just as heavily as it did on her.

"Why didn't either of you come to me sooner?" Emma asked, her voice softer now, laced with hurt.

"We were scared," Jaxon admitted. "I didn't know what to do. I thought... I thought if I told you, it would destroy everything. I didn't want to lose you. Nana said she would handle it, not to worry. So..."

Emma's heart ached at his words, but the reality of their situation was too overwhelming to offer any comfort. A big part of the truth was out now, and there was no going back.

Detective Ross's revelation about Domingo Carmona had changed everything. The man she'd been married to was a dangerous criminal, a murderer. And worse, he wasn't the only one keeping secrets.

"We have to figure out how we move forward, away from this." Emma said, more to herself than to Jaxon. Her mind was spinning, trying to process the enormity of what had happened, what their next steps should be.

As Emma sat in her chair in silence, her thoughts circling back to the dark secret she'd been carrying, one that had been buried for almost two years, hidden from her mother, and even from Jaxon. Detective Ross's revelation about Domingo Carmona had cracked open something deep inside her, forcing her to confront the horrifying secret that she'd kept locked away since her husband's disappearance.

THE NEXT EVENING, EMMA walked through the hospital's sliding doors, her heart still pounding, her mind replaying the events of that fateful evening like a broken record. She nodded at the night receptionist, offering a weak smile, and headed straight to the elevator. Her hand clutched her purse, feeling the weight of the empty vial inside it.

The hum of the hospital seemed distant as she pressed the button for the basement. The morgue. The one place where people never asked questions, where things were meant to disappear.

The elevator doors slid shut, and she was alone with her thoughts. She could feel her pulse in her throat, each second ticking louder than the last. A part of her felt like she was dreaming, like none of this was real. But the cold glass of the vial pressed against her gloved fingers reminded her that this was very real.

The doors opened with a soft ding, and the fluorescent lights of the basement flickered to life. The sterile smell of disinfectant hung heavy in the air, mingling with something faintly metallic — blood, perhaps. The hallway was eerily quiet, deserted at this late hour, with only the distant hum of machinery to break the silence.

Emma moved quickly, her footsteps echoing off the linoleum floors. She knew the morgue well, having worked the night shift long enough to learn its every corner, its every shadow. The double doors at the end of the hall stood closed, but the key card hanging from her scrubs would get her inside.

She glanced around, ensuring she was alone. Not that anyone ever came down here after hours, but she couldn't afford to be seen. Her hand shook slightly as she swiped the card through the reader, the green light blinking as the door clicked open.

The morgue was colder than the rest of the hospital, the chill biting into her skin as she stepped inside. The metal drawers lining the walls seemed to watch her with silent judgment. She wasn't here for the bodies, though. She was here for the incinerator.

In the far corner of the room, beneath the stainless-steel table used for autopsies, stood the large steel furnace. The hospital used it to burn medical waste, the final destination for anything that needed to disappear without a trace. Emma knew the procedure—staff disposed of used gloves, soiled linens, and even expired medications here, all reduced to ash.

Her hand tightened around her purse as she approached the incinerator. She opened her bag and pulled out the vial, her fingers brushing its smooth surface one last time. For a moment, she hesitated. This was the point of no return.

She bent down and pulled open the incinerator door, its creak breaking the dead silence of the room. The heat rushed out in a wave, the flames licking at the edges, hungry for what she had to offer. She tossed the vial and her gloves inside, watching as they vanished into the inferno, swallowed by the heat in an instant.

The glass shattered, consumed by fire, leaving nothing behind but ash and the faint smell of burning plastic from her gloves. Emma stood there for a moment longer, staring into the flames. It was done. The last piece of evidence, gone.

She closed the incinerator with the edge of her scrub top and wiped her sweaty hands on her scrubs, the cold returning to the air around her as the heat faded. Her heart still raced, but the weight of the vial in her pocket was gone, replaced by a hollow emptiness she couldn't quite name.

With one final glance at the silent morgue, Emma turned and walked out, the heavy door clicking shut behind her. No one had seen her. No one would know.

As Emma stepped out of the morgue, wiping her hands on her scrubs and trying to steady her breath, the sound of a cart's wheels squeaking down the hallway made her heart skip a beat. She froze in place, her pulse thudding in her ears as the janitorial lady rounded the corner, pushing her cleaning cart. The older woman, wearing the hospital's standard janitorial uniform, stopped abruptly when she saw Emma.

"Evenin'," the janitor said, raising an eyebrow. "What brings you down here this late?"

Emma's mind raced. She couldn't afford to panic. She forced a calm smile, keeping her voice steady. "Oh, hey," she said casually. "One of the night nurses asked me to check on some lab samples stored down here. She thought we might've sent them to the wrong place."

The janitor tilted her head, clearly curious but not overly suspicious. "Lab samples, huh? Thought that was more of a day shift thing."

Emma shrugged, the tightness in her chest easing just a little. "Yeah, normally, but they've been swamped upstairs. Thought I'd help out since I was already on break."

The janitor nodded slowly, wiping her hands on the towel she had tucked into her waistband. "Well, these late-night shifts can be strange. Always somethin' going on. You find what you were looking for?"

"Yeah," Emma replied quickly, "everything's sorted now."

The janitor smiled, giving Emma a knowing look. "Glad to hear it. Be careful around here, though. This place gives me the creeps sometimes, all these bodies tucked away. Feels like they're watchin' us, you know?"

Emma chuckled softly, her nerves still buzzing. "Yeah, it can be a little eerie. Thanks for the heads-up. I should get back upstairs."

"Take care, now," the janitor called after her, resuming her cleaning duties as Emma walked away.

As she headed back toward the elevator, Emma kept her pace steady, her hands still trembling slightly. She had dodged the question for now, but the encounter left her rattled. She couldn't afford any more close calls.

As she stepped back into the elevator and pressed the button for her floor, Emma exhaled a long, shaky breath. She was back in her world now, the world of patients and doctors, of saving lives. The morgue was behind her. Carlos was behind her.

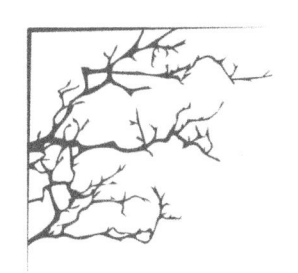

# Chapter 43

Jaxon was having the nightmare again.

It was always the same — reliving the night he and Martha did the unthinkable. In his dream, everything slowed down, each detail sharp and vivid, even more real than it had been that night. The thick smell of blood, the heavy weight of guilt, and the sound of Carlos's choking breaths haunted him.

He saw himself standing there, shovel in hand, while Martha tightened the rope around Carlos's neck. The man's eyes bulged with fear, his face twisted in confusion. Jaxon's heart pounded as he replayed it all, the warmth of Carlos's blood hitting his skin when they started cutting. The metallic smell filled his senses. In the dream, it seemed like it would never end—Carlos's body jerking and thrashing before finally going limp.

But in the nightmare, Carlos always fought harder than he had in real life. His body refused to stay still, his limbs jerking back to life, grabbing at Jaxon and Martha, his fingers clawing at their arms, trying to pull them down with him. The blood wouldn't stop, flooding the room, thick and endless.

Jaxon could see it all—Carlos slumped over, too drunk to notice them at first, muttering to himself, a glass of bourbon in hand. Emma had poured it for him earlier, and now the bottle was almost empty, its amber liquid spilling over the white tablecloth, soaking everything around it.

Martha nodded to Jaxon, her face hardened, eyes cold with resolve. They moved in unison, quiet and deliberate, like shadows creeping across the dimly lit room. Jaxon reached for the heavy nylon rope they had brought, his heart pounding in his ears as he slowly unfurled it.

In one swift, brutal motion, Jaxon looped the rope around Carlos's neck from behind, yanking it tight with every ounce of strength he could muster. Martha quickly took the other end, pulling in sync with Jaxon, making sure it was tight enough to suffocate him. Carlos jolted forward in shock, his hands scrambling toward his throat, his eyes wide with terror as the realization hit.

He gasped—a horrible, wet sound that barely escaped his throat. There was no scream, just the sickening gurgle of a man desperate for air. His fingers clawed frantically at the rope, trying to pry it away, but it was too tight. His strength was no match for the two pulling at either side.

"Help me!" Carlos's rasping voice sliced through the tension, the sound fragmented, weak. "Help me, Jaxon."

Jaxon winced at the words, his muscles straining against the resistance. But the nightmare only intensified.

Martha moved quickly, her hands pressing down on Carlos's shoulders, forcing him back into the chair. His body convulsed, hands still scratching at the rope in a sluggish, futile effort. His eyes bulged, his face a deepening shade of red, but there was no coordinated fight left in him, no burst of strength to throw them off.

"Nana," Jaxon grunted, sweat dripping down his face, "why isn't he fighting harder?" His voice was tight, strained, as he pulled with all his might.

"Because he's drunk," Martha snapped, glancing at the half-empty bourbon glass on the table and the slow, uncoordinated jerks of Carlos's body. "Keep pulling! We have to finish this."

Jaxon tightened his grip, but the resistance was fading. Carlos's body twitched, his efforts weakening until his hands fell limp at his sides. The room fell into a heavy, oppressive silence, broken only by the rasp of their breathing.

They stood frozen for a moment, the weight of what they'd done settling in. Jaxon's hands still gripped the rope, his knuckles ghostly white, trembling as the adrenaline coursed through him. Martha stepped back from Carlos's lifeless body, her breath coming in short, heavy bursts, but her expression remained firm.

The deed was done.

Jaxon let go of the rope, Carlos's head slumping forward onto the table with a dull thud. For a moment, neither of them moved, staring at the lifeless body before them.

"Oh my god, we did it," Jaxon whispered, his voice barely audible, as if speaking too loudly would break the fragile silence that had settled over them.

Martha's gaze was cold, clinical. "Yes, but we're not done yet."

With practiced precision, they carried Carlos's body from the dining room to the garage, where the tarp and tools had been laid out earlier. The smell of oil and dust clung to the air, mixing with the metallic tang of blood as Martha picked up the saw. She glanced at Jaxon, who looked pale, sweat beading on his forehead.

Jaxon tried to scream, tried to run, but he couldn't move, paralyzed by fear, guilt, and the weight of what they had done. In his dream, it didn't matter how many times they buried him. Carlos always came back.

Suddenly, the dream shifted. He was standing in the backyard, at Martha's house, staring at the headstone. The oak tree loomed above him, its branches reaching out like skeletal fingers. The grave was freshly dug, the earth loose and unsettled. Jaxon knew what was under there. He knew what they had buried, but in the dream, the ground started to crack, shifting as if something—or someone—was trying to claw their way out.

The headstone crumbled, and he could see the outline of Carlos's hand, fingers breaking through the dirt, reaching for him. He tried to back away, but his feet wouldn't move. He was rooted to the spot, forced to watch as Carlos emerged from the grave, eyes wide and lifeless, staring straight at him.

"You can't hide forever," Carlos whispered, his voice cold and hollow. "I'll find you."

Jaxon woke with a start, gasping for air, drenched in sweat. His heart pounded in his chest as he lay there in the dark, the nightmare still clinging to him. The room was silent, but the echoes of Carlos's voice lingered, sending chills down his spine.

He sat up, running a hand over his face, trying to shake the images from his mind. But even as he stared into the darkness, Jaxon knew the nightmares wouldn't stop. Not as long as their secret remained buried, festering beneath the surface, just like Carlos's body beneath the ground.

"I'll do it," Martha said, her voice hard. "Hold him steady but close your eyes."

The first cut was brutal, the teeth of the saw biting into flesh and bone with a sickening crunch. Jaxon recoiled at the sound, bile rising in his throat, but he forced himself to hold Carlos's arm in place as Martha worked, her movements methodical and unflinching.

Blood splattered across the concrete floor, pooling beneath them on the tarp, the garage filling with the grotesque sounds of dismemberment. Jaxon's gloved hands were slick with sweat and blood, his mind reeling, but he couldn't look away. Each cut, each motion felt surreal, like a nightmare he couldn't wake up from.

Martha's face was set in stone, her eyes narrowed with grim focus. She had no room for hesitation, no time for second thoughts. This had to be done, and there was no turning back.

By the time they were finished, Carlos's body was unrecognizable, reduced to pieces that would be easier to dispose of. Jaxon slumped against the wall, his body trembling, his mind numb.

Martha wiped the sweat from her brow, her eyes scanning the blood-soaked garage. "We need to clean this up," she said, her voice steady.

Jaxon nodded, his hands shaking as he pushed himself to his feet.

As the night pressed on, thick and heavy, Martha and Jaxon loaded the dismembered remains of Carlos into thick, black garbage bags, carefully tying them off. The smell of blood, sweat, and gasoline lingered in the air as they placed the bags in the trunk of Jaxon's car, each thud of a bag settling in the trunk sounding like a hammer pounding the final nail into their guilt.

Neither of them spoke during the drive. The sound of the engine and the rhythmic hum of the tires on the road were the only things breaking the oppressive silence. Martha sat in the passenger seat, staring out the window, her face expressionless, while Jaxon's hands gripped the wheel, knuckles white from tension. He kept his eyes straight ahead, focused on the road, trying to block out what they had just done.

They arrived at Martha's house just past midnight. The old farmhouse stood still and silent, its weathered exterior illuminated faintly by the moonlight. The backyard, where William's headstone rested beneath the old oak tree, looked eerie in the darkness, the gnarled branches casting long shadows across the grass.

"This is it," Martha said, finally breaking the silence as they pulled the body bags from the trunk. Her voice was steady, but there was a tightness in her tone, a weight that hadn't been there before.

Jaxon nodded, swallowing hard. The reality of what they were about to do hung between them, but neither of them acknowledged it. They were too far gone, too deep into this nightmare to stop now.

The headstone marked the spot where Martha's husband, William, had been laid to rest—his ashes scattered in the soil beneath the old oak tree. It had been almost two years since his passing, and now, the same earth that held his memory would become the final resting place of a man whose life had been a lie. A man who had terrorized their family and left them no choice but to take his life.

Martha handed Jaxon the shovel, and together they began to dig. The sound of the shovel breaking through the earth was slow at first, then faster, more desperate, as the hole grew deeper. Sweat poured down their faces, mixing with dirt as the grave widened, inch by inch. The weight of their actions pressed harder with each shovel of soil tossed aside.

Jaxon's breath came in ragged gasps as they worked, but he didn't stop. He couldn't stop. He had to finish this.

Finally, the hole was deep enough. They emptied the black bags into the ground, each one landing with a hollow thud that seemed to echo across the empty yard. The sight of the dismembered body hidden beneath layers of soft soil made Jaxon's stomach churn, but he forced himself to keep moving. He couldn't afford to think about it now.

Martha stood above the grave; her face illuminated by the pale moonlight. She looked down at the hole, her expression unreadable, but Jaxon could see the slight tremble in her hands as she took a deep breath.

"We need to burn the bags in the garbage, tonight."she whispered, almost to herself.

They shoveled the dirt back over the grave in silence. The soft earth covered the body parts quickly, erasing any trace of what they had done. As the last of the soil was spread over the hole, Martha knelt down, her hands smoothing the dirt over like a caretaker tending to a garden. The headstone above them stood tall, marking the spot where William's ashes rested—and now, where the remains of Carlos lay hidden forever.

The air was thick with the scent of freshly turned earth, and Jaxon felt a heaviness settle in his chest, a suffocating weight that no amount of soil could bury. He stared at the headstone, the name "William Dawson" etched into the stone, feeling the finality of their actions sink in.

"Will anyone notice?" Jaxon asked, his voice barely above a whisper.

Martha stood up, brushing the dirt from her hands. "No one will notice. William's been gone a long time. No one comes out here. As far as anyone's concerned, this is just an old grave, nothing more."

Jaxon nodded, though he couldn't shake the feeling that they hadn't buried just Carlos—they had buried a part of themselves too.

"Let's go burn the trash now," Martha said, her voice calm, but her eyes betrayed her weariness. "We've done what we had to do."

They walked back to the garbage cans to burn the last of the evidence, leaving the grave behind, the headstone standing as a silent witness to their crime.

They finished and went in through the kitchen. Inside, the house felt impossibly quiet, the weight of the night's events hanging in the air like a storm waiting to break.

Jaxon glanced back through the window at the backyard, the faint outline of the grave barely visible under the oak tree. He could still feel the weight of the shovel in his hands, the sound of dirt falling onto the bags, the knowledge of what lay beneath the soil.

But as Martha turned off the porch light and locked the door behind them, it was as though the outside world no longer existed. The grave, the body, the crime—they were all buried, hidden beneath the earth where no one would find them.

At least, that's what they hoped.

The room was silent as they stood there, side by side, bound together by the weight of their secret. They had done what they set out to do. Carlos was gone. But the question lingered in the air, unspoken but undeniable: How long could they live with what they had done?

Jaxon woke up from his nightmare, realizing that his mother had not come to check on him. He got out of his bed and went to the kitchen, the cold floor stinging his warm feet as he went.

The sun came up as Emma pulled into the driveway from her night shift at the hospital. Jaxon reached over and flipped on the coffee pot to make her some fresh coffee.

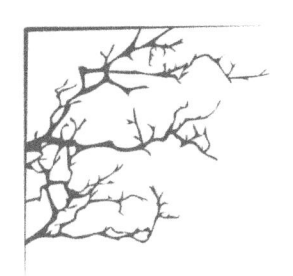

# Chapter 44

Jaxon paced the room, his anxiety palpable. "Mom, what are we going to do? If this comes out... about him, about *us*..." His voice trailed off, unable to complete the sentence.

Emma barely heard him. The weight of her own guilt was suffocating, pressing down with a force that made it hard to breathe. She had been so focused on Carlos—or Domingo, as he was truly called—never realizing that her own secrets would eventually surface too.

"We can't let them find out," Emma finally whispered, her voice shaking. "No one can ever know what I did."

Jaxon froze mid-step, staring at her. "Wait, what do you mean? What are you talking about, Mom?"

Emma lifted her gaze, meeting her son's eyes. She saw the fear in them, but she couldn't tell him what she had done, not now. Her secret had to stay buried.

"Just know that I wasn't always the victim, Jaxon," she confessed, her voice barely above a whisper.

Jaxon's eyes widened, his confusion turning to horror. "Mom, oh my gosh, Mom. Wha-What did you do?"

Emma took a deep breath, the words tasting bitter in her mouth. "I did something... well, covered up something. Something awful. And now, with everything coming out... I'm terrified it'll link it back to me."

Jaxon stood frozen, trying to absorb her words. "Wait, y—you covered up one of his crimes?" His voice cracked, as though he couldn't comprehend the reality of what she was saying.

Emma shook her head, her face pale. "No, it was something else.... something that I did."

The room fell into a tense silence. Jaxon sank into the chair across from her, his face drained of color. They were caught in a web of secrets and lies, and the more they struggled, the tighter it seemed to pull.

"We need to figure out how to keep this from coming out," Emma muttered to herself. "No one can know what I did. Not now, not ever."

Jaxon watched his mother, realizing that whatever truth was about to unravel, he had to tell his Nana, she would know how to approach this, how to hide it better than either of them would. "Alright, Mom. But what did you do? You've got to tell me."

Emma shook her head, "I can't... No, it won't do anyone any good for anyone else to know about this." She sat in a daze, muttering to herself.

They had survived Domingo Carmona's deception, but now they had to survive their own.

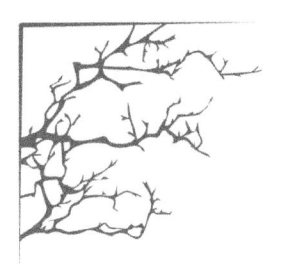

## Chapter 45

Martha's living room felt like a courtroom as Emma stood by the fireplace, her fingers tracing the cool bricks. She called them in with a voice that allowed no room for argument, each syllable weighed with an unspoken ultimatum. Jaxon entered first, his tall frame seeming to loom even larger in the tension-thick air, while Martha followed, her red hair a fiery contrast against the pale walls.

"Sit down," Emma's words were not a request but a command, and they obeyed, finding their places on the worn-out sofa that had hosted years of family gatherings, now a silent witness to their fracturing bond.

She studied them for a moment, Jaxon's guarded eyes and Martha's firm set jaw, memorizing this tableau before the storm. Then, taking a deep breath, Emma let the dam break.

"I've spent my life caring for people," she started, her voice steady despite the tremor of emotion threatening to break through. "Healing wounds, easing pain... because I believe every life is precious." Her green eyes glistened, but she held the tears at bay. "But now I have to tell you something. Something horrible that I have done."

She paused, letting the question hang heavy between them. The silence was oppressive, filled with the weight of unsaid confessions and the echo of her own heartbeat. Emma loved them, more than she could ever articulate, yet that love now tasted bitter with betrayal.

"Family means everything to me," she continued, the words scraping raw against her throat. "But I can't ignore the darkness of what's happened, what I've brought into our home." Emma's hands clenched involuntarily, her knuckles whitening as she fought the anger mingling with her grief.

"Tell me, please," her plea was both a whisper and a scream, "how do I move forward from here and keep you both out of what I have done?"

The moment stretched, taut as a wire ready to snap. Jaxon's eyes skittered between the two most important women in his life, the air around him charged with unspoken truths. He sat rigid on the edge of the faded sofa, every muscle coiled like a spring. His long, wavy hair, usually a curtain hiding his thoughts, now pushed back revealing the raw unease in his hazel gaze.

"Mom," he began, but the word was strangled, barely escaping his throat. He cleared it, trying again. "Emma..." The use of her first name felt foreign on his tongue, a desperate attempt to bridge the chasm that had suddenly yawned open between them.

Martha, standing statuesque beside the hearth, interjected before he could continue. Her voice, typically a blade honed sharp with sarcasm, now carried an unfamiliar tremble.

"Emma, what are you talking about? I don't think... you just don't understand—" She broke off, swallowing hard. The defiance that always marked her demeanor was there, in the steel of her posture, but her eyes betrayed her, shimmering with something akin to regret.

"Understand?" Emma's response sliced through the tension. "I understand more than you think." Her voice, though controlled, vibrated with contained energy, a coil winding tighter within her. She kept her stance rooted, unwilling to show the quake that threatened to unravel her from within.

"Nana," Jaxon said, turning toward Martha, his tone pleading for some sliver of guidance. But the woman who had raised them both—the one who faced down life with unflinching resolve—seemed momentarily stripped of her armor.

"I know what we did..." Martha continued, fixing her gaze on Emma, "but it was never meant to hurt you." Her voice cracked on the last word, the facade of the indomitable matriarch crumbling as she grappled with the enormity of their shared secret.

A silence fell over the room, deep and dark as the secrets they harbored. Emma watched them, her expression unreadable, her heart waging a war between the instinct to nurture and the horror at the betrayal that pulsed like a malignant shadow through the veins of her family.

"What you did, Ma? What do you mean what you did?," Emma finally said, her voice low but resolute, her green eyes reflecting a depth of pain only a mother's love could endure. "I am talking about what I did."

Jaxon stood in the doorway, his heart pounding in his chest as he watched the scene unfold before him. His mother sat frozen at the table, her face pale, eyes wide with the kind of realization that changes everything. Across from her, his Nana stood with her hand extended, shaking slightly, as if she wasn't sure whether to comfort or confess.

The air in the room felt heavy, like it was thickening with every unspoken truth. Jaxon's breath caught in his throat. He could feel the tension between them, a silent battle being fought with glances and half-swallowed words.

"Mom? Nana?" Jaxon's voice was barely a whisper, but it sliced through the air like a knife.

Emma didn't answer right away. Her eyes darted between him and Martha, as if she were trying to make sense of something too horrible to accept. "Ma? What... I—I didn't know," she finally murmured, her voice shaky. "I didn't want to know."

Martha's hand hung in the air, trembling. "Emma..." her voice was strained, but there was no more hiding. "We did what we had to. You have to understand that."

Jaxon saw it then—the understanding creeping into his mother's eyes. She knew what he and Martha had done, and worse, she knew why. It was the same reason Jaxon had stood by Martha all this time. They both thought they were protecting her, shielding her from the darkness that had wrapped around their lives.

But now, there was no more pretending. Emma wasn't the only one with secrets.

Jaxon felt his chest tighten again, like the weight of their collective sins was too much to bear. He watched as his mother's hands clenched into fists on the table, her knuckles white with the effort of holding herself together.

"You knew," Emma whispered, her voice hoarse. "All this time... you knew what I did."

Martha's eyes shimmered with unshed tears, her hand still reaching out, though now it seemed more like a plea. "No, but I suspected you had done something. It was too easy, what Jaxon and I did. But, baby girl, we both did what we had to."

For a moment, Jaxon thought his mother might crumble right there, under the weight of everything—the lies, the guilt, the truth. But instead, she straightened in her chair, her chin lifting just slightly, like she was trying to hold on to the last shreds of control.

Jaxon wanted to speak, to step in, to do something to stop the unraveling. But what could he say? What could any of them say when the unthinkable had already been done?

The room felt like it was closing in on them, the silence stretching out as they all sat on the brink of something too big to name.

Finally, Martha lowered her hand, letting it fall limply to her side.

"There's no going back now." she said softly, her voice barely audible.

Jaxon swallowed hard, his throat dry. He didn't know if that was true anymore.

Emma just watched, her own hands limp at her sides, the healer within battling the storm of betrayal and the relentless pull of blood ties. The Dawson living room, once a sanctuary of laughter and warmth, had transformed into a theater of psychological warfare where the next move could mend or forever mar the fragile tapestry of their lives.

Emma paced before them, each step echoing like a verdict in the stillness of the room. The air was thick with anticipation, as if the very walls were holding their breath. She paused and fixed her son and mother with a gaze that cut through the tension.

"Jax," she began, her voice quivering as if she were trying to hold the world together with mere syllables, "and you, Mom." Her words were laced with a profound sadness that seemed to fill every corner of the room. "Did you... How did you know?" She swallowed hard, fighting the lump in her throat. "I had to, it was for us, — to protect us all."

Jaxon's Adam's apple bobbed visibly as he swallowed, his eyes never leaving Emma's face. He looked like a boy again, vulnerable and seeking assurance from the one person who had always been his haven.

"Mom, I—" he started, but the words crumbled before they could take shape.

Emma raised a hand, halting his attempt at confession. "Don't," she said, a sharp edge of anger slicing through her sorrow. "What we've done, it... it has to stay between us. Just us. Tearing each other apart in front of the world won't heal us and it won't undo what has been done." Her declaration hung between them, heavy with unspoken consequence.

Jaxon's shoulders, which had been taut as bowstrings, slumped suddenly, relief washing over him in an almost visible wave. His eyes glinted with unshed tears—tears of a child who had escaped punishment, yet still carried the weight of his misdeeds.

"Thank you, Mom," he whispered, his voice barely audible, but the gratitude within it echoed louder than any spoken word. Guilt shadowed his features, etching lines of self-reproach that might never fully fade.

Emma watched her son, the depth of her forgiveness mirrored in her weary green eyes. They stood there, a family bound by love and marred by secrets, each bearing scars that would shape their paths forevermore.

Martha's hand, trembling and pale, extended across the void of the living room, her fingers reaching for Emma with a desperation that belied her usual stoicism. The red tendrils of her hair seemed to quiver in the silence, an echo of the turmoil that ebbed and flowed beneath her skin.

Emma watched the outstretched hand, a silent symbol of all the sacrifices they had made for one another, a ledger of debts both paid and owed. She could see the glistening onset of tears crowning Martha's eyes, those steely pools that had once been impenetrable fortresses, now breached by the gravity of their reality. Slowly, as if moving through water, Emma reached back, her own hand a whisper against her mother's.

Their fingers interlocked, a lifetime of unspoken words passing between them. Martha's grip tightened just enough to convey the strength that had once defined her, the resilience that she had ingrained in Emma with every sharp-tongued lesson and protective embrace.

"Ma," Emma began, her voice threading through the tense air, stronger now, more certain. "I don't want to know what you did; I won't tell you what I did. But I need you to understand; this... this has to just disappear." Her green eyes, usually so warm and inviting, took on a steeliness that mirrored Martha's own. It was clear that the nurturing nurse, the daughter raised under Oakdale's simple skies, had evolved into something more formidable, more resolved.

"Emma," Martha started, her voice a rasp, but Emma pressed on.

"Protecting you is part of who I am, Ma. But so is remembering. I can't forget what we've done, what lines we've crossed." Her grip on Martha's hand was steady now, a lifeline amidst the tempest of their creation. There was love there, a fierce, burning love that could weather the darkest of storms, but also a new edge—a keen awareness that the veil of ignorance had been lifted, never to be drawn again.

"Consequences will come, Mama. Maybe not from the law, maybe not today or tomorrow. But they will come. And we have to face them, carry them, learn from them."

Martha's mouth opened, then closed, no words finding passage. Her gaze didn't waver, though, meeting Emma's with an intensity that acknowledged the truth in her daughter's words. The matriarch of the Dawson family, the woman who had faced life's cruelties with biting sarcasm and unbending will, understood the weight of their shared secret, the burden of guilt that would shadow them forevermore.

In that moment, as their hands remained clasped, Emma knew the path ahead was fraught with shadows and echoes of a past that would always nip at their heels. But with the clarity of her resolve and the bond that tethered their fates together, she felt the stirrings of a grim determination settling in her bones.

They were fractured, yes, but unbroken. They would forge a new way forward, traversing the twisted landscape of their choices, seeking redemption in a future where the light of forgiveness might someday overcome the darkness of their deeds.

Jaxon's breath hitched; a sound barely audible above the thrumming silence that had settled over the room like a shroud. He sat rigid, his spine pressed hard against the back of the couch, as if bracing against an unseen force. Emma watched him closely, her gaze unyielding—a sentinel to their shared truth.

"Jax," she whispered, the single syllable heavy with resonance.

His face, once flushed with the heat of confrontation, now drained of color, leaving his skin ghostly pale in the dim light filtering through the closed curtains. The shadows seemed to cling to him, accentuating the sharp angles of his jaw and the hollows beneath his eyes. Those hazel orbs, which often held the world at bay with their intensity, now reflected only the torment of a soul caught in the cross hairs of its own making.

"Mom, I—" His voice cracked, a testament to the burden he carried, the weight of actions too heavy for shoulders so young.

Emma reached out, her fingers grazing the air between them before retreating, knowing that touch could not absolve the chasm that yawned wide and dark between intent and deed.

"Jaxon," Martha interjected, her voice a thread of sound that wove through the tension. She stood, her posture erect, every inch the matriarch who had weathered storms and spit in the eye of adversity. But now, her steel was tempered by the tremble in her voice, the vibrato of vulnerability that underscored her conviction. "We... we've made our bed, haven't we? And it's lumpy and cold and will never let us rest easy."

Emma observed as Martha moved closer to Jaxon, her movements deliberate, each step a testament to the resolve that had defined her life. She crouched beside him, her hand finding his knee, gripping it with a strength that belied the tremors running through her.

"Listen to me, Jax, and you too, Emma," Martha said, her voice gaining power, rising from the quiver of acknowledgment into the clarion call of defiance. "What's done is done. We can't change it, can't turn back the clock on choices that are etched in stone. But I'll be damned if I let it eat us alive."

Her eyes, fierce and unblinking, locked onto Emma's, then shifted back to Jaxon, who stared at her with a mix of awe and fear. "We're Dawsons," she continued, her words carving a path through the despair. "We stick together, come hell or high water. I'll stand by you, both of you, through whatever comes next. That's my promise."

In that living room, where family portraits watched from the walls, silent witnesses to the unfolding drama, a new pact was forged—one not of blood, but of shared culpability and the relentless pursuit of redemption. Emma felt the ground shift beneath her feet, a tectonic realignment of their familial landscape, as they prepared to navigate the treacherous terrain that lay ahead.

Emma's hands were steady as she reached out to extinguish the last flicker of candlelight that had been their only witness. A soft click echoed in the living room, and shadows clung to the corners like specters of the secrets they harbored. Her eyes, vibrant green pools reflecting a maelstrom of emotion, moved from Jaxon to Martha, locking onto each in turn.

"Ma, Jax," Emma said, her voice low and resolute, almost a whisper but laden with a fortitude that resonated through the silence. "This darkness... it won't define us. We have to leave these secrets here, right here and never let them escape from this room."

Jaxon, his youth etched with lines of premature wisdom wrought by their shared ordeal, swallowed hard, nodding imperceptibly as if afraid any larger movement might shatter the fragile hope his mother offered.

Martha, her red hair a fiery testament to the fierce spirit that had weathered countless storms, let out a breath she seemed to have held for an eternity. It was a silent surrender to the vow that now tethered them, a pact of perseverance amidst the wreckage.

The room settled into a heavy silence, the kind that presses down like the weight of the world, thick with unspoken thoughts and the aftershocks of truth laid bare. The family portrait on the wall, its smiles frozen in time, seemed to mock them with the normalcy they had lost.

Jaxon stared at his hands, knuckles white where he gripped the armrest, while Martha closed her eyes, her chest rising and falling with the labor of introspection. They were adrift in their own minds, navigating the murky waters of remorse and resolve.

Emma watched them, her heart aching with a love that both shattered and soldered her soul. She too was lost in contemplation, wrestling with the paradox of protecting those she loved from the world while condemning them to the purgatory of their conscience.

"Whatever comes," she whispered, more to herself than to the others, "whatever comes..."

Emma rose from the edge of the pristine couch, a silent sentinel in the dimly lit living room. The clock on the mantle ticked away moments that felt as heavy as the silence they bore, each second stretching out like an accusation. She moved towards the window, her reflection staring back at her through the glass—a woman torn between the jagged edges of love and justice.

Jaxon shifted in his seat, the shadows under his eyes betraying the turmoil within. He glanced up at Emma, searching for an anchor in the storm that was their lives. His gaze held a question, one that begged for reassurance in a world that suddenly seemed devoid of certainties.

Martha's fingers traced the lines of her palm, reading them as if they were a road map to absolution. Her posture remained rigid, a fortress built over years of battles fought and scars accumulated. But her eyes, those conduits of raw emotion, shimmered with unshed tears, a crack in her armor.

"Mom..." Jaxon's voice broke through the silence, tentative yet seeking.

Emma turned from the window, her green eyes reflecting a resolve forged in the crucible of their shared confession. "We start by acknowledging every choice, every mistake," she said, her tone not just offering a direction but demanding accountability.

Martha stood, her movements deliberate, drawing herself up to her full height. "And we face what comes," she added, steel lacing her voice.

Their three figures, cast in the soft glow of the room, formed a tableau of contrasting emotions. Relief mingled with guilt on their faces, the relief of being understood, of being accepted despite it all, and the guilt of knowing the cost of their silence.

Emma reached out, her hand hovering in the space between them, an invitation to unite. Jaxon took it, his grip speaking volumes of the gratitude and shame he carried. Martha's hand joined theirs, her touch solid, grounding them in the reality of their pact.

As they stood there, connected by the gravity of their promise, the weight of the past and the uncertainty of the future seemed to converge upon them. Yet, beneath it all lay a fierce determination to rise above the ashes of their actions, to forge a path lined with the shards of their brokenness.

AS THE WEEKS TURNED into months, then years, the dark cloud of secrets continued to loom over Martha, Emma, and Jaxon, but they had learned to live beneath it. Their unspoken pact, forged in the fires of murder and lies, bound them closer than they ever could have imagined.

Life went on. From the outside, they looked like any other family—grieving the loss of a husband and father but pushing forward. Emma returned to her work at the hospital, her hands steady as she cared for patients, though her mind was never quite free from the weight of what she had done.

The poison that ended Domingo Carmona's life, the man she had once known as Carlos, was a secret she would take to her grave. It ate at her sometimes, especially in the quiet moments, but she silenced those thoughts, burying them as deeply as the body that now rested in an unmarked grave.

Martha, ever stoic, carried on with her life as well. Her secret—what she and Jaxon had done to protect Emma—was a burden she bore without complaint. She knew they had done what was necessary. Carlos, or Domingo, was a threat. His lies, his violence—it would have only gotten worse. She would not allow herself to feel guilt. To her, it was survival, plain and simple.

Jaxon, though young, had grown old in the span of those fateful weeks. The burden of their crime weighed heavily on him, more than he let on. He had nightmares sometimes, but he never spoke of them. Instead, he threw himself into his studies, into work, anything to drown out the echoes of that night. He knew the truth, and though it haunted him, he kept it locked away, just as his mother and grandmother did with their own truths.

The three of them lived with their secrets, and in time, they became like the air they breathed—heavy, but essential to survival. Detective Ross had long moved on, the case of Domingo Carmona a tangled web of crime and deceit, but never once pointing in their direction. The real Carlos Martinez was long dead, and the man who had taken his name was just another criminal in a sea of unsolved mysteries.

As for the three of them, they lived on, not with innocence, but with a kind of peace. They had done what they had to do to protect each other, to survive. The world would never know what truly happened, and perhaps that was for the best.

In the end, they had all three gotten away with murder, but the real victory was their silence—the unbreakable bond of family forged through shared darkness. They were free, but they would never be free of each other. The secrets they kept were buried deep, but they would always remain, silent and still, like the shadows that lingered in the corners of their lives.

And that was how it would stay, for as long as they lived.

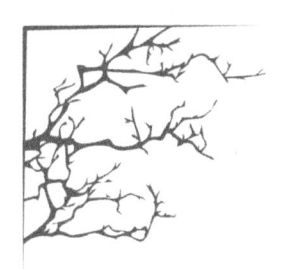

# Epilogue

Eight years later...

The sun dipped low over the horizon, casting a warm golden glow across the Dawson family farm. The old house, with its familiar weathered boards and wraparound porch, stood as a testament to the years that had passed. It looked peaceful, almost untouched by the dark secrets that once threatened to tear the family apart. But to those who knew its history, the calm was deceptive. Beneath the surface of this serene life, the scars of the past lingered, buried but never forgotten.

Emma and Jaxon moved in with Martha. The silent support of each other helped them withstand the bouts of uncertainty.

Emma stood on her mother's porch; her hands wrapped around a mug of coffee. The breeze was cool and carried the faint scent of pine and earth. She inhaled deeply, letting the air fill her lungs, feeling the weight of the past settle more lightly on her shoulders now. It had taken years—years of therapy, of quiet contemplation, of careful lies and hidden truths—but she had finally found a semblance of peace.

She had never told anyone about the poisoning—not Jaxon, not Martha, not the police. The secret remained hers to keep, locked deep inside where no one could touch it. It still haunted her on sleepless nights, but she had learned to live with it. In a strange way, it had given her strength. She had done what she had to do to protect herself and her family. She destroyed the small bottle that was hidden beneath her father's headstone, just as an extra precaution, she put it in the hospital's incinerator. And in the end, they had all moved on.

"Mom?" Jaxon's voice broke through her thoughts. He stood at the edge of the porch, taller now, more mature. His eyes—those same crisp hazel eyes she'd always loved—were filled with the warmth and ease of someone who had grown into himself.

"Yeah, honey?" she answered, turning toward him with a soft smile.

"Dinner's ready. Nana made her famous roast." He grinned, and for a moment, Emma saw the boy he once was. But Jaxon was no longer the child who had been dragged into a web of lies and violence. He was a man now, strong and capable, and—thankfully—free from the shadows that had once threatened to consume him.

Martha's voice floated from inside, calling them to the table. Emma watched as Jaxon walked back toward the house, his steps sure, his posture relaxed. He had moved on from what happened. Martha had too. They had never spoken again about that terrible night, about the man they had left in the past, or the lies they had constructed. It was as if they had made an unspoken pact—what was done was done, and there was no point in dredging it up.

Inside, the house was warm with the smells of home-cooked food and the sounds of family. Martha bustled around the kitchen, her hands steady and sure as she set the table. Her hair had turned silver, and her once sharp eyes had softened with age, but her spirit remained unbroken. If she carried any guilt or regret, she never showed it. Martha had been the one who taught Emma how to move forward, how to live with the weight of their shared sins.

As they sat down to dinner, Emma glanced around the table. It was a simple meal—roast chicken, mashed potatoes, fresh vegetables from the garden—but it felt rich, filled with the quiet joy of family. They were all here, together, despite everything that had happened. Despite the lies, the violence, and the secrets, they had survived.

And yet, as Emma picked up her fork, she couldn't help but wonder if survival was enough. Was it enough to live in this quiet life, pretending that the past hadn't nearly destroyed them? Or was there something more—something she still hadn't grasped, even after all these years?

She pushed the thought away. Tonight was about family, about the present. The past had no place at this table.

Jaxon looked at her from across the table, his eyes filled with a question he never asked aloud. He knew—he had always known—that there was more to what had happened than what they had admitted to themselves. But like Emma, he had learned to live with the uncertainty. They were all bound together by that night, by the unspoken truths that connected them in ways that would never fully unravel.

As the meal went on, laughter filled the room, soft and genuine. Emma smiled, feeling the warmth of it all settle around her like a blanket. For the first time in a long time, she felt content. The future was uncertain, but for now, this moment was enough.

Later, as the sun dipped below the horizon and the stars began to twinkle in the clear night sky, Emma stepped out onto the porch again. She leaned against the railing, looking out at the land that had been her sanctuary and her prison. The wind whispered through the trees, carrying with it the faintest echo of the past.

But she didn't fear it anymore. The secrets she had buried, the things she had done—they were a part of her, but they no longer defined her. Emma had made her peace with the past, with herself.

And as she stood there, the darkness folding in around her like a soft embrace, she knew that she, Martha, and Jaxon would be all right. They had survived the storm, and now, they could finally live in the calm that followed.

In the end, they had gotten away with it. But more importantly, they had gotten away *from* it. And that, Emma realized, was all that truly mattered.

The End, or is it?

# Don't miss out!

Visit the website below and you can sign up to receive emails whenever Bekka Scott publishes a new book. There's no charge and no obligation.

https://books2read.com/r/B-A-UBPLC-WNUAF

BOOKS 2 READ

Connecting independent readers to independent writers.

# Also by Bekka Scott

Fractured Reflections
Reflejos Fracturados
Divine Design: Unlocking the Secrets of Prayer and Manifesting!
Bajo las Cenizas
Beneath the Ashes

Watch for more at https://authorbekkascott.com/.

# About the Author

Bekka Scott is married to her high school crush, mother to three daughters and a bonus daughter, and Nana to ten grandmonsters.

She has two dogs, Sally Barbara Jean, Walter Mitty, and a cat, Sammich. In addition to writing, she has been a crocheter since the age of three.

You can find her on Instgram, Facebook, X, Tiktok, Linkedin and Goodreads.

Her author website is here: https://authorbekkascott.com/ Follow for new releases and updates.

Thank you for reading.

Read more at https://authorbekkascott.com/.

Milton Keynes UK
Ingram Content Group UK Ltd.
UKHW040352111224
452348UK00001B/88